Beyond Res

Part Three of The Ransom Series

By A.T. Douglas

Copyright © 2014 by A.T. Douglas

All rights reserved.

ISBN: 1502382512
ISBN-13: 978-1502382511

Without limiting the rights under copyright reserved above, no part of this book may be reproduced, transmitted, downloaded, distributed, stored in or introduced into any information storage and retrieval system, in any form or by any means, whether electronic or mechanical, without prior written permission from the author, except by a reviewer who may quote brief passages for review purposes.

This book is a work of fiction. References to real people, events, establishments, organizations, or locations are intended only to provide a sense of authenticity. The author acknowledges the trademarked status and trademark owners of various products referenced in this work of fiction, which have been used without permission. The use of these trademarks is not authorized, associated with, or sponsored by the trademark owners.

Contents

Chapter	Page
Prologue	1
1	4
2	9
3	14
4	19
5	28
6	36
7	41
8	46
9	56
10	62
11	71
12	78
13	85
14	95
15	102
16	109
17	118
18	131
19	146
20	153
21	162
22	170
23	184
24	192
25	199
26	210
27	215
28	230
29	238
30	245
31	253
32	263
33	270
Epilogue	275
Author Notes and Acknowledgements	285

Other Books by this Author 286
About the Author 287

*To my readers
for loving this series enough
to be desperate for book three.*

This one's for you.

Prologue

The emblazoned sun fills the sky above me. It's the same sun I've known all my life but feels completely different here with its dry heat over this barren desert terrain. I'm far from home, and I know it's dangerous to be here, but this is something I have to do. My family needs this. *I* need this.

And he needs me, too.

We've only had this raging celestial body in the heavens to connect us all together, but its pull on the Earth is nothing compared to the pull of family. Resisting the primal need to be together is something we can't do anymore. There is no moving on with life knowing that the final piece of our family is out there.

We understand the risks. We know what's at stake. We're ready to face whatever the hell life decides to throw at us, because honestly it can't be worse than the difficulties we've already endured. It's time for happiness and love to bring our family back together after being apart for so long.

It's time.

I can feel the sweat beading on the back of my neck as I watch closely for any movement from the massive building in front of me. I'd like to think my body's reaction is from the heat of leaning on this black car in the full sun of mid-afternoon as I wait, but I know nerves are playing their part. While our plan is well underway, this moment is where it could all fall apart. The next few hours will tell me just how risky this self-created situation is.

A blaring buzzer sounds from the building before a metal side door opens. For the intensity of the sound, I would have expected an army to emerge from inside, but only one man with a plastic bag in hand walks out before the door closes abruptly behind him.

He walks with his eyes trained on the ground and no urgency to his movements. Even at this distance I can see the worn lines of age that travel across his skin. His hair is wiry and gray with white patches throughout. As he walks down the path toward the massive barbed wire fence that separates us, I fear the life within him has been as drained as it appears to have affected his body.

Even after the guard at the gate unlocks a door in the fence and allows the man to leave, there is no purpose to the man's steps. He glances up only briefly to acknowledge that there is a car waiting for him as expected, though I see his expression long enough to recognize the look of confusion there.

When he's within feet of me and the car, he finally looks up to meet my gaze and clears his throat. "You're from the cab company?"

It pains me to hear the hopelessness in his voice. Given what this man has endured and what just happened to change his life around, he should be elated, full of anticipation, ready to take on the fucking world.

I smile and avoid his question completely. I won't lie to the man. I will never lie to him. "I'm here to take you home."

He laughs under his breath, a guttural sound full of sarcasm and discontent. I'm on the verge of putting it all out there right at this very moment to make him feel better and understand, but I have to wait until we're on the road. I can't risk anyone seeing his reaction.

Before I can move to do it for him, he opens the front passenger door and takes his seat, slamming the door shut behind him.

I take a brief moment to breathe and remember who I've just met and how long I've waited to meet him. There is no room for anger or frustration between us.

He will understand.

I move around the car and buckle into the driver's seat, glancing only briefly next to me to confirm the scowl I expected would be on the man's face. Without another word, I start up the car and get us on the road.

The car's radio is silent. Only the sound of the air conditioner combating the heat of the summer sun fills the space between us, though the car feels thick with tension.

I need to make him understand, to put his worries to rest. Though I've been ready to do this for an eternity, now that the moment is finally here it's almost impossible to know what to say.

I turn to face him, fully intent on opening my mouth to speak and get the words out with no stopping until he realizes just how great of a turn his life has really taken, but there's no need for me to say a thing. Understanding is written all over his face as his eyes remain fixed on my left hand on the steering wheel.

"Oh my God," he whispers in disbelief. Tears and sparks of life fill his eyes as he raises them to look at me. "It's you, isn't it?"

My heart momentarily jumps to my throat as I glance down at my left wrist and the small black symbol of infinity tattooed there. I slowly bring the car to a stop on the side of the desert road before turning to meet the man's gaze again, swallowing hard before speaking.

"It's good to finally meet you, Grandpa."

1

Three months earlier...

The crumpling of leaves beneath my feet is strangely calming as I walk. I know every step of this route beneath the trees, each rock standing its ground and the occasional fallen log forever rotting away back into the dirt. My mark on this place is clear as I tread further down the worn path I've inadvertently been working on since I was old enough to walk.

The forest is the stereotypical sanctuary for mankind, a place where the worries of daily life disappear and nature takes over in its exquisite and generally untouched beauty. The cacophony of cities and civilization is non-existent here, replaced by the sweet harmony of running water, the wind brushing through the trees, the birds going about their daily business. The forest is my own sanctuary but is also my prison.

I've lived in the backwoods of Maine for my entire life.

As I step out of the narrow path into the small clearing, the sound of the nearby creek is even more pronounced. The spring runoff is running its course, washing away any remnants of the frigid winter we've been stuck in for months. It's a relief to return to this place, to know that it's always here waiting for me from season to season and year to year. It's the one constant in my life that I can always rely on.

The rush of water calls to me, getting louder as I cross the clearing and follow the continuation of my forest path on the other side until it comes to parallel the creek. The large rock shaded by trees and hidden from the world comes into view. Seeing it immediately calms my nerves, and I can't help the quickening in my steps to get there.

Pulling myself up onto the rock, I take a seat at the top where its irregular round shape transforms into a perfectly flat surface. It's nature's bench above the creek, its gift to me within the only place I've ever called home.

My heart rate quickly steadies. My breathing becomes even. Minutes or hours go by filled with silent thoughts and the freedom of solitude. I find focus despite the worries that desperately try to creep into my mind. It's almost game time, and I need to get my shit together.

I will not let my family down.

The sound of water whisking down the creek isn't enough to mask the traveler approaching from the clearing. I've spent too many hours in these woods not to recognize every possible sound from the individual instruments that create the symphony playing the forest's orchestral composition.

My eyes remained trained ahead of me, though my focus is waning and my temper is flaring, at least it wants to. These footsteps are quick and close together. They are the footsteps of my worried mother, and I could never be angry with her, despite her interruption of my time alone in this place.

"Dante?"

The last bits of my focus shatter as I turn my head in response and give my mom a small but genuine smile. "Hi, Mom."

She smiles back, though it's only a tentative gesture. I can see the worry in her eyes despite the aura of reassurance she's clearly trying to portray as she approaches me. A gust of wind sweeps her long hair behind her shoulders. It looks darker and more brown than blond under the shade of the trees.

"Can I join you? I know you like to be here alone, but–"

"It's okay. Let me help you up," I interrupt and immediately extend my hand to her. Nature's bench at the top of the rock is just barely long enough to fit two people, though I'm usually its only occupant.

When my mom is fully seated next to me, it takes only once glance of her eyes meeting mine before she grabs my hand in both of hers and grips on to me as if this may be the last time we ever see each other. The slightest shaking rocks her fingers as she stares down at our connected hands. Silent sobs start to rack her chest, and I can't let her fall down this slope any longer.

The beautiful sounds of nature around us snip out to silence and my entire focus and being become concentrated on the loving, caring person next to me. I pull my mom into my embrace and let her crumble around me. She grips me back just as tightly as she cries away her worries into my shoulder.

It's unnerving to see her this way. Despite everything she's been through and the unusual life she's had to live, she's taken it all in stride, finding happiness and contentment with a smile on her face regardless of life's difficulties. She's been strong for me all my life. I guess it's my turn to take on that responsibility and be there for her.

"Everything will be fine, Mom. It's a solid plan. I know it'll go smoothly," I try to reassure her, though my words seem to have the opposite effect. She immediately withdraws from our embrace.

"What if it doesn't? It was my idea. It's my plan to succeed or fail, and I will never forgive myself if it fails. If I lost you…"

"No," I reply definitively, shaking my head to dispel even the thought of failure from my mind. "I won't let anything bad happen. You and Dad have prepared me for this my entire life without even meaning to. I can do this."

Mom wipes away a wave of fresh tears, keeping her eyes forward instead of looking at me. "What we've prepared you for is the possibility of someone finding us, not us throwing you out into the world to be found. It's dangerous, Dante."

"For you and Dad it is," I counter. "The world has no idea who I am. No one will recognize me. No one will question why I'm there."

"We should at least come with you. If something goes wrong, you'll need backup."

I love my mother, but I can't deny the frustration swelling within me at this conversation. With a quick run of my hands over my face and through my dark hair, I try to tuck away those feelings, reminding myself just how difficult the upcoming days will be for my mom.

Taking her by each shoulder, I turn her to face me, not speaking until her reddened eyes have met mine completely so I know she's listening. "You and Dad can't be seen anywhere near Arizona. I know it's been over twenty years, but you could still be recognized. Hell, your faces were on TV and social media for years after you disappeared with me."

It's hard to do, but I manage to hold Mom's gaze. Acceptance slowly works its way into her features, but I don't have her fully convinced yet.

"I know you're, um, older now," I continue with an unavoidable awkward pause at describing my mom like this even though she only just turned forty last fall, "but honestly you don't look that much different from those pictures in the old news reports. Same goes for Dad, and you know all his tattoos make him stand out if he's not careful to hide them. I know you're worried about me, but there is no way you can go on this trip. I need to do this by myself."

"Damn it," Mom curses as her eyes fall from mine to her lap. "Okay. We'll stick to the plan, but if you find yourself in any kind of trouble or think for even a moment that someone knows who you are, you get yourself out of there immediately, got it?"

I nod my understanding. "I'll be careful."

The meek smile she offers back at me is completely overpowered by the weary look on her face, an expression that is only going to worsen when I get on the road tomorrow morning. She sighs deeply before pulling me into her arms and kissing me on the side of the head.

"Bring our family back together," she whispers beside my ear.

I discreetly swallow the lump forming in my throat at the thought of what I've been asked to do. "I will."

2

It's been a long four days. I've seen more of this country and its busy population in the last four days than I have in my entire twenty-one years of life.

My limited amount of driving between our hidden home in the forest to the nearby towns in Maine left me completely unprepared for the experience of driving across the country. Traveling through bustling cities and seeing a thriving world outside of my protective bubble in Maine was incredible. Even driving through farmland and desert and a whole lot of nothing was exciting and different.

I didn't mind that I was alone for the drive and sleeping in my car at rest areas. I couldn't care less about the angry drivers passing me on the highway and flipping me off for sticking to the speed limit and strictly obeying every traffic sign and stoplight. While everyone else was intent on getting from one place to the next as quickly as possible, my only concern was not garnering attention. My fake identity is not something I could explain to the police if they figured out the fraudulence behind my driver's license and other records.

Sleep was a challenge last night, not entirely due to the difficulties of resting while reclined in a small car at a rest area parking lot. My nerves stayed relatively under control the entire drive until I got here, just outside of Phoenix, within miles of my final destination.

Though the drive here was the first step in this journey, my actions today mark the actually beginning of our plan. The risk of getting pulled over by a cop while driving is nothing compared to the risk I'm about to face. Today could be the start of something amazing. It could also mean the end for me.

I need to at least smell good if I'm going to face my potential end.

I'm awake early enough to make a detour to get cleaned up at a nearby truck stop that has showers available. By the time I leave the truck stop, I'm quite presentable for a kid who spent his entire life hidden away in the backwoods of Maine.

My nerves hit a peak as I make the turn past the guard booth and into the prison complex. The large parking lot and front of the building are just as I remember from researching everything I could find about this place. I know exactly what door to watch and where to park the car so that I have an unobstructed view of the door.

After almost two hours of constantly looking between the inactive door and the exceptionally slow movement of time on my prepaid cell phone, the door finally opens. An armed female guard steps out and holds the door for the person behind her.

Adrenaline shoots straight to my heart and races throughout my body the moment I see her. I've only seen pictures of her before, glimpses of the media's portrayal of a woman who gave up everything to protect her daughter and her family. She has aged significantly since that time, her long dark brown hair much shorter and almost completely gray at this point, but there's no mistaking the woman exiting the prison with a large purse on her shoulder is my grandmother.

I quickly turn on the car and peel out of the parking space. My eyes immediately connect with Cindy's as I pull up to the sidewalk in front of the building, and what I see there confuses me.

There's recognition in her eyes.

As she seems about ready to crumble into tears, I throw the car in park and jump out of the vehicle to meet her up the sidewalk. A rising panic overtakes my body at her reaction to seeing me, and I feel like I'm losing all control. This was not part of the plan. She's not supposed to know who I am. She hasn't seen me since I was an infant.

With as unforced of a courteous smile as I can muster toward the armed guard at the door still watching our every move, I wrap my arm around Cindy's shoulders and guide her toward the car.

"You need to wait," I whisper to her, maintaining my plastered-on grin and barely moving my lips. "They're watching."

Her eyes only widen in response as I open the passenger-side door and offer a hand to help her in. Through our grasp I can feel her entire arm shaking slightly. I give her what comfort I can, squeezing her hand lightly before letting go to close the door.

By the time I'm back in the driver's seat, my entire focus turns to getting us out of the parking lot and away from the guard booth at the entrance. There will be plenty of time for explanations and emotions and catching up. For now I just need to get Cindy away from this prison and deliver her to freedom.

When the female guard emerges from the guard booth and blocks our exit, my heart sinks. For a moment my foot dithers between the brake pedal and the gas pedal, but I can't floor it out of this fucking parking lot. They'll instantly suspect something and move to chase, and everything will be ruined.

Reluctantly, I slowly compress the brake pedal and bring the car to a stop a few feet away from the guard. She approaches the passenger-side window, so I push the button to lower the window and pray to God that our plan doesn't blow up in my face before it even gets started.

The guard leans down to the window and gives me a quick glance. She's clearly taking me in, wondering who the hell I am. The question has to be on the tip of her tongue.

Her focus shifts to my passenger, and a broad smile emerges on her face. "Your day is finally here, I see. Congratulations, Cindy."

Cindy's breath seems to catch in her throat before she can manage a response. "Thanks. It's been a long time coming."

The guard nods in agreement. "You'll be missed, though I'm sure you won't miss any of us." She gives Cindy a wink and flashes her smile once again. "Get out of here. Enjoy your freedom."

With a couple pats on the car, the guard stands up and reenters the guard booth. I don't waste any time putting the window back up and getting us moving forward again. In my rearview mirror, I catch a glimpse of the guard watching us drive away for only a moment before she turns her attention to something else.

I can't help the huge sigh of relief that escapes me as I turn the car out of the parking lot. The adrenaline fueling my veins from the last few minutes finally catches up to me, erupting out of me in a ridiculous, victorious series of laughs. The smile on my face could not be any wider as I turn to see Cindy sitting next to me, apparent tears of joy staining her wrinkled but grinning cheeks.

It suddenly hits me. Even though we've met before when I was a baby, Cindy and I are only now meeting for the first time, and I'm acting like a complete idiot.

"Sorry," I immediately blurt out, keeping my attention on the road ahead of us. "That was just a little exhilarating, and by exhilarating I mean absolutely frightening."

Cindy remains quiet for a long moment. I can feel her eyes on me as I drive. I can practically hear the unspoken questions gathering in her mouth ready to pour out at me. She clears her throat instead, causing me to jump slightly in my seat.

"You look just like him," she says quietly. "I could have sworn you were Leo pulling up in this car to meet me."

"Believe me, Dad wanted to come. Mom did, too." I pause a moment, shifting in my seat and glancing briefly at Cindy next to me. "I mean, your daughter wanted to be here."

"She's your mom," Cindy interrupts with a dismissive wave of her hand. "You can call her that. I got used to the idea of Morgan being a mom even before you were born."

I can only manage a slight grin. It's strange to talk to someone other than my parents who is my own flesh and blood, especially a person who knows my parents as well as I do.

"I'm glad I could be here," I offer in an effort to change the subject. "I have a lot to tell you, and in the end you'll have some decisions to make. If it's okay with you, I'd like to take you to a motel outside the city so we can talk. I need to lie low while I'm here."

She nods in agreement. "Of course. I go where you go. I don't want to miss a minute with my grandson."

3

By the time we're settled in at a motel not far from Phoenix, the exhaustion from the day starts to hit me. The lack of sleep last night and the large doses of adrenaline from picking up Cindy at the prison have taken their toll on me, but my task here for today has only just begun.

I give Cindy enough time finish eating her lunch before I start up this conversation. I'm not ashamed to say I downed my food in less than two minutes. Giving her the time she needs to eat gives me time to think about how I'm going to do this even though I've already spent countless hours planning this conversation in my head. No matter what words I use, she's not going to like some of what I have to say.

Cindy throws away her trash from lunch before taking a seat on the bed next to me. She wraps her arm around my shoulder and gives me a squeeze. "I still can't believe you're here, Dante. Look at you all grown up."

I can feel the heat of embarrassment in my face at her comments. I shouldn't be overly surprised, I guess. This must be standard grandmother practice, but my natural inclination is to move past these emotional moments and get right down to business.

"I'm here, well, first and foremost, to finally meet you," I begin, giving myself a mental slap in the face at how poorly I'm starting this important conversation, "but also because we have a plan."

Cindy's face contorts sideways in confusion. "I don't understand."

"Let me explain." I take a deep breath and will the right words to come out of my mouth. "We want you and Robert to come live near us. We want to bring the family back together again."

Tears instantly form in Cindy's eyes as she tries and fails to speak. She only nods instead.

"My parents and I have safely lived in our house in the woods all these years," I continue. "We know you lost everything to pay your legal bills during the trial. We want you to start over near us. We have a small house picked out and ready for you. It needs a lot of work, but it's secluded and not too far from us."

I'm quickly surprised and a little overwhelmed as Cindy pulls me into her embrace and cries uncontrollably on my shoulder. I do my best to return her gesture, though I still find this grandmotherly affection difficult to accept. I've always been that way with my mom's signs of affection toward me, too.

Cindy pulls back from me and tries to manage the tears still escaping her eyes. I take the opportunity to grab some tissues from the bathroom and offer them to her.

"Thanks. God, I'm a mess," she says with a small laugh as she runs the tissues over her eyes and nose.

I return to sitting on the bed next to Cindy, cracking my fingers in my lap as a distraction while I wait for her emotions to calm down.

"I'm okay now," she says after a few minutes, sounding more like she's trying to convince herself than convince me. "I would love to come live near you. I'm sure Robert would, too."

My expression turns uneasy, causing concern to flash across Cindy's face. "Robert is where this plan becomes a little more complicated."

"How so?"

"My parents are worried," I begin to explain. "Even though you and Robert will have completed your entire sentences in prison, there's no telling what interest the authorities will have in your lives after you're released, especially for Robert given his history on the police force."

Understanding works its way into Cindy's face. I can see the lines of concern deepening in her features. "You think they'll follow us to you."

I nod slowly. "We don't think the authorities have actively looked for us in years, but given all the past media coverage about my parents and about your trial, we can't be certain that some crazy FBI agent or reporter won't try to follow you to solve the great mystery of where my parents and I disappeared to. We need the world to believe that you and Robert have moved on with your lives." My eyes meet Cindy's and hold her gaze. "We need the authorities to believe that you've moved on from each other."

"What are you saying?" Cindy asks in a whisper. The look on her face is as if I just pulled out her entire world from underneath her.

"It's not as bad as you're thinking," I try to reassure her. "We don't want you two to actually split from each other; we just want everyone to think you have. You were friends with the wives of other police officers who worked with Robert, right?"

Cindy only nods at me.

"We want you to reach out to some of them. Meet them for lunch and explain that you're leaving Robert to start a fresh life somewhere else. Let them believe that you want nothing to do with your past and your family after the twenty years you've spent in prison because of them."

I can't help wincing slightly at my last words. It's painful to think how my grandparents have suffered because of us while my parents and I have remained free.

My words slowly register with Cindy. She looks away for a moment, clearly lost in thought. "So this is all you need me to do? You want me to gossip to the wives so they'll tell their husbands?"

"You have the idea, yes, but it's not the only thing we need you to do." I take a moment to clear my throat and rub my hands together in my lap before I continue. "We need you to tell Robert."

"Excuse me?" Cindy stands up from the bed and starts to back away from me. I immediately stand up to follow her, but when she extends her hand in front of her body as if she wants nothing to do with me, I sit back down on the bed. "You want me to tell my husband while he's still in prison that I want nothing to do with him for the rest of my life? After all we've been through? How can I–"

Her hand flies to her mouth as she turns and makes for the bathroom, slamming the door abruptly behind her.

My first reaction is that I've failed. I've asked too much of this woman who has sacrificed the last twenty years of her life for this family already. I'm only adding to her devastation at a time when she should be elated to be free.

"Fuck," I mutter under my breath, running my hands over my face with the temptation to punch myself for being such an asshole to my grandmother.

Part of me wants to knock on the bathroom door to make sure Cindy's okay. Another part of me wants to call my mom and tell her the plan is off, that we can't make Cindy do this.

I settle with grabbing a motel room key and stepping outside, pacing across the empty parking spaces just outside our room's window with nothing but the thoughts in my head to keep me company.

The door to our room opens some time later and Cindy appears with no sign of emotion on her face. She motions me back inside, and at this point I'm almost reluctant to follow. I hate that I've made her upset with all this.

"I'll do it," she says before I can even close the door behind me. "I'll do as you ask, but you have to promise me you'll make Robert understand as soon as he is out of prison."

I give her a quick nod. "We want the inmates and prison staff to believe the family is broken. That's all."

"The only one who will be broken is Robert. This will devastate him."

"I know. We just want his reaction to be genuine." Cindy looks about ready to cry again, so I try to give her some support and pull her into a hug. "Thank you for doing this. It'll be hard for a while, but once we're all back together, you'll see that it's worth it. I hope Robert will realize that, too."

"He will. He'd do anything for you and your parents. You already know that."

Though I've only known Cindy in person for less than a day, I can feel that familial bond that we already share. I'm getting a glimpse of what it will be like to have our family back together again, and I know for certain now it will all be worth it.

4

Silence. It's filled the space between me and Cindy for the last four days. Since the moment she emerged from visiting her husband in prison, she has barely said a word to me, but the tears she's shed all over the place have told me enough.

There's nothing like tearing your grandmother's heart out then having to drive the entire length of the country with her.

If we had unlimited amounts of phone minutes and battery power, I'd let Cindy talk to my mom the entire drive. Those are the only moments she seems to brighten up and forget that she just broke her husband's heart into a million tiny jagged pieces. To see her smile and laugh in the few times we've called my parents since we got on the road from Arizona has been such a relief but only makes me feel worse when the calls end and we're back to the nothingness, just the stale silence and heavy heartache and the endless road before us.

Thank God we're almost there.

As we make the final turns through the twisting roads deeper into the woods of Maine, my heart rate inevitably picks up. My palms are clammy. I suddenly feel claustrophobic in this car. I shouldn't be nervous about reuniting Cindy with my parents, but for some reason it scares the shit out of me. The hard part of the first half of this plan is done. This should be fucking easy.

The turn into our driveway appears ahead, and something clicks in my brain, a perfect understanding of my current uneasy state.

Our lives will never be the same.

The dirt driveway to the house is long. I can feel the wheels of the car struggle to get through a few patches of mud left over from recent rain. I'm quickly reminded of the difficulties we've had getting up and down this driveway over the years and the countless times we've had to dig out the tires when Dad got overly ambitious about making a supply run before the next snow storm.

We've had so many memories together here, in our house and in these surrounding woods. It's always been just me and my parents, but that's all about to change, and change is scary, even if it's a good change.

I feel some amount of relief the moment I see home. After all the time I've spent cooped up in that small brown box of a house, I never thought I'd miss it and its pointed roof and white shutters around the windows, but it's such a welcome sight.

Seeing my mother run out the front door of it careening toward us makes it all that much better.

Cindy's hands fly to her face as she bursts into tears at seeing her daughter for the first time in over twenty years. As I bring the car to a stop, I can't deny the lump threatening to form in my throat at the sight of Cindy getting out of the car straight into her daughter's embrace. Mom's crying now, sobbing into Cindy's shoulder as they grip on to each other.

I take a deep breath and step out of the car, willing my emotions to stay under control. It helps to see Dad step out of the house, the signature stoic look on his face reminding me to man up and not let myself get mushy about this reunion. Seeing him after hearing Cindy say that I look just like him makes me realize just how right she is. Though my hair doesn't quite reach my ears, it has the same dark and tousled look as my dad's, and there's no mistaking I have his slate blue eyes.

He gives me a nod before grabbing my hand and pulling me into a hug. "Damn fine job, son," he compliments, giving my back a hearty pat.

I pull away from him and return his gesture with a smile. "All that worrying for nothing," I tease, nodding toward Mom and the mess of tears she's sharing with her own mother. "Everything went perfectly."

When Mom and Cindy finally pull back from each other, they immediately come toward us, Cindy pulling Dad into a hug as I am quickly enveloped by Mom's arms. She squeezes me tightly before pulling back to look me up and down. She releases a deep, relieved breath. "You're home and in one piece."

I can't help laughing at her. "Of course I'm in one piece. I just went for a long drive, remember?"

The familiar look for a mother wanting to school her son on the dangers of life plays on her face for only a moment before she bursts into a smile and hugs me again, whispering, "I'm proud of you."

"I'm glad I could bring her back to you," I whisper back, that damn lump in my throat desperately trying to make a reappearance.

She pulls back and looks me directly in the eyes. "Back to us," she says firmly. "This is for all of us, Dante. You need more than just your parents in your life."

If only she knew how true her words are. I won't let it show in my face, but I can feel the happiness and relief within me slipping away, opening up just enough of a crack to let the thoughts lingering in the back of my mind creep in.

I need a lot more of everything in my life. *I need a life.* I can't spend the rest of my days holed up in this house hidden away in the woods. This past week of being out in the world–the actual world that exists beyond the small surrounding towns of Maine– has shown me just what I've been missing, all the places and experiences that most normal people take for granted. Friends packed into a tiny car already half-drunk on their way to a party. Couples holding hands as they walk out of a fancy restaurant after dinner. Families playing at the park seemingly without a care in the world. They may all have their ups and downs, but there is vibrancy in their lives. They have the potential to hold meaning and purpose.

It makes me feel fucking empty.

Dad grabs our bags from the back seat as Mom leads Cindy toward the house, and suddenly I just don't feel like being here anymore. The place that brought me such relief just minutes before is now pushing me away.

"I think I'll go for a drive," I call out to them.

Mom and Cindy are already deep into conversation, so only Dad hears me. He turns around, completely confused. "You've been driving for days. You really want to do more of it?"

I can't hide the dumbfounded look on my face as I realize how stupid this idea sounds. "You three need some time to get reacquainted," I explain, proud of myself for thinking that one up on the fly. "I won't be gone long."

Dad shrugs. "If you insist. Be back before dinner?"

"Deal."

With a quick nod, I hop back in the car and wait for my family to get all the way inside the house before starting the engine and turning around to brave the sinking mud puddles of the driveway again.

It takes only a few minutes of being back on the main road for me to realize just how stupid of an idea this really was. My place of refuge is back in the woods, the clearing and the rock by the creek that bring some amount of peace and solace to my isolated life. I'm just wasting gas driving myself down the endless roads of Maine with no destination, no purpose. Once this grand scheme to bring my family back together again is over, I'll have no purpose again.

I don't know if I can go back to living like that.

The steering wheel quickly becomes the receiving end of my rage. I slam my hand against it as hard as I can, over and over until an achy feeling from my fingers to my wrist tells me I've gone too far. I need to reset my thoughts, to get back on track, to either bring me back in focus or distract me enough not to care.

I need alcohol.

It takes thirty minutes to get to the nearest bar, a place I've eyed up on every supply run I've ever gone on but have never actually visited. Its isolated location on the back roads instead of in the center of town has always made it appealing.

By the time I pull into the parking at CJ's Tavern and park the car, I've committed myself to going inside despite the tiny voice in the back of my mind telling me to turn around and get the hell out of here. The list of reasons why I shouldn't be here is long, but at this moment I don't really give a shit. I'll have one harmless drink and be out of here in no time.

When I step inside, I immediately notice that the tavern is a lot quieter than I expected. Sure, there are only about four people at the bar and a few scattered throughout the tables that take up the majority of the remaining space, but I expected rowdiness and loud music and demands for another drink to be shouted into the air. Instead everyone looks about as miserable as I feel, drowning away their sorrows in the beverages before them in a dark and dreary establishment.

I've apparently come to the perfect place.

Wanting to avoid any and all conversation, I opt for a table in the corner instead of sitting at the bar. I've barely sat down before I hear someone approach me.

"What can I get you?"

The woman's voice comes across like a radiant beam of light through this depressing space. My head tilts up to see the owner of the voice, the perfect mouth that spoke her words, the dimples that sit at the tips of the smile on her face, the shoulder-length brown hair that frames her face. And her eyes. God, her dark brown eyes are the finishing touch on the friendliest and most welcoming face to greet me in as long as I can remember.

I clear my throat and look away for a moment, completely taken off guard by my reaction to this woman who only asked what I want to drink. After quickly composing myself, I reply, "Sam Adams. Lady's choice."

Somehow her smile manages to go even wider as she nods in reply before walking away.

My heart thuds rapidly in my chest as I settle back in the chair and take a deep breath. What the fuck is wrong with me? The last bits of my control after my outburst in the car seem to be scattering away from me. Mentally I'm scrambling to get them back, to refocus and get my shit together before that lovely creature comes back to my table.

I'm acutely aware of the woman's approach as she returns to my corner of the room. My eyes remain focused on her, my posture confident. I'm ready to make up for my strange reaction just moments before.

She stops a foot away from my table, holding the bottle of Boston Lager out in front of her but not extending it to me. She gives me a suspect look. "You look pretty young. Are you sure you're old enough to drink?"

I'm speechless. She's going to scrutinize me for my age even though she can't be much older than me. Given her job here, she's probably been trained to spot underage drinkers. Though I am genuinely of legal drinking age, there is nothing authentic about my ID. My family has lived with fake papers for my entire life.

After a few seconds of her staring at what I'm sure is a horrified look on my face, her doubtful expression dissipates into a huge grin. "I'm just messing with you. Here's your beer."

She offers the bottle to me, and I have to will my hand not to shake as I accept it. "Thanks."

My tentative smile is not nearly as enthusiastic as the beaming look on her face. She studies me for a moment before turning around and calling out over her shoulder, "Let me know if you need anything."

I cup the bottle between my hands, immediately feeling the soothing effects of the cold glass against my sore hand as a sort of calm overtakes my body. The effects may be less the bottle's doing and more from my inability to stop watching my waitress weave through the tables on her way between other customers and the bar. Her body almost bounces as she walks, as if the life within her is so vibrant that it shows through in every move she makes. She's almost always smiling, her expression contagious to the patrons she serves and even to the woman behind the bar helping her serve up drinks.

When she disappears behind two swinging doors next to the bar, my focus returns to where it should be. I take turns between swigs of beer and holding the bottle to my injured hand. I don't dare look to see if my waitress has returned to the room. My eyes instead stay trained on the wall or on the bottle or the front door, anything to keep my mind away from that walking welcoming distraction that does crazy things to my brain.

I grip the bottle a little tighter as I hear her approach. Jesus, I can recognize her footsteps now.

"Here," she says quietly, and I have no choice other than to drag my eyes away from the bottle to look at her. She's holding a small bag of ice toward me. "Much better option than the bottle."

For a moment I'm not sure what to say or do. She was clearly keeping an eye on me just as much as my eyes were following her. She looked closely enough to notice me nursing my injured hand with the cold bottle. She cared enough to get me ice for it.

In my lack of response, she slowly prics the bottle away from my hand and replaces it with the small bag of ice, cupping both the ice pack and my hand between her palms for a couple moments before beaming another smile at me.

Her aura is infectious. I can't hold back the grin on my face as I look away to hide the reddening I can feel working its way into my cheeks. God, this is fucking embarrassing.

"You should see the other guy," I offer in a desperate attempt to laugh it off.

She nods, clearly impressed. "I'm sure your car learned its lesson. Let me guess. Steering wheel?"

Though my pride should feel shaken at being called out like this, I can only laugh. My eyes close and my head falls back and I let the effects of the alcohol or this woman's presence take me away into a fit of laughter before I finally pull myself together enough to respond to her. "That fucking steering wheel."

She gives me a thoughtful look before turning away to tend to the other customers, and the moment she's gone I already miss her. She is clearly affecting me way more than the bottle of beer I've all but finished. Can I not bottle up the energy this woman exudes and bring it with me, let it nurture me and pull me out of the status quo that is my life?

Then I remember the reality of my life, the reason I have no friends and why I was homeschooled by my parents and why there is nothing normal about my existence.

My parents are criminals who have been hiding from the world for over twenty years. We can't make social connections with people who can never know us. Isolation is the price we pay for freedom.

But what point is there to being free if we cannot truly live?

I have to stop this train of thought. I need to get out of this bar and away from the woman who brings life out in me that I haven't felt since I was a kid, back when I didn't fully understand my family's past and the reality of our situation. Ignorance is total fucking bliss. What I wouldn't give to go back to that.

    I toss the ice pack down as if it's on fire and abruptly stand and grab the first paper bill I can find in my wallet. After throwing a twenty down on the table, I make for the door, not daring to look behind me as I take the first steps backward to status quo.

5

It took over two months, but the house is finally complete.

There is an amazing amount of work involved in renovating a house. With the help of their attorney friend, my parents anonymously purchased the structure that looked like nothing more than a beat-up forgotten shack in the woods. I don't think they realized the amount of work that would be required to make it a livable space for my grandparents, but luckily they had me. Throughout the entire project they continually reminded me just how grateful they were for my help.

What they didn't realize is I was grateful for the distraction.

From the moment I picked up Cindy the day she was released from prison almost three months ago, I've been feeding off the feeling of having a purpose to my life. My parents relied on me to bring Cindy back to them. They let me lead the effort to rebuild the house my grandparents would settle in nestled away in the woods of Maine within an hour of our own home.

That feeling of purpose has filled the emptiness inside me. It's only temporary, but I'll take any distraction to put off what I know is going to come crashing down on me eventually. The full realization that I will never lead a normal life is not something I'm ready to face yet. I'm keeping my distance for now, refusing to acknowledge that it's coming.

I need to remain in this beautiful state of denial.

Endless hours poured into replacing broken floorboards, painting walls, and fixing wiring were just what I needed, the ideal means to distraction. When the work ran out and the house was as perfect as Cindy wanted it, my focus immediately shifted to what's next. It rests on me now to bring this plan to completion, to go get Robert and bring him home to us.

Letting me go to pick up Cindy three months ago was almost too much for my parents to bear, but it wasn't as tearful of a goodbye this time. They know I can do it again. I have to believe I can, too, but I know the risk is even higher this time. Robert is the prime target for anyone who will scrutinize his release.

The drive back to Arizona was bittersweet. Exploring the country again and seeing the life and potential that is out there for anyone to grasp but me was almost hard to witness this time. The heavy feeling it placed on me dulled my nerves the entire trip until I finally made it to the enormous state prison surrounded by desert. Its tall barbed wire fence and guard towers were all the reminders I needed that I was willingly throwing myself into the lion's den.

An array of thoughts swirl through my mind as I wait in the car just outside the prison. It's giving me the unwelcome opportunity to reflect on my past and look forward to my future, and I'm realizing that I'm losing sight of what I'm here for. The purpose of this plan is fading from me. I'm forgetting the reason my parents let me come out of hiding and risk my life to do what we've wanted to do for as long as I can remember.

I've stayed in this damn car for far too long. I don't know if it's the cramped walls of the vehicle around me or my current train of thought that seem to be suffocating me, but I have to get out. Throwing the door open, I inhale a deep breath and step out of the car as if there's something deadly inside it. In the short amount of time I have left before today's part of the plan gets underway, I try desperately to reset my thoughts and focus again on my purpose for being here.

The emblazoned sun fills the sky above me. It's the same sun I've known all my life but feels completely different here with its dry heat over this barren desert terrain. I'm far from home, and I know it's dangerous to be here, but this is something I have to do. My family needs this. *I* need this.

And he needs me, too.

We've only had this raging celestial body in the heavens to connect us all together, but its pull on the Earth is nothing compared to the pull of family. Resisting the primal need to be together is something we can't do anymore. There is no moving on with life knowing that the final piece of our family is out there.

We understand the risks. We know what's at stake. We're ready to face whatever the hell life decides to throw at us, because honestly it can't be worse than the difficulties we've already endured. It's time for happiness and love to bring our family back together after being apart for so long.

It's time.

I can feel the sweat beading on the back of my neck as I watch closely for any movement from the massive building in front of me. I'd like to think my body's reaction is from the heat of leaning on this black car in the full sun of mid-afternoon as I wait, but I know nerves are playing their part. While our plan is well underway, this moment is where it could all fall apart. The next few hours will tell me just how risky this self-created situation is.

A blaring buzzer sounds from the building before a metal side door opens. For the intensity of the sound, I would have expected an army to emerge from inside, but only one man with a plastic bag in hand walks out before the door closes abruptly behind him.

He walks with his eyes trained on the ground and no urgency to his movements. Even at this distance I can see the worn lines of age that travel across his skin. His hair is wiry and gray with white patches throughout. As he walks down the path toward the massive barbed wire fence that separates us, I fear the life within him has been as drained as it appears to have affected his body.

Even after the guard at the gate unlocks a door in the fence and allows the man to leave, there is no purpose to the man's steps. He glances up only briefly to acknowledge that there is a car waiting for him as expected, though I see his expression long enough to recognize the look of confusion there.

When he's within feet of me and the car, he finally looks up to meet my gaze and clears his throat. "You're from the cab company?"

It pains me to hear the hopelessness in his voice. Given what this man has endured and what just happened to change his life around, he should be elated, full of anticipation, ready to take on the fucking world.

I smile and avoid his question completely. I won't lie to the man. I will never lie to him. "I'm here to take you home."

He laughs under his breath, a guttural sound full of sarcasm and discontent. I'm on the verge of putting it all out there right at this very moment to make him feel better and understand, but I have to wait until we're on the road. I can't risk anyone seeing his reaction.

Before I can move to do it for him, he opens the front passenger door and takes his seat, slamming the door shut behind him.

I take a brief moment to breathe and remember who I've just met and how long I've waited to meet him. There is no room for anger or frustration between us.

He will understand.

I move around the car and buckle into the driver's seat, glancing only briefly next to me to confirm the scowl I expected would be on the man's face. Without another word, I start up the car and get us on the road.

The car's radio is silent. Only the sound of the air conditioner combating the heat of the summer sun fills the space between us, though the car feels thick with tension.

I need to make him understand, to put his worries to rest. Though I've been ready to do this for an eternity, now that the moment is finally here it's almost impossible to know what to say.

I turn to face him, fully intent on opening my mouth to speak and get the words out with no stopping until he realizes just how great of a turn his life has really taken, but there's no need for me to say a thing. Understanding is written all over his face as his eyes remain fixed on my left hand on the steering wheel.

"Oh my God," he whispers in disbelief. Tears and sparks of life fill his eyes as he raises them to look at me. "It's you, isn't it?"

My heart momentarily jumps to my throat as I glance down at my left wrist and the small black symbol of infinity tattooed there. I slowly bring the car to a stop on the side of the desert road before turning to meet the man's gaze again, swallowing hard before speaking.

"It's good to finally meet you, Grandpa."

A look of shock remains plastered on his face as he is speechless in response to my greeting. For a moment I'm not sure what to do. This man has been through countless ups and downs in this life. His mind has to be jarred from the experience.

After a moment, he seems to come back to reality, glancing me up and down before looking away to discreetly wipe his eyes. Robert laughs to himself before speaking, his voice raspy. "I can't believe I didn't recognize you. You look–"

"Just like my father," I interrupt with an unstoppable smile broadening across my face. "Cindy thought so, too."

"Cindy…" Robert's voice fades away as he stares out the windshield.

"It's not what you think," I quickly chime in. "You need to understand what's going on now that you're away from the prison. I have a lot to tell you, I just need you to listen."

"Is she okay? Is she happy?" Robert's gaze finally returns to me, though his eyes seem reluctant to meet mine as if he's afraid of the answers I'm going to give him.

"She's waiting for you." I pause a moment, letting the weight of my words sink in as a look of disbelief overtakes the worry on Robert's face. "My parents are waiting for you, too."

Robert shakes his head and brings his hand to cover his mouth. I see the understanding work its way into his face. From what my parents tell me, he was a damn fine detective before he was thrown in prison for helping me and my parents evade the law. It seems to have only taken my few words for him to put the pieces together.

He looks away from me, clearly trying to compose himself, and I give him the time he needs. It's uncomfortable to see a grown man break down like this, to see my own grandfather fall apart and be put back together again all in the course of a few minutes.

"You had a plan," he finally manages to say, though he still won't look at me. "You wanted everyone to think the family would never be back together again."

"We wanted the lowest possible chance that there would be interest in the family after you and Cindy were released. We had to reduce the risk."

Robert nods his understanding and takes a deep breath, but it doesn't feel like I've explained enough or apologized enough for what he's gone through.

"Cindy got word to the wives of your old police force about the breakup," I continue. "We're sure they spread the news. Having the prison staff and other prisoners believe it too was the final piece, and that's where you came in. I'm sorry you bore the brunt of that, but we had to make you believe."

A tentative smile breaks out on Robert's face. "Boy, did I believe. Just when I was about to get my life back, it was all taken away from me that day Cindy visited and told me it was over."

It's hard to hear the effect our plan had on Robert and to know that I played a direct part in making him feel that way. "She was devastated after she visited you. I wasn't sure she'd ever speak to me again after that."

With a genuine laugh, Robert turns to look at me, his face finally forming a complete smile. "That sounds like Cindy."

As I see some of the life returning to Robert's features and demeanor, I feel some of the weight and unease lift from my chest. At this moment, it seems like everything might be okay.

My focus shifts to the road ahead of us, the seemingly endless desert that paves the way for the rest of our trip to Maine, the path to beginning the rest of our lives. "Let's get back on the road and get you away from this place."

Robert nods his agreement just as I hear his stomach grumble, its sound amplified in the silence between us. He gives me an apologetic look, but my own stomach is on the same page with his.

"Perhaps a real meal would be in order?" I offer. "We have a long drive ahead of us."

"Where are they?" Robert asks, his eagerness clearly more tied to getting information about the location of our family rather than anything to do with food.

"Maine. We've been in Maine this whole time."

Though Robert seems satisfied with my answer, he still has the look of a million questions all over his face.

I begin to reach behind me, digging around for the cell phone I know to be on the back seat. "We can call them if you'd like to talk–"

"No," Robert abruptly stops me. "Not yet. I can't." He shakes his head and looks at me, the pleading look on his face trying to make me understand. "I need to know more first. I need to process this."

After my best attempt at a reassuring smile, I abandon the search for the cell phone and focus instead on getting the car on the road. "We can talk over lunch, then."

Relief smoothes out Robert's face as he settles back in his seat. The day has only just begun and he already looks exhausted.

Whatever it takes, I'll help him understand.

6

Robert has been quiet during lunch, though I can tell he's deep in thought. He keeps glancing at me then peering around the diner we're in with this strange look I can't quite place. It makes me worried that he sees some danger I don't. It makes me wonder if we should throw money down on the table and get the hell out of here.

I've almost completely finished my sandwich before I can't take it any longer and whisper across the table, "What is it? Do we need to leave?"

Robert waves one hand dismissively in front of him and sets down his coffee mug. "Sorry, it's nothing." There's more he wants to say, but he seems reluctant to proceed.

Setting what's left of my sandwich down on the plate, I try to relax back against the booth seat to let my appetite come back to finish lunch, but I'm finding it hard to get past Robert's strange behavior.

I'm tempted to bring up the subject with him again, but he speaks first. "Your father and I sat in a diner much like this back when we were working together, back when we were looking for your mom when she was taken from both of us."

Anxiety pools in my stomach at Robert's mention of the past, filling whatever space was left of my appetite for lunch.

Robert fiddles with the coffee mug between his hands, the uneasiness rolling off him seeping into me the longer it takes for him to continue speaking. "Did your parents tell you how they met? Did they explain how this all began?"

I shift uncomfortably in my seat and find it impossible to look Robert in the eye when I reply, "They've always believed in being truthful with me, though they didn't tell me the full story until I was a teenager."

I take a moment to look around the almost empty diner, noting a family of four at a booth near the window on the opposite side. The two kids can't be more than five and eight years old as they decorate their placemats with bits of their lunch and pictures drawn in crayon. They look young and innocent, untouched by the troubles of the world and the pains of life. I've been tainted since the moment I was conceived.

"When I was much younger, I'd hear my mom crying and sometimes screaming in the middle of the night. At the time my parents explained she was just having nightmares, but when I was old enough to ask why she had them, they started to explain more of my family's history." I glance at Robert, gauging just how far I should go into this explanation. His face is stoic, his focus completely on me and seemingly ready to accept more, so I continue. "As a teenager I couldn't understand why I had to be homeschooled and could almost never leave home. My rebellion against our reclusive way of life got so bad that my parents had no choice but to tell me their whole story."

Robert nods solemnly, and it suddenly occurs to me the look on his face is one of pity, but I don't want his pity. He has suffered just as much as a result of what happened to my parents as all of us have.

"It was fine," I quickly say to try to dismiss the regretful look on his face. "It was better they told me everything. It was my wakeup call. If I didn't know the full details of what they went through and the danger they faced if they were caught, I never would have got my act together." In this moment of reflection, I'm reminded again why I can never have a normal life. "Ever since that day I've dedicated myself to protecting my family and learning how to survive like my parents. They've taught me everything they know."

Concern and regret lace every line of Robert's face. "I wish you didn't have to live this life. I wish they didn't, either."

"We've accepted it," I reply automatically. "It's the price we pay to remain free, and it's worth paying. We've at least had each other, and now we have you and Cindy."

"There's no one else? What about Jack?"

I can't help my visible reaction to Robert's question, my gaze darting around the room again as I fidget in my seat. This is the part of the conversation I've been dreading. It's one that I left to my parents to explain to Cindy when I brought her home three months ago, but I can't wait that long this time. I promised Cindy I would tell her husband everything when he was released from prison. "Jack is dead. A lot happened after you and Cindy were arrested."

"Tell me," Robert pleads. Even though he must know our story had as happy of an ending as it could given our circumstances, he still looks completely worried about the explanation I'm about to give.

"My parents turned to Jack after our family picture went up all over the news and social media. They had nowhere else to go, and Mark knew they'd go there." Robert's face twists in disgust at the mention of Mark's name. I can't deny the man's name tastes like poison rolling off my tongue. "He's the one who reported you and Cindy to the authorities and told them the location of the house my family lived in. He followed my dad there from a graveyard he was visiting."

The disgusted look on Robert's face quickly turns to shock. "Mark was alive?" As I nod, I can see the wheels turning in his head as he again puts the pieces together. "He came after you."

I nod reluctantly. "He stabbed Jack and tried to steal me in the middle of the night. My parents fought back, but Jack managed to take Mark down enough for my dad to finish the job. Jack died shortly thereafter but not before giving my parents instructions to take all the cash he had and to call his attorney who helped them get settled in their new home."

"In Maine," Robert completes the thought for me. "And you've been living there ever since?"

"We're well-hidden in a small house in the woods. My parents were careful with the money Jack gave them. They've only ever bought the most basic food and supplies for us to survive, and anything else they buy is second-hand. Even after all these years they had more than enough money left to buy you and Cindy a small home not far from us in Maine."

Robert's eyes instantly seem to perk up. "You got us a house?"

"Well, it was more like the basic frame of a house at first, but we've been working hard on it these past few months. My parents and I fixed it up after I brought Cindy to Maine when she was released. The past few weeks she's been busy putting her own finishing touches on it. It's nothing fancy, but–"

"It's going to be perfect." Robert reaches across the table and takes my hand in his. It feels like the first real moment we've connected as family. "Thank you for everything you've done. Thank you for getting me and telling me all of this."

I nod simply because there are no words for me to reply to his gesture. I've accomplished the hard part of what I needed to do. Robert understands. Now I just need to get him home.

"I think I'm ready," Robert says confidently as he squeezes my hand and releases it. "I need to talk to Cindy. I–" He stops to take a breath, seemingly having trouble keeping his emotions in check. "I need to speak with my daughter."

I smile widely in response, trying to let happiness and relief wash over my own swirling emotions at the conversation we've just had and what today means for my family. Pulling the phone out of my pocket, I offer it to the man whose life is about to change in an incredible way. "It's the first saved number. They're waiting for your call."

There's a slight shakiness to Robert's hand as he takes the phone from me. I stand up to offer him a hand getting up from the booth, but he waves me off. "I may look like an old man, but I can still get around just fine." He smiles at me once he's fully to standing. "Thank you, Dante."

I'm left in a bit of unexpected shock at Robert calling me by name for the first time as he makes his way out the door of the diner. Taking my seat again in the booth, I watch through the window as Robert paces the dirt parking lot of the diner and dials the number on the phone.

When he collapses to his knees and puts a hand to his forehead I know the call has connected.

He's reunited with his family again.

I smile even wider and let him have his moment as my appetite returns to finish the rest of my sandwich.

7

The drive back to Maine was just as long as before though not nearly as quiet.

It helped to not have a grieving, emotionally distraught grandparent next to me.

Robert seemed to enjoy our days of driving together. He was eager to get to our destination, insisting that he take the wheel for large portions of the drive to give me a chance to rest and to get us home with as few stops as possible.

It was never addressed out loud between us, but there was a look of reflection on his face as he'd glance over at me in the seat next to him throughout the trip. I know he spent countless hours driving around with my dad when they were an unlikely pair working together to find my mom all those years ago. I wonder if he experienced that sense of déjà vu again with me in this car.

We hit the Maine border after less than three days of being on the road. It's late evening, well past dinner time by the time we drive by the road that leads to my house, but in speaking with my mom an hour before, she said the family would wait to eat dinner until we arrived. Cindy insists on welcoming Robert to their new home with an amazing home-cooked meal that she refuses to let him eat reheated from the microwave.

It makes me smile inside to think these are the kinds of dilemmas my family will have to face going forward.

Robert is awake but quiet next to me, apparently nervous out of his mind as the light of the dashboard shows him twisting his hands in his lap and staring out the windshield at the empty road surrounded by trees and brush ahead of us. The debate in my mind whether to say something to him to calm his nerves is cut short by something catching my eye just as we're making a fast turn around a curve. There's movement on the dirt shoulder of the side of the road.

My throat collapses in a gasp when I see her brown hair whip behind her as she raises her head. The headlights catch her eyes looking at the car–looking at me–and I yank the steering wheel to the side to give plenty of clearance so that I don't hit her.

Robert curses and grabs the dash in front of him as I straighten out the car to finish the curve. I can feel his stare on me as he asks, "You okay?"

"Everything's fine," I quickly reply, daring a glance at the rearview mirror, but she's already gone from my view. "Just wasn't expecting someone walking on the road this late."

Despite my attempts to keep my voice even, I'm sure Robert can sense that seeing that woman on the side of the road has put me completely out of whack. I refused to let myself go back to CJ's Tavern to see the waitress who had such an effect on me the one time I went there three months ago. I busied myself with rebuilding my grandparents' house, not letting my mind linger on her and the life she exuded in every step. As much as I tried to block her from my mind, there was no stopping her from entering my dreams.

Dreams can be beautiful, showing us that which is so incredible and amazing that it can only exist in dreams. They can also be torture, reminding us of the past and of futures we can never have.

I'm still trying to get my head screwed back on straight when we pass by CJ's Tavern only a few minutes later. The irony that it's on the way to my grandparents' house is not lost on me. I've had to pass by it–to be reminded of it and the experience I had with the woman working inside it–each day that I went to work on my grandparents' house as part of my efforts to forget about her and my dead-end life, and I'll continue to pass by it each time I go to visit my grandparents from this day forward.

I never should have gone to that damn tavern in the first place.

Less than twenty minutes and a few side roads later, we're pulling into the driveway to my grandparents' house. After not seeing it for a week, I can more fully appreciate how much better it looks now than it did when we first got the keys to it.

Hanging lanterns on each side of the covered front porch highlight the vertical light blue plank board siding of the one-story house. Two sturdy rocking chairs and a small coffee table fill one side of the porch and planters full of flowers fill the other. I see movement through the window as we approach the house, and within moments the front door swings open.

Cindy is the first to emerge, quickly tearing off her apron and throwing it aside as she takes the few steps down from the porch and practically runs toward the car. Robert is out of the vehicle before I even turn off the engine, and I sit back and watch as my grandparents truly reunite for the first time in over twenty years.

By the time my mom is outside and within Robert's embrace, I almost can't watch anymore. I've hardened myself emotionally, trying to be strong and not let my feelings overwhelm me, but it's difficult to maintain my composure while experiencing this long-awaited reunion. I may not remember or have been part of all the hell my family went through, but I still feel the effects of it right along with them. I've seen my mom suffer and struggle over the years to get past everything that happened to change her life. She never thought she'd have her family back together again, yet here we are.

They embrace each other in tears for a long moment until it appears Cindy has decided to prod her husband toward the front door, no doubt to get him seated at the dining room table for his first home-cooked meal in decades. I can't hide in the car any longer as Mom motions me out of it to follow her.

Before I can even get out of my seat, she has her arms around me. The wetness on her cheeks sparkles from the light from the porch, making the broad smile on her face look even brighter.

"You did it, Dante," she whispers in my ear. "You brought them both back." I can feel the silent sob in her chest as she pulls me even closer to her.

Dad walks up behind us, pulling us both against him for a moment before we all pull back from each other. "You did great."

She nods in agreement with him, grinning with an easy and impenetrable happiness that I'm not sure I've ever seen from her before, and for a moment I feel absolute satisfaction in what I've done with my life. My goal has been fulfilled. My family is back together again, and I've served my purpose. This is the first day of the rest of our lives.

Lives that will still be lived in seclusion. Lives that will never be normal.

I swallow away the tightness in my throat. My emotions are running wild now. Between seeing the woman on the side of the road, to seeing my family back together again, to realizing I've accomplished everything I've set out to do since the moment my mom came up with the idea to reunite our family, I'm left with nothing but an empty feeling.

I don't know what tomorrow will bring. It's the bad kind of blank slate. The entire world is out there for me to embrace, but I'm forced to watch it from a distance. It's this damn snow globe in the palm of my hand that I can clearly see inside but never truly experience. I have nothing to grasp on to, nothing to hope for.

"You had better get inside before Cindy scolds you for being late for dinner," I say with a forced smile and a nod toward the house. Mom is still wiping away tears but laughs at my comment as Dad wraps his arm around her and leads her toward the front door.

I'm left in the silence and darkness of the night as I grab our bags from the trunk of the car. The sharp sound of the trunk closing echoes out into the sky, marking the definitive end to this part of my journey.

This part of my journey. My journey isn't over. It doesn't have to end here. My parents taught me everything they know. They've lived as wanted fugitives these past twenty-one years and managed to survive their interactions with the outside world without being caught. I know exactly how to blend in, how to remain under the radar and avoid attention. If I'm careful, I can have a life outside these woods. The world has much to offer. I only need to embrace it.

Turning to the warm and inviting home in front of me, I resolve to enjoy this night with my reunited family, to bask a little in what we just accomplished, and to daydream about what comes next.

The next step is right there in front of me. All I need to do is take it.

8

I feel a bit like a stalker. I'm not going to lie.

After spending much of the next day with my parents and grandparents, the first in a long series of days to make up lost time from these past twenty-one years, I've opted to go for a drive, which really means I'm going to CJ's Tavern. I have no idea what days or hours this woman works, but I'm hoping she'll be there.

After pulling into the parking lot, I step out of the car with purpose to my steps. The last time I was here was for alcohol. This time I'm here for her.

The smell of cigarette smoke practically bellows out the door as I open it. It's not difficult to find the source. Four gruff-looking men are seated near the door, each with a tall glass of beer in front of them and cigarettes hanging from their mouths as they laugh much louder than necessary about something.

I look past them in search of who I'm here for, the woman haunting my dreams whose name I didn't even catch the last time I was here. My heart sinks a little when I don't see her smiling face and lively movements around the tables, but I opt to take a seat in the same corner table I sat at before anyway.

While many of the tables remain empty, the seats at the bar are completely full, and there's no question why. The bartender tonight is a young blond woman with a tight white T-shirt that doesn't leave much to the imagination. When she leans over the bar, each customer is clearly getting more out of her service than the drink she has in her hand.

Yes, I've been attracted to beautiful women and should be just as attracted to this busty bartender right now as the men lined up to order drinks from her at the bar, but my mind is completely elsewhere, stuck on a certain lively brunette I don't even know.

After a few minutes I begin to realize how stupid I am for being here, for stalking this poor woman in her workplace and being one of hundreds of other men who surely come to this tavern to drool over women they can never have. Despite this realization, I find myself still planted firmly in this seat with no intention of moving.

My persistence is rewarded when the door next to the bar opens and the brunette comes bustling out, her hands completely full with trays of food balanced delicately on her open palms above her. I watch with amazement as she glides between the tables to drop off each tray of food to its appropriate set of patrons seated at tables on the other side of the tavern. She still has that bounce to her step and that vivid smile on her face.

She glances in my direction with a sly grin before making her way toward my table. With each step she takes toward me, my heart beats just a little faster and I feel myself becoming more alive.

Without saying a word, she grasps my hand from the table and holds it between both of hers, inspecting it thoroughly and hesitating only briefly when her thumb runs over the lines of the small infinity tattoo on my wrist.

After setting my hand back down on the table, she eyes me up with a satisfied grin. "I was afraid you picked a fight with your car again."

I can't help the laugh that escapes me or the broad smile on my face. "We've been getting along better for the most part."

"Good. Your car must have learned its place." She glances away from me and almost nervously tucks a piece of hair behind her ear. "So what brings you back here? Haven't seen you in a while."

"You," I reply simply, but when her eyes return to mine, their strange shyness is replaced by a look of annoyance like she's heard this a thousand times before. I find myself scrambling to explain. "I mean, I saw you last night on the road. It was dark and you were walking alone."

"I don't live far from here," she replies defensively as she grabs for her notepad and pen, clearly ready to move on to business. After scribbling something on the notepad she stops and slowly lifts her head back up toward me. "Wait. Were you in that car that swerved away from me last night?"

I bite my lip and nod reluctantly. "I wasn't expecting anyone on the road. I'm sorry if I scared you."

"That was really dangerous, you know. Another car could have been coming around the curve and hit you." She shuffles her feet beneath her awkwardly. "I appreciate you not wanting to hit me, though."

"Honestly you shouldn't even be walking on that road at night. A drunk driver could hit you. Someone could attack you."

She shrugs off my comments and straightens her stance. "It's not that far to walk. I'm perfectly capable of taking care of myself, but thank you for your concern…" she pauses, looking at me expectantly for my name.

"Dante," I fill in for her, extending my hand.

"Dante," she repeats thoughtfully as she shakes my hand with a warm smile. "I'm Lily."

I'm trying to keep an even face as our hands release, but inside my mind is reeling over how perfect her name is. It's only appropriate that someone as stunning and lively as she is would have such a beautiful name.

Lily and I both turn at the sound of her name being yelled from the door next to the bar. I've clearly kept her at this table longer than she should have been.

With a rushed smile, Lily returns her attention to me and asks, "You want the same as last time? Sam Adams, was it?"

I nod, unable to hide the impressed look on my face. "Thanks, Lily."

She tucks away the pad of paper and pen in her back pocket as she turns and quickly weaves through the tables to the bar. She gets my drink and quickly returns with it, leaning her arms on my table as she sets it down and whispers within inches of my face, "Don't disappear on me this time."

I don't know whether I'm more shocked by what she's said or the glimpse she's inadvertently giving me to the cleavage showing in the crook of her V-neck shirt. I acknowledge her with a silent nod as she straightens up and leaves my table to go through the door next to the bar.

The rest of the tavern is only a blur to me as my mind remains focused on Lily even when she's out of my sight. I mindlessly drink my beer as I watch her do her thing, taking drink orders and clearing empty plates from tables. The smile never leaves her face as she works, and it brightens just a little when she steals glances at me. I'm not sure what to think of how she's interacted with me tonight other than I know from watching her work that she's treating me differently than her other patrons. Something warm swells within my chest to receive that kind of attention from her when I've spent my entire life moving in the shadows and blending into the world around me.

Within seconds of my beer bottle being empty, Lily is at my table offering me another.

"I'm all set," I politely decline.

The hint of disappointment plays on Lily's face as she tears off my bill from the notepad and sets it on the table.

"What time do you get off work?" I ask impulsively.

"We close at nine o'clock."

I glance at the clock encircled with blue neon lights that hangs above the bar. It's a half-hour until close. "Let me drive you home tonight?" I offer. She looks at me with only partially feigned skepticism, but I explain myself anyway. "I don't like the idea of you walking home alone this late."

She opens her mouth to speak but seems to catch herself before the words actually make it out of her. "Deal, but I'm driving," she counters. "What if you look all sweet and innocent but you're actually some crazy person trying to steal me away?"

My face blanches a little at her comment. She's completely right in what she's saying, but she has no idea that she just touched on multiple uneasy subjects for me. I'm not innocent in the eyes of the law, living with my fugitive parents under a fake name, and the only reason I exist is because both of my parents were ultimately brought together after being taken away from their families by a psychopath.

"What if you're just as crazy and want to steal *me* away?" I fight back with a teasing smile, doing whatever I can to recover and hide my discomfort.

She tries and fails to hold in a small fit of laughter. "You got me there. I guess you'll just have to take the risk."

Take the risk. That's exactly what I'm already doing. My presence in this tavern bringing attention to myself with this woman is completely against every directive my parents have given me since I was old enough to understand my family's situation. I think that's what my life is lacking, though. I've never taken risks, never dared to step outside the neatly marked box my parents created for my life. I may never know true freedom, but I'll be damned if I don't at least get the opportunity to live a little.

"You can drive," I decide. "I'll take my chances."

A pleased, victorious grin spreads across Lily's face. "Great. I look forward to it."

As she walks away, I can't help the increasingly rapid beat of my heart against my ribcage. What have I agreed to do? I've hardly even spoken to other women before, let alone tried to court one of them. Is this whole song and dance my pitiful attempt at flirting with my waitress at a bar? She agreed to go with me, though. I guess my effort isn't so pitiful if it actually works?

It's only now that I realize I'm watching Lily move around the room with a different pair of eyes. I'm noticing the way the other men in the bar interact with her, from motioning for her to bend down closer to speak to her, no doubt to get a better view down her chest, to clearly checking out her ass as she walks away.

A strange feeling of jealous rage builds inside me with each interaction I see. To anyone else, even to Lily, these actions must seem completely benign and insignificant, but to me they trigger some kind of internal protective beast that wants to drag Lily away from these men and this tavern forever.

By the time nine o'clock rolls around and the place is emptying out, I've calmed down significantly from the chaos that was erupting inside me. Knowing that I'd be the last patron to leave the tavern and that I'd be leaving with Lily in my car gives me a strange sense of pride and accomplishment.

Lily emerges from the door next to the bar with a purse on her shoulder. "Ready for a ride?" she asks, though I swear I hear a hint of playfulness in her voice as she says it.

I don't quite know how to respond to that, but I manage to nod and stand immediately to follow her out the front door.

It's completely dark outside as we walk into the almost empty parking lot. The air is a bit crisp for a summer evening, but I find it refreshing. It doesn't seem to bother Lily either in her short-sleeved shirt and jean shorts as I lead her toward my black sedan.

Lily stops in front of the vehicle and holds her hand out to me expectantly. "Keys, kind sir?"

I pull them from my pocket, noting how warm the metal is as I place them in Lily's hand. My fingers inadvertently brush the soft skin of her wrist as I pull my hand away, and in that moment our eyes find each other through the relative darkness surrounding us.

Her expression makes it impossible for me to read what she's thinking. I'd give anything to know whether our touch affected her as much as it affected me. I'm still trying to wrap my head around it as I take a seat in the passenger side of the car and watch Lily buckle into the driver's seat. She settles in and starts up the car as if she's driven it a million times before.

The dashboard lights up and the radio comes to life, the speakers blasting the local classic rock station louder than I would have liked. I scramble to turn down the music, but Lily's hand covers mine and she stops me, her fingers slowly entwining with my fingers around the volume knob to leave the music on but not nearly as loud as it was. Our hands remain there as our gazes meet, and this time there is no room for interpretation in the expression on Lily's face.

She's going to kiss me.

Her hand leaves mine to cup my cheek as she moves her upper body forward and presses her lips to mine. She's in complete control, her entire body moving with each kiss as she finds my lips over and over again with a subtle intensity likes she needs this more than air to breathe.

My heart races as she unbuckles her seatbelt and pushes herself over the center console to straddle me, her lips barely leaving mine in the process. I've never done anything like this before, but I don't stop her. It's an exhilarating feeling to let her do exactly as she pleases, to throw myself into this primal experience I've dreamed about for years.

As her hand leaves my face to trail down my neck and chest, I become acutely aware that my hardness is pressing up against her bare thigh, but strangely I'm not embarrassed by it. It only encourages me to become more involved in this completely spontaneous exchange between us as I grab Lily's hips and slowly grind against her.

Our lips part briefly as the breath of a moan escapes Lily's mouth, but that's all the time it takes for the passionate moment between us to dissipate. She presses on my shoulders to push herself back, putting as much space between us as my car will allow. She's practically panting, her cleavage pressing in and out of her shirt with each movement of her chest as she hovers over me.

"I have to stop," she whispers, sounding more like she's trying to speak to herself than me. Her eyes meet mine, and in the soft glow from the dashboard, I can see the apologetic look in them. "I'm sorry, Dante. I got a little carried away."

I'm not sure how to respond. I'm not sorry it happened, though I'm not sure how far I would have let her go anyway given we just learned each other's names less than two hours ago and I've never been intimate with a woman before.

Lily works herself off my lap and settles back into the driver's seat, the pink in her cheeks from our exchange or from her embarrassment clearly present even in the dim lighting of the car. I want to reach out to her and relieve her worry, but I keep my hands to myself and give her my best comforting smile instead. "I think we were both getting carried away."

"Maybe." A look of relief crosses her face as she clears her throat and runs her fingers through her hair nervously. With a deep breath she puts the car in reverse and backs us out of the parking lot.

Luckily she wasn't kidding about living close to the tavern. It takes only five minutes to drive there. Any longer and the awkward avoidance of conversation between us would have been unbearable. Lily pulls the car into a development of small two-story homes in a less wooded area not too far off the main road.

As she pulls into the driveway of one of the small white buildings, a spotlight above the single garage door automatically turns on. Lily wastes no time opening her door and hopping out of the car, so I do the same.

She walks around the front of the car to me, and I swear I see a flicker of debate cross her face as she meets my gaze. "Thanks for letting me drive," she says, biting her lip momentarily before adding, "both times."

My breath catches a bit as she says this, and my response comes out as more of a laugh. "Believe me, I enjoyed the ride."

The look of indecision makes a reappearance on her face as she grins and turns toward the front door. She only gets a few steps closer to it before she stops abruptly and turns back to me. "Coffee tomorrow?"

"Coffee?" I reply, dumbfounded at her suggestion.

She laughs at my response, seeming to relax a little. "Yes. You, me, and two cups of coffee coming together somewhere other than the tavern or your car."

"Sure," I accept before I realize what I'm saying. I'm not supposed to be interacting with people like this. Getting close to people is not conducive to my family's lifestyle.

It's only coffee, though. How harmful could a cup of coffee be?

"Great. Pick me up at ten o'clock?"

I nod, my mind racing at the implications of what I've just done.

I've made out with a woman for the first time.

I've scheduled my first date.

I've broken every rule my parents ever taught me.

But I'm living. I feel the effects of it pulsing through my veins. The residual exhilaration from tonight and my anxiety about tomorrow will make it impossible to sleep, but I welcome every second of it, because this is what I've been waiting for my entire life.

The bright look of anticipation on Lily's face as she turns toward her front door only confirms that I've made the right decision. My face almost hurts from smiling as I watch her disappear across the threshold and close the door behind her.

9

By the time I pull into the driveway at home, it hits me how exceptionally late it is for me to be out. My parents will question where I've been, and my dread at facing this only deepens when I park in front of the house next to the old forest green SUV we bought off Craigslist for my grandparents to drive.

I reluctantly turn off the engine and step out of the car into the refreshing night air. With a deep breath, I make my way toward the front door, though each footstep feels heavier the closer I get to it.

The sound of laughter from within the house greets my ears as I fiddle with my keys in the front door. When the lock finally releases, I swing the door open to find my parents and grandparents in full-on smiles sitting across from each other in the living room, a couple bottles of liquor and a few empty shot glasses resting on the wooden table between them.

Mom gets up from her chair to approach me as the laughter in the room dies down at my sudden appearance. She pulls me into a hug and holds me there. "We were getting worried about you."

Returning her embrace, I smile to the rest of my family over her shoulder. "Sorry, I was gone later than I expected."

"I'm just glad you're home." She squeezes me just a little harder before finally releasing me.

"What were you up to?" Dad asks, shattering the fragile bubble of relief that surrounded me just a moment before.

I glance around the room as if the response I'm looking for may be written clearly on the walls in front of me. Instead of finding a way out, I face the issue with my dad head-on. "I stopped for a drink at the bar." It's not the full truth, but it's not a lie, either.

Dad's face remains expressionless while Mom jabs my shoulder and frowns with disapproval. "You shouldn't be spending money like that. You should know better than–"

"You met a girl."

Everyone turns to Robert at his comment before the entire room stills. My heart races in my chest–its pounding probably audible across the room at this point–but I don't otherwise make a sound.

Mom is the first to turn to me, looking me up and down as if something may be seriously wrong with me. "I don't understand."

"I've seen that look before," Robert explains as studies me with a penetrating gaze. "It's the same look I saw on Leo's face all those years ago." He stops and thinks for a moment, and I fear the next words to come out of his mouth because I can clearly see the wheels turning in his head. "The woman on the road last night. We passed a bar not long after we saw her. She's the one you're seeing?"

My hand involuntarily moves to my temple. I can almost feel the headache coming on in the wake of this conversation that is getting way out of hand too quickly. I need to contain this wildfire before it spreads any further. "I'm not seeing anyone. I offered her a ride home from work today so she wouldn't be walking in the dark." It takes me a moment to clear my throat and work up the courage for what I'm about to say next. "I'm also meeting her for coffee in the morning."

"What are you thinking?" Mom asks, her voice practically begging me to deny the whole thing. She pulls me to look at her, and I can barely meet her gaze. "You know the rules. You can't get too close to people. You're not supposed to bring attention to yourself. We need to remain invisible."

My heart sinks at her words even though I know each one is true. Is it selfish of me to bring more risk into our lives for the sake of actually living my life?

"I…"

The words start and fail to come out of my mouth, the debate in my mind over what's right and wrong overpowering my ability to explain myself. As I look around the room and meet the concerned gazes of each of my family members, I absolutely lose it. My temper flares within me, igniting some hidden part of me that has been repressed since back when I was a rebellious teenager ignorant of my family's unique situation.

"Look at us," I burst out in a fury. "We're here together now as a family. No one is looking for us. No one is following us. No one gives a damn about our fucked-up family anymore." My blood is boiling at this point, the rage within me overpowering its banks and about ready to overflow even more than it already has. "Why can't we be more normal now?"

"It's too risky," Dad growls, and in that moment I can see my own rabid temper mirrored in my father as he stands up from the chair. "You have no idea what this family has been through. Each one of us has sacrificed everything to be here. Our friend died to give you this chance at a life of freedom, and you just want to throw it all away!"

Dad's mention of Jack Pearce–the aging doctor who brought me into this world and sacrificed his life to save my family–brings my tirade to a halt, and suddenly it feels impossible to be in the same room with these people any longer. I'm caught up in an inescapable whirlwind of guilt and anger and indecision as I turn and bolt down the small hallway to my room and slam the door behind me.

Just as I turn the lock, I feel the doorknob jiggle and clank loudly before loud pounding starts up against my wooden door.

"Dante. Open this damn door!"

Dad's verbal and physical assault on my door continues, and for a moment I wonder if he's going to break the door in. It's not until I hear Mom's voice outside that everything stops.

I can't make out what my parents are saying in their hushed discussion just outside my room, but eventually heavy footsteps move away from me down the hall and my mom's voice is all that remains.

"Enjoy your coffee tomorrow. We'll talk when you get home."

I don't know what to say. No response seems appropriate. I feel like a fucking child in how I just acted. It was wrong and I was disrespectful to my family, but how else was I supposed to react? The way my life was before just isn't enough now. I need to do more than just exist. I need to actually live.

Someday they'll understand.

I know I should go out there and apologize. I should ask the people I owe everything to for forgiveness, but I'm not ready to face them yet. It's stupid of me, but I'm going to stay tucked away in my room, ready to face a restless night torn between a life of safety and a life worth living. There are two clear paths I can take, one with significantly more risk than the other, and I can't take them both.

Until now I've never known the turmoil of true sleeplessness. Being stuck in the conscious world amidst silence and darkness for hours with my only my jumbled thoughts to accompany me is agonizing.

The morning comes painfully slow as last night's fight with my parents left me with too much to think about. In these hours I've been lying awake in bed, I've reflected on the past I remember and the past I've only heard stories about. I've looked to the future, to who I want to be and what I want to do with my life. The possibilities are endless, all laid out before me awaiting my move, and I don't have a fucking clue what to do.

The moment I see the hint of brightening outside behind the curtains over my window, I'm out of bed and getting dressed. The twilight of morning is barely introducing itself to the sky, but I need to get out there. I need to put some space between me and this house that has essentially encompassed my entire life.

I remain as silent as possible as I leave my room and stop at the bathroom across the hall. Glancing at the closed door to my parents' room only fuels me to get out of this house faster. I'm not ready to talk to them about my explosion of emotion last night. I'm not sure I'm ready to even think about it yet.

After grabbing my keys, I slink out the front door and lock it quietly behind me. It takes only seconds of being out in the open air for me to feel better, as if the weight on my chest has finally been lifted just enough for me to breathe again.

There's barely enough light now to guide me through the forest, but I hardly need it to get me to my destination. I've been down this path to my sanctuary in the woods too many times before.

With each step I take closer to it, I start to feel better, but at the same time I wonder whether this is what I should really be doing. I'm effectively running from something that I should be standing up to face head-on. I'm hiding my issues deep inside and reverting back to a state that is comfortable and safe by coming back to this place of solitude in the woods.

By the time I reach the large rock perfectly nestled amidst the trees next to the creek, the sky has brightened significantly in its preparation to fully greet the sun. I take my usual seat on the flattened natural bench at the top of the rock and bring my knees to my chest, fully expecting my presence in this almost sacred place to immediately wash me over with the comfort and clarity this spot of nature can provide, but something is off. I find it does nothing for me.

I feel nothing.

This was enough before. Just being here in this place where the rest of the world was irrelevant made me feel better. Out of the entire planet, I had at least this one place where it was okay to be all alone and not a part of anything larger than me or my family.

A slight bit of panic rises up within me at the realization that I can't find that relief now. For whatever reason, it's not enough for me anymore. The world has everything to offer yet it all feels beyond my grasp. I feel like I belong nowhere.

Absolutely fucking nowhere.

I can't sit here a moment longer. I don't want these thoughts and this moment to scar my good memories of this place any more than they already have. After hopping down from the rock, I glance back at it and wonder if my sanctuary that has helped keep me sane for years is finally lost to me. It feels tainted now, a bad moment in time that has seeped into my brain and ruined the beauty and comfort of this spot from this day forward.

As I make my way back through the woods, it seems an ironic gesture that time has chosen this moment to allow the sun to fully rise, to bathe the sky above me in radiant morning sunlight when I feel overwhelmingly drenched in darkness. I press on back toward the house, though I have no intention of reentering it. I'm not ready to face my parents. I'm not sure I'm even ready to face Lily, but the desire to smile and laugh and forget about my strange place or lack of place in the world is enough to overpower my reservations about going forward with the coffee date.

Today is a test. By the end of the day I want to choose a path for my life and be confident in the direction I've chosen.

10

It feels like the morning has lasted for ages already, but it's finally close enough to ten o'clock for me to make my way to Lily's place and put an end to my aimless driving around the area to kill time before our coffee date. I'm ready for a reprieve from being alone with my thoughts. I'm ready for distraction and the refreshing shot of life that Lily is about to inject into my day.

As I pull into the housing development where she lives and park outside her garage door, some of the pain and difficulty that have weighed me down since last night start to lift. When I see Lily's beaming face emerge from the house and her brown hair bouncing all around her as she turns to lock the front door, everything about me and this day seems to lighten even more. She is exactly the person I should be with at this moment.

I get out of the car and run around it to the other side. Lily's zipping along so quickly from her front door to the car that I'm starting to wonder if she's had a few cups of coffee already.

"Hey," I greet her with an unstoppable smile on my face as we meet up by the passenger-side door.

She seems to sigh a little in relief. "So glad you're here." When I give her a sideways glance in confusion at her comment, she waves her hand dismissively between us. "Sorry, I was just a little worried you might not show up after how I practically attacked you in your car last night."

Heat courses through me at the reminder of my first kiss that progressed much further than first kisses should. It's hard to keep a straight face when I respond to her. "You'll have to try harder if you're looking to scare me away."

She pushes my shoulder playfully before opening the passenger-side door. "You're one of the good ones. Why would I want to scare you away?"

Though she's clearly joking around, a glimpse of seriousness plays out on her face as she takes a seat. I debate whether to ask her about it further as I make my way around the front of the car to the driver's side but opt to keep my mouth shut. I'd rather keep the tone of our morning light and fun as I take a seat next to her. "Well, you're letting me drive now. I consider that a good sign."

"If you wanted to take advantage of me, I think you would have tried when I gave you the perfect opportunity last night." Her cheeks seem to redden just a shade with her words. "Sorry again about that. It's just a bit of a turn on to find a guy who looks at me like more than a walking piece of meat."

I'm a bit taken aback by her bluntness and am left dumbfounded at how to respond, but once the shock of it passes, I finally realize what she's trying to say.

She's into me. This girl might actually have a thing for me.

I buckle in and turn on the car with renewed vigor pulsing through me, suddenly feeling more than okay about my decision to accept this coffee date and step outside my safety bubble.

"So… coffee," Lily bursts in before I can even put the car in reverse. "Do you even know where we're going?"

My reply is immediate. "Lady's choice."

"I was hoping you'd say that." She buckles in as we hit the stop sign before the main road. "I know there are cute little coffee shops in town, but I have to admit I'm a Starbucks girl."

"Starbucks it is, then," I declare, taking us in the direction of the nearest Starbucks just outside of the nearby town.

Lily seemed to like having the radio on last night, so I fiddle with the volume until the local classic rock station is just loud enough to hear without overpowering any conversation. She smiles and moves her head back and forth just enough to tell me she recognizes this song and is clearly enjoying it.

I can't help my curiosity. "You know this song?"

"I know all these songs." She closes her eyes for a long moment and seems to absorb every note of the music and word of the lyrics. It's hard to keep my eyes on the road when all I want to do is watch her experience this music. "My dad was a huge fan of classic rock." Her eyes open and some of the pure joy that was there a moment ago seems lost from her expression. "I know you're going to ask the question, so I'm just going to get the answer out of the way now. He died in a car accident when I was three. You don't have to say anything about it or feel sorry for me. I'm just glad I can hold on to the pieces of his life that I can."

Our light and fun morning just took a morbid turn. I'm glad she alleviated my need to reply, because no words would seem appropriate at the moment to talk about her dead father.

We remain immersed in the music until I notice the tavern up ahead. "You have the day off today?"

She shakes her head. "Working from two o'clock until close unfortunately." She pauses a moment, though her upper body doesn't stop its small movements to the music. "Do you have to get to work at some point?"

"Not working today."

"Not working just today, or any day?" A playfully skeptical look crosses Lily's face. "Are you sure you're not playing hooky just to hang out with me this morning?"

This girl is something else. It's difficult to hold back the laugh building inside me, but I manage to restrain myself. "I can assure you that I have nowhere else to be today."

"Oh no. Don't tell me." She looks horrified for a moment and slinks away from me in her seat. "You don't live in your parents' basement, do you?"

The car keeps moving us forward, but all thoughts and emotions within me come to a screeching halt. I direct my attention to the road for a moment before chancing a glance back at Lily. How do I approach this topic honestly without sounding like a total loser? "I do live with my parents," I begin to explain, "but that's mostly because I don't really have anywhere else I can go at this point."

A new song starts up on the radio, a slower tempo that seems to bring down the energy of the entire car, the perfect complement to my admission.

"I get that," Lily finally acknowledges after a few moments of silence between us. "I think you'll like breaking away from them, though. Once you're finally out on your own, you'll realize it was well worth the wait."

"I hope so." Though I should know better than to go any further into this conversation, I let more honesty seep out of me. "I'm at an interesting point in my life," I continue, though I can't look at her as I say these words. My gaze remains straight ahead of me, only looking forward. "I've accepted the way things were for a long time, but I'm not sure I can do that anymore. It's just not enough for me now."

The somber melody on the radio fills the space between us. Lily doesn't respond to me. I don't know if she's even still paying attention to me and my random ramblings about life. I know I need to turn to see her, to read the expression on her face to understand just how stupid of an idea it was to open up to her like this, but I'm afraid of what I'll see there. Other than with my parents, I've never opened myself up to anyone like this.

"Here's the deal," she finally speaks up, her tone completely serious. She doesn't continue, forcing to me to look at her to see why she's not talking when she clearly has something to say. When I glance over and our eyes meet, I realize the expression on her face is kind and genuine. She's really trying to help me here. "You, sir, need a new beginning. You need to do what makes you happy, otherwise what's the point to life?"

"I wish it was that easy," I blurt out before immediately wishing I could retract those words that I have no desire to explain. Though this conversation is definitely uncomfortable for me, it feels good to talk about this subject with someone who clearly understands my point of view.

Luckily Lily doesn't press me on what I've said as she points straight ahead of us. "There it is. The happiest place on Earth."

I'm thoroughly confused by Lily's excitement until I see the Starbucks appear up ahead. Relief almost immediately washes over me at seeing our destination and knowing this difficult conversation is at an end.

As I'm pulling into the parking lot, a more upbeat song comes on the radio, gratefully easing away even more of the heaviness in the air of the car from just moments before. I hope we can take some of that energy with us to liven up this coffee date that was meant to be much more relaxed and carefree than this.

Lily's natural bounce to her step is back as she gets out of the car and moves to the entrance of the Starbucks.

"Are you sure you didn't have a cup or two already before I picked you up?" I tease.

After a scolding look and a quick stick of her tongue out at me, Lily disappears behind the door and looks me straight in the eye as she purposefully neglects to hold the door open for me.

The laugh I was holding in earlier that I thought had been extinguished by our previous conversation finally does escape me, and the feeling I get along with it is addictive. With a few long strides, I make it to the door and practically chase Lily the rest of the way inside.

"I've learned my lesson," I concede when I finally join Lily in the ordering line. "Never make fun of a girl's addiction to coffee."

"Don't even joke about coffee," she admonishes me with a serious tone that is completely betrayed by the slight grin on her face. "You must treat coffee with the utmost respect, for it is the greatest substance to exist on this Earth. It is the fuel behind mankind."

I throw my hands out in front of me in defeat, easily giving in on this fight as we take a step forward as the next in line at the register.

Lily greets the employee behind the counter before placing her order. "I'll have a grande half-skinny extra hot triple shot latte with whip, please," she recites with absolute ease.

The employee doesn't bat an eye at taking the order from her before turning to me, eagerly awaiting my order. A quick glance at the menu only serves to intimidate me more. I can immediately tell it will be no help. I don't have a clue what to say, so I stick with what I know. "I'll just have a small black coffee, please."

That's when everything seems to stop. It feels like the entire population inside this Starbucks is looking at me like some kind of freak.

"Wait. Hold on." Lily repositions herself in front of me, putting herself between me and the employee behind the counter and pointing her finger to my chest. "You did not just order a small black coffee." She doesn't even give me a chance to reply before swinging around to the employee with a decisive nod over her shoulder at me. "He'll have what I'm having."

Everything seems to go back to normal–the end of the world no longer imminent–as the employee rings up the order at the register. I fish some cash out of my wallet before Lily even has a chance to open her purse, and she doesn't fight me when I pay for our drinks.

She leans toward me and whispers, "You owe me for bailing you out on your drink order anyway. We need to have a discussion about that."

I collect my change just as Lily drags me by the elbow toward an empty table next to the window.

"Small black coffee? What planet are you from?" she questions in disbelief as we take our seats. "This is Starbucks. You get extra points the more complicated your order is."

"Sorry, I'm not fluent in whatever that language was you were speaking."

"Hopeless." Lily throws her hands up in the air in mock frustration before returning her eyes to meet my gaze, her look becoming more serious. "Have you really never been to Starbucks before?"

In the direction of this conversation, I can sense the reemergence of that uncomfortable exchange from the car. "I'm used to Folgers at home and gas station coffee on the road. That's just who I am as a coffee person. Take it or leave it."

"I will convert you yet," Lily declares with a look of absolute determination in her eyes. "Though I'm starting to feel like your waitress here. You let me choose your beer for you at the tavern and now I'm ordering your drinks at Starbucks." She gives me a playful shove. "I'm off the clock, damn it."

"Okay, you got me there," I admit. "But think about it, you're doing a good deed keeping me hydrated and preventing my total humiliation at the same time."

"I prevented nothing of the sort. I bailed you out, but you were well past the embarrassment stage at that point."

She gets up from the table, leaving me with my slightly bruised ego as she makes her way to the pickup area just as our drinks are set out on the counter. When she returns with the cups and sets mine down in front of me, the delicious smell of coffee wafts in the air around us. I'll admit my mouth is salivating at the smell of it.

Lily holds her cup between her hands and seems to study it, or maybe she's just not sure what to say now that she's proven how inept I am at making a worthy drink order. Her eyes never leave the cup even when she finally starts to speak. "You know I never did catch your last name, Dante."

There's a slight twist in my heart at being indirectly asked this question. The world only knows me by my fake name, though I at least got to keep my real first name. Even when my grandparents were ruthlessly questioned by the authorities after they were arrested, they never revealed my first name. Their lack of cooperation was the majority of the reason why they were dealt such harsh sentences and served their full time.

Something deep inside me screams to tell her my real last name, to beam with pride over who my parents are and where my family came from despite the world's opinion of them as criminals.

"Martes." I give her the answer she needs to hear, though it's hard to hide the disappointment in my voice at saying it.

"Dante Martes." She holds her hand out to me as if this is the first time we're actually meeting. "I'm Lily Alistair, short for Liliana."

I never could have imagined her name being more beautiful and appropriate than Lily, but there it is, making her shine even more brightly before me. "Pleasure to meet you, Liliana."

After our formal introductions–taking a step back to get this started the way it should have been in the first place–I find myself enjoying every minute with this woman in front of me even more. My face hurts from laughing the further we get in conversation. In the hour it takes us to sip through our ridiculously fancy coffees, I find myself leaning more toward a certain path and wondering how I ever thought to even consider the other path this morning.

I won't settle for the status quo. I choose something more: happiness, life, potential.

A future that is my own, not based off the hand fate dealt me.

11

Time is an interesting thing. It keeps going and going, plowing ahead with nothing to stand in its way while the entire world with which it coexists is constantly changing. From the stories of my family I know how easy one's life can change in just a few hours or minutes or seconds. I never experienced it for myself until this morning.

Pulling into my driveway after dropping Lily off at her house, I feel like a completely different person than the lost and indecisive nobody who left here just hours before. Clarity and direction came to me much quicker than I expected, all thanks to one person.

Lily.

I thought I would dread the impending conversation with my parents more as I park the car and approach the front door of our house, but I find myself strangely calm. Confidence swells within me as I unlock the door and step inside. My nerves remain completely unaffected as I see my parents sitting together on the couch in the living room, my sudden entrance clearly having interrupted whatever conversation they were just having. Their expressions are difficult to read. This conversation is either about to go spectacularly well or go up in flames.

"Hey," I greet them to break the heavy silence between us. I throw my keys on the kitchen counter and take a seat in one of the chairs across the coffee table from my parents in the living room.

Dad's arm around Mom's shoulder tightens just a bit as Mom replies for the two of them. "Hey, sweetie."

I lean my elbows forward on my knees and try to prepare myself for what's coming next. Before we discuss anything about the revelations I've had this morning, I need to address what I did last night. "I'm sorry about blowing up yesterday. What I said was completely disrespectful not just to you, but to Robert and Cindy and even to Jack's memory."

Mom's face softens into a smile. "It's okay. We understand."

I'm not sure how to take what she's said. "You understand?"

"We've done a lot of talking since last night," Mom continues but abruptly stops speaking as she looks to her side at Dad. She keeps her gaze on him, her eyes never leaving his as I can clearly see her emotions getting the best of her. Dad settles his free hand over Mom's wrist and gently rubs it where her only tattoo still resides: the black circle forming an almost complete letter C that mirrors my dad's own tattoo, the symbols together creating infinity. It was only natural that I wanted to have my own version of their combined tattoo inscribed on my wrist when I turned eighteen, though my parents insisted that it be more discreet in size.

When Mom turns back to me, tears fall from both of her eyes, but somehow she's still smiling. "We've been hiding for so long, Dante. We almost lost everything. We almost lost you." She stops to take a deep, calming breath before continuing. "I think somewhere along the way we forgot to stop running and start living."

She's not scolding me. She's not yelling or making feel like I'm threatening the safety and stability my family has fought to keep for so long. She actually understands me.

"I promised your mother the world," Dad interjects, his voice low but completely unwavering. "When we first arrived in Maine, I promised her a full life and so much more, but I should have made that same promise to you. We gave you an existence and a home to reside in, but we haven't given you an opportunity to truly live."

I'm speechless, my throat instantly clenching as feelings of relief overwhelm me that my parents actually understand. My eyes dart to the floor as I take a moment to pull myself together so I don't unravel completely.

By the time I look back up at my parents across from me, Mom is wiping away silent tears from her cheeks. Dad's face remains stoic, though I can see the hint of his emotions wanting to emerge from just below the surface.

"I appreciate all you've done for me," I finally manage to say. "And I'm really glad you understand. I don't want to put this family in danger–that's not even close to my intent–but I'd like to get out more and maybe have a social life."

"Maybe have a girlfriend?" Mom's sudden suggestion is immediately followed by a burst of a half-laugh, half-cry as my stunned eyes shift to her. "Tell us about her. Who's this girl who caught your eye?"

I can't help shifting uncomfortably in my seat at even the thought of talking to my parents about Lily, but I need to reward their trust in me by trusting them right back. "Her name is Lily. She works at CJ's Tavern just like Robert figured out, but her true passion is in writing. She studied creative writing at the University of Maine but hasn't made a career out of it yet, which is why she's stuck waitressing for right now."

My parents watch me intently and hang on every word I say, clearly having no intention of interrupting, so I continue.

"She has a lot of energy and life in her. You can see it in every step she takes. It makes everything around her seem brighter. I think that's why I'm drawn to her. I've only met her a few times, but each time she's made me laugh and smile more than I can remember in years."

"She sounds wonderful." Mom finishes another swipe of her fingers beneath her eyes before giving me a huge smile.

"Don't take this the wrong way," Dad suddenly speaks up, "but I have to ask the question. What did you tell her about yourself? About us?"

I try to do exactly as my dad says and not be upset by his question, remembering that he's just looking out for the best interests of our family as he has for years. "I told her I've lived in Maine my entire life and that I live with my parents. I told her I was homeschooled growing up and didn't go to college. She thinks I work construction and am in between jobs right now."

The serious look on Dad's face fumbles just enough that I can tell he's trying to hold back a laugh at something I've said.

"What?" I ask with my own unavoidable hint of laughter in my tone. "It's mostly the truth. I've helped you fix up this place over the years and worked on Robert and Cindy's house for over two months not that long ago."

A full grin finally manages to creep into Dad's face as he nods at me in agreement. "That's true. Clever way to stick to being mostly truthful." His smile suddenly fades. "What happens if you get more serious with this girl, though? You can't be completely truthful with her. She can never know who you really are or the family you're a part of. Can you live with that?"

It's a devastating question my dad has asked and something that I haven't really let myself think on yet. I'm extremely early in this process. I've never dated or even really socialized with the outside world before. Lily and I seem to be hitting it off well, but we've only really met a few times. For the most part I've been able to get by with half-truths about my life, but what happens if we do get closer? The questions will inevitably become more invasive into my past. She'll expect to see where I live, something that will never be allowed to happen. Hell, she'll want to meet my parents eventually, and it would raise all sorts of red flags if I deny her the opportunity to meet them.

I'll just have to hope she understands. Given Lily's reluctance to talk about her parents and her stepfather during our coffee date, it would seem she's an ideal candidate to be understanding of my need to keep certain parts of my life hidden away.

"I think it'll be okay," I conclude. "I know I can't tell her everything, and I think she'll understand. She seems to be battling some of her own demons about her past."

Mom looks at me curiously. "What do you mean?"

"She wouldn't talk about her childhood other than she grew up in Connecticut and lived with her mother and stepfather until she graduated high school. They were too focused on their relationship while she was growing up, and she was never really close to them. She barely keeps in touch with them now. Her biological father died when she was three."

A tinge of sorrow plays across Mom's face while Dad immediately looks away from me at my comment. He knows exactly what it's like to lose a father at a young age. Both of his parents were murdered in front of him when he was eight years old. It's hard not to wonder how much I constantly remind him of his father given that I bear his name.

When Mom notices his discomfort, she entwines her arm with his with a supportive smile. Dad looks down at her and nods, just barely, before they both return their gazes to me.

"What's next, then?" Mom inquires. "Do you have plans to see her again already?"

I nod. "She has a day off from work in a couple days. I offered to help with a few projects in her house."

Mom's eyes go wide. "You'll be spending time in her house already? Are you sure that's such a good idea?" She looks to her side, gauging Dad's expression, but he doesn't seem overly concerned. "I remember what it was like to be your age and attracted to someone. It's easy to let your hormones make your physical relationship progress faster than it should."

My hands immediately move to my face before I run them through my hair, wishing I could simultaneously rake what my mom just said out of my head. "I'd rather not hear about my parents' physical relationship if that's okay." I peer up at them, feeling the rush of embarrassment in my heated cheeks. "I know what you're trying to say, and I need you to trust that I won't get carried away."

Neither of my parents seem overly convinced, but they don't push me on the subject any further.

"We trust you," Mom confirms. "Just remember what you've learned over these years. We want you to have this opportunity to explore this new part of your life, but don't forget to keep protecting what you already have."

"She can never know your real last name," Dad adds. "This house must remain hidden from her. We'll never be able to meet her."

"I understand. I'll be careful," I reassure them.

Dad nods in acknowledgement as Mom gets up from the couch and approaches me with a tearful look in her eyes. "Come here. I need to hug you."

The moment I stand up, I'm immediately swept into my mother's embrace. She holds me tightly as my arms encircle her back comfortingly. I can feel her attempts at deep, calming breaths.

"You're all grown up now," she says quietly, her voice cracking slightly. "Actually, you grew up a long time ago, but the day has finally come that we need to acknowledge it and let you start living more of your life." She pulls back and beams at me, though her cheeks are stained with tears. "We want you to be happy."

"Thank you," I reply, but those two words seem too insignificant to properly express my gratitude for this extra freedom and trust they are granting me. "This means a lot to me. I won't let you down."

"You're a Marini," Dad says proudly as he stands up and wraps each of his inked arms around me and Mom to pull us against his chest. "The Marinis are fighters. Our road is never easy, but we make it through. You're living proof of that."

In this moment, everything becomes clear in my mind. I have to do this right. I will not stain my family's legacy by screwing up everything we've worked toward for the sake of embracing a social life.

I will be careful about this, every step of the way.

But I will also enjoy it. Every fucking minute of it.

12

It was hard not going out to CJ's Tavern the night of my coffee date with Lily when I knew exactly what hours she'd be at work. It was almost impossible to stay away from that place the next day when I was stuck at home knowing she'd be there again and probably walking to and from work by herself on that dangerous winding road.

Thank God it's finally her day off.

Desperate for anything to keep myself busy the last day and a half, I focused on painstakingly gathering and organizing every possible tool and useful material I could think of that we had in the house and loaded it all into my car. I practically have a home improvement store ready and waiting for me in the trunk, prepared to take on whatever projects Lily has planned for me.

I can't deny my nerves are on edge the entire drive to her place. Anxiety is rolling through me in waves, hitting its peak by the time I pull into the section of houses where Lily lives. It's funny, though. The moment I pull up to Lily's house and see her standing in the open garage waiting for me, the worry pulsing rapidly through my veins seems to lessen. When I'm backing the car into the driveway to make my mobile home improvement store more accessible and I see her beaming a smile in my rear-view mirror, the rest of my anxiety seems to dissipate.

God, I love the effect this girl has on me.

After turning off the car, I step out of it to find Lily approaching me looking completely different from how I've seen her before. Her shoulder-length brown hair is tied up in a messy bun at the back of her head. Her face is completely void of makeup, though her skin is still smooth and her dark brown eyes are shining as bright as ever. She's wearing thin gray cotton shorts dotted with paint stains and a light pink tank top that fits snugly to every curve of her chest and stomach. She is absolutely stunning to me just as she is without even trying to make herself up to be beautiful.

"You look amazing." My lips can't help speaking the words. It's the first thing that comes to mind when she stops in front of me, and I feel compelled to relay this to her.

Lily glances down her body then returns her attention to me with a goofy look on her face. "That's clearly what I was going for here."

"I'm serious." Again, my mouth speaks without letting my brain catch up. "Don't discount your natural beauty."

Lily's eyes dart around me, avoiding what must be an overly penetrating gaze on my face. "You're very sweet, and though I'd love to stand here and let you compliment me all day, we have some work to get to, don't we? I'm not letting you inflate the hours I'm paying you for with praising my looks instead of actually working."

I shake my head with a defiant grin. "I already told you before that I'm not accepting a dime from you for this work. I'm happy to help."

As I'm about to move toward the trunk of the car, Lily grabs me by the arm. "Not so fast."

Our eyes instantly meet. While we continue to stare at each other, Lily's thoughts are unreadable on her face while my thoughts are clearly focused on wishing I could place my lips on hers at this moment, but I know better than to make that kind of move. Spending time with Lily on her home turf will be a huge test of my restraint, and I refuse to fail in that respect.

She cups the side of my cheek with her hand and brings our faces even closer together. When her lips open, I'm convinced she's going to lean in and kiss me, but instead she says, "You're in between jobs. I'm going to pay you for the work you're doing here."

My head tilts to the side as I struggle with how hard to fight her on this and how to respond. "You can pay me by keeping me hydrated while I'm working and maybe feed me every so often. That's more than enough." Lily lets go of my face but continues to look at me, indecision and unease at my suggestion written all over her face, so I try to alleviate her concern even more. "Seriously, my expenses are almost non-existent right now. I'll be fine."

After a moment, she nods reluctantly. "Okay. I don't like it, but you have a deal."

Relieved to be past that little battle over compensation, I open the trunk of the car to grab a work bag and a plastic bucket both filled with the most basic tools I'll need for this endeavor.

Lily's eyes widen at the almost completely full trunk. "Wow. We're not tearing down any walls, you know."

I laugh and set the bucket down on the pavement next to me so I can close the trunk. "I just like to be prepared. If I've learned anything about home improvement projects in the years I've been doing this, it's that you can never have enough tools, and despite being prepared, you'll almost always end up needing a tool you don't have."

Lily grabs for the bucket I set down and motions me toward the open garage. I reach out to take the bucket from her, but she dismisses me with a wave of her other hand. "I got this."

In my hesitation to help her, she slips in front of me and leads the way into the garage past a small red hatchback car to a door just a little further inside. It opens into a small kitchen with worn wooden cabinets and dated white appliances, their presence completely contrasting the beautiful granite countertops that cover each side of the kitchen. As we move further into the dining room, I note she has the potential for a nice open floor plan but there's a strange partial dividing wall separating the dining room from the living room on the other side. To the left of us is a small bathroom and stairs leading up to the second floor. Pergo flooring runs the length of the floor, another nice upgrade she already has in place.

"Not bad at all," I comment as I set the work bag down on the floor. "I see you already have a few decent upgrades in here."

"They were working on some renovations before I started renting here, but I guess the money ran out before they could finish everything. The landlord doesn't care what I do in here as long as the place looks better in the end."

In some ways I wish her place was more of a disaster so I'd have an excuse to spend inordinate amounts of time here working to improve it for her. I could, of course, make a few suggestions to prolong my overall time spent here. "So, where should we begin?"

Lily's eyes light up as she motions toward the kitchen. "I'd love to get these cabinets refinished. Maybe stain them white to brighten up the room." She drifts over to the dining room table and regards the gaudy bright gold chandelier hanging above it with a clear look of disgust on her face. "This thing definitely has to go."

I can't help laughing and nodding in agreement with her as we make our way up the stairs to the second floor. She turns on the light inside the first door in the hallway. The vanity in this bathroom is covered with beautiful granite counters similar to the kitchen but with a different pattern, more greens and purples throughout the rock instead of oranges and browns. The other fixtures are clearly dated but not in horrible condition.

Lily swings back the translucent shower curtain to reveal a plain white bathtub with simple white tile going up the length of the wall. I immediately notice a small droplet of water dripping down from the showerhead every few seconds. "The showerhead obviously needs to be replaced. I wouldn't mind getting the temperature knobs and sink faucet done at the same time."

As she turns away to walk out of the bathroom, my eyes remain on the empty tub and how easily I can picture myself stepping into it with Lily and letting the water rush down over us as we get lost in each other's bodies. With extreme difficultly, I push the thoughts from my mind and focus on following Lily down the hall.

She stops outside two doors directly across from each other and quickly closes the door on our right. "That's my office. It's a bit messy and doesn't really need any work, so we'll leave that alone for now." I'm directed instead toward the other door, stepping inside as Lily turns on the light. "This is my bedroom, but that's all it is: a bed in a room. It's not much of a retreat."

I take in the plain white walls around me, the simple wooden furniture, and the lack of artwork or color or anything interesting on the walls, and I have to agree with her. "Yeah, this room sucks."

Lily crosses her arms and glares at me for a moment before I see the concession in her face. "Okay, you're right. It sucks." She glances around the room and sighs heavily.

"It's strange," I begin to say, and Lily looks at me curiously. "You are the complete opposite of this room."

"What do you mean?"

Crap. I've opened my big mouth and now I'm expected to explain myself. How do I say this without sounding like a total creep? It takes me a moment before I realize that being completely honest is the only way to go. "You're just so vibrant all the time. You're color and light in a world that is otherwise bland and gray."

Lily looks like she wants to turn her focus away to anything but me, but she continues to hold my gaze. "That may be one of the nicest things anyone's ever said to me."

I see the change in her expression immediately after she says it. It's that look from in the car, in the moment before she dipped her lips to meet mine to engage me in that exhilarating kiss.

Then I remember where we are: in Lily's bedroom.

We need to get out of this room.

"I have an idea," I scramble to throw out there, failing to hide the awkwardness in my voice at breaking the strange intensity that was building between us. Lily's stance becomes more relaxed and relief floods her face as I continue. "I know you said we weren't tearing down walls on this project, but what if we did?"

"Tear down walls?" Her lips curve up into a slight smirk. "You construction workers are just as bad as the guys at the auto shop. Always looking to fix what isn't broken."

I hold out my hands in front of me, my declaration of innocence. "Hey, I'm just giving you my professional opinion here."

Lily ponders my offer for a moment. "What exactly did you have in mind?"

I can't help the satisfied grin on my face as I motion toward the hallway. "Let me show you downstairs."

Stepping out the door and away from the bedroom brings me instant relief. As we make our way downstairs, I realize that working on her bedroom may not be a good idea–not now and maybe not ever. The risk of us getting carried away like we did in the car the other night is just too great with us both in the same room with her bed only feet away.

When we reach the first floor, Lily stands aside with her arms crossed as I make my way to the strange partial dividing wall that separates the dining room from the living room.

"If we took out this wall, you'd have a much more open floor plan," I explain as I run my hand over its surface. "You'd also get to play with a sledgehammer during the demolition. That right there should make it well worth doing."

"Sledgehammer, huh?" She approaches me and stops in front of the wall, observing it and contemplating what I've offered. With a final glance from the dining room to the living room, she turns to me and extends her hand. "Damn you and your professional opinions. You have a deal."

I take Lily's hand in mine, beaming a smile at her which she instantly reciprocates. We're both in no rush to release our grip of each other. I'm on the verge of lifting her hand to my mouth to give it a gentlemanly kiss when a cell phone rings from across the room.

Lily curses under her breath as she releases my hand. "Sorry, let me check my phone."

The little bubble of perfection that surrounded us pops abruptly as she walks away from me to dig through her purse on the counter. She pulls out her cell phone and glances uneasily at it before making her way toward the stairs.

"I need to get this if that's okay?" she asks, her voice sounding a bit strained and uncomfortable. "It's work calling."

"Sure, no problem."

With a brief smile, Lily bolts up the stairs and answers the call. I hear her talking quietly until a door closes upstairs and I'm left in silence.

I look to the space around me and can't help thinking how much I'm going to enjoy this project. Talk about a win-win situation. It's not just a way to spend time with Lily and get to know her better, but it's something I can apply myself to. I like the idea of being needed, of having a new purpose, at least for the time being.

I don't have a clue how long this will last, but I'm going to enjoy it. Every single minute of it.

13

I've been watching Lily struggle with the pizza dough she's trying to make from scratch since the moment she opened the packet of yeast. After the two times she declined my offers to help her along the way, I gave up and kept myself tasked with cleaning up the mess in the dining room from our long day of work.

"How does Pizza Hut sound for dinner?" Lily suddenly asks from the kitchen. She sighs heavily as she stares down in defeat at the solid clump of dough that refuses to flatten into the pizza pan. "This dough may have uses as a paperweight or a dangerous projectile, but I think it's a lost cause for pizza."

I offer a sympathetic look, feeling slightly guilty for not pushing more to help her along the way. She made it clear all day that she had every intention of making something from scratch for us for dinner, so I didn't want to ruin that for her before, and I have no intention of ruining it now.

After throwing the last few tools in the work bucket, I stand up and move toward the kitchen. "Let me help."

Lily immediately shakes her head. "No way. You've been working like a fiend in here all day. The least I can do is get you something edible for dinner."

She catches my arm just as I reach the sink to wash my hands, but I don't stop what I'm doing as I turn on the water and wash away the dust and grime from my skin. "I don't mind helping. Besides, you've been working right along side me all day."

Despite the determined look in Lily's eyes, she lets go of my arm and steps back. "Okay, okay. I give in." She huffs a frustrated breath. "I may be good at serving food, but I'm not particularly skilled at making it."

The small grin on my face at her admission is completely inadequate to show the elation I feel inside at having this opportunity to show off some of my cooking skills. "Don't worry. We'll work on that."

"Oh come on." Lily nudges my shoulder in a playful shove. "You're already fixing up my place. I'm not letting you take on fixing everything else that needs work in my life."

Her words cause a strange feeling to stir within me. It's familiar from the night I saw her walking alone on the dark road and the night I offered her a ride home. This girl in all her brightness and beauty deserves the entire fucking world. If there's anything I can do to make her life better, even something as insignificant as replacing shower fixtures in her house or giving her some cooking tips, I'm all for it.

After ignoring Lily's comment, I place myself in front of the counter that contains the chaotic remnants of the previous attempt at pizza dough. "Do you have a clean bowl?"

Lily fetches a large mixing bowl from one of the cabinets and sets it on the counter in front of me as I open a new yeast packet. I'm on autopilot as I go through the motions of making the dough, something I've done numerous times before at home with my parents over the years. Lily seems in awe as she watches me, acknowledging every step I explain to her along the way.

By the time I have the dough pressed out in the pizza pan, Lily looks seriously impressed, and I'm beaming internally with pride.

"That was amazing," she comments as I spread pizza sauce over the dough. "You didn't even follow any instructions."

"Family recipe," I explain before reaching for the mozzarella that Lily shredded for me. "I learned a lot from cooking with my parents over the years. I suppose that is one benefit of living with them for so long." *And having absolutely no friends and nowhere else to go each day,* I want desperately to say, but I keep those thoughts to myself.

"You're lucky. No one ever taught me a damn thing about cooking from scratch."

"I guess I am lucky, then. I'll get to teach you instead." I finish sprinkling the mozzarella over the sauce and put the pizza in the oven before looking up to meet Lily's gaze. I love the content expression on her face. She looks genuinely happy, exactly the way I want her to be.

A flicker of an idea sparks across Lily's face, and she steps around me to open the fridge. "I know of at least one thing I can do for you in return." The beautiful sound of glass coming together strikes through the air around us as she pulls out two frosty bottles of Sam Adams Boston Lager.

"You've been holding out on me," I tease.

"I didn't want the man who's tearing up portions of my house with dangerous tools consuming alcohol on the job."

"Fair enough," I concede as she opens both bottles and offers one to me. I turn the bottle around thoughtfully in my hand as something occurs to me. "You got these just because of me? You don't strike me as the Sam Adams type."

"I'm not sure I'm any type when it comes to alcohol. I don't drink it much really."

I almost choke on my beer at hearing this. "Isn't it a requirement for people our age to drink in one form or another?"

Lily narrows her eyes at me, studying me carefully. "How old are you, anyway?"

"Twenty-one."

The urge to ask for her age is almost overpowering enough to make me risk insulting her by asking, but I don't even get a chance to act upon it as she says, "I got a few extra years on you. I'm twenty-six."

I don't know why this revelation shocks me, but it does. It takes me a moment to respond. "I never would have guessed you were twenty-six."

Lily laughs. "You can pick your jaw up off the floor now. I'm not *that* old."

"You're practically an old lady," I comment, hoping desperately that sarcasm will overpower my feeling of embarrassment at my reaction to her age. "How could I possibly have grouped myself in the same age category with you?"

"Okay. You've had your fun." She leans back on the counter and crosses her arms in front of her.

"In all seriousness, though," I begin to say, "the way you've talked about just getting out of college recently made me think you were closer to my age. That's why I'm surprised."

"I relocated and worked for a few years to save money before I actually started college. Other than some financial aid I received for tuition, I paid my own way through school."

"That must have been hard. That's a lot to take on by yourself."

Lily shrugs my comment off. "Hey, at least I got the opportunity. Have you thought about going to college? This old lady is living proof that it's never too late to start."

I can't help smiling at her continuing my tease from earlier. "No college plans for me, at least not in the near future. I'm still figuring out what the hell to do with my life."

It's quiet for a moment between us until Lily reluctantly asks, "You've lived with your parents this entire time? You've never ventured out to do your own thing?"

This conversation is quickly moving toward topics that I simply can't discuss, but I press forward anyway, nodding my answer to her.

"What do you parents do for a living?"

I take a long swig of my beer, knowing that I'll need the infusion of alcohol to get me through this part of the conversation. "My parents took an early retirement. They inherited a decent amount of money from a friend and have been living off it ever since."

Lily's eyes go wide. "Wow. Lucky them."

Internally I'm wincing at her reaction. If only she knew the circumstances of how my parents inherited that money. They lost their most trusted friend that day. The man who brought me into this world and saved my life did so much more for my family than give us his money.

A meek smile is all I can manage as I veer my response away from my current train of thought. "It's not like they won millions in the lottery or anything, but it helped my family a lot, and they've made it last. My parents are probably the most frugal people you'll ever meet."

The moment the words slip out of my mouth, I know I've screwed up. Lily's expression brightens. "You think I can meet them sometime?"

I take the opportunity to set my beer down and peek inside the oven at the pizza to delay my response as long as possible, because I don't know how she's going to take this. "I don't think so. My parents enjoy their seclusion. They aren't much for socializing with the outside world."

"That's not fair to you." Lily steps directly in front of me with a defensive gleam in her eyes. "They've kept you in their isolated bubble, haven't they? Homeschooling you, not letting you explore the world…" Her eyes dart away as she seems to ponder this for a moment. "What do your other friends think about this?"

I'm shocked into silence, unsure of whether the cause has more to do with hearing Lily indirectly calling herself my friend or realizing that I'll have to acknowledge to her the sad truth of my lonely existence.

"Wait." Lily puts a finger out of in front of her in pause as she looks away for a long moment. It confuses me at first until I realize she's struggling to keep her emotions under control. She finally looks back to me and reluctantly says, "You don't have any other friends."

I won't confirm or deny it, but my silence is all the answer Lily needs.

"Dante." She closes the remaining distance between us, grasping the sides of my biceps. The moment her skin touches mine, I swear I'm on fire, a flaring heat shooting throughout my entire body. Her hands slowly run up my shoulders to my neck. By the time they make it to the sides of my face, my eyes have closed automatically, and in that moment I feel all of that heat and adrenaline pool into my heart.

She cares about me. She's practically a stranger, but she actually gives a damn about me.

"Hey."

It only takes that one word from her lips to prompt me to open my eyes. She's peering up at me with a simple but perfect smile. I remain completely still as she leans up to kiss me, her lips not moving with the raging passion and desire of our first impromptu exchange in my car a few nights ago, but instead treating my lips with tender care. Her hands move away from my face to encompass my back as her soft kisses trail along the side of my cheek until she pulls me into a hug.

Everything about this feels right. As she continues to hold me, I can feel my throat tightening at this sign of compassion and caring that I've never felt from anyone else besides my family.

"You shouldn't have to live like that," Lily says after a long moment. She finally pulls away from me and searches my eyes, begging me to focus on her and truly listen to what she's saying.

"I'm realizing that now," I manage to respond while keeping my emotions in check. "That's how I've been able to spend time with you."

"You've talked to them about this?"

I nod. "They understand. They acknowledge they've been holding me back more than they should have." I think back on the conversation we've had and the picture I've painted of my parents and find that I need to clarify something. "They're good parents. They thought they were doing what was best for me all these years, but they recognize that things need to change now."

Some of the light works its way back into Lily's expression. "Good. Do they know about me?"

"They do."

"Did they know about today and your plans to help me work on this place?"

"I've told them everything."

Lily squints her eyes slightly as a sly look overtakes her face. "Did you tell them about me practically attacking you in your car?"

A half-laugh, half-cough erupts from my chest at her question. "Okay, fine. I guess I didn't tell them *everything*."

Lily laughs at my response as she moves to the other side of the kitchen and leans against the counter, studying me curiously. "I think I know how I can make it up to you."

A million thoughts race through my head, some much less innocent than others. "Make what up to me?"

"In exchange for you helping me renovate this place and giving me cooking lessons, I'm going to help you live a little. And by a little, I mean a lot."

"Okay," I reply with a laugh and some obvious skepticism in my response. Lily's face remains completely serious, though.

She moves to the fridge and removes a small magnetic whiteboard with a black marker attached to it. "What's on your bucket list?"

"Aren't I a little young to have a bucket list already?"

Lily dismisses my question with a wave of her hand. "Come on. Spill it. What have you always wanted to do but have never tried?"

I look away from her, reengaging my beer bottle to give me time to think and get another infusion of alcohol into my system. This seems like such a strange conversation to be having, especially with Lily. Beyond the conversation I had with my parents after my coffee date with Lily, I haven't spoken to anyone about my hopes and dreams and desires.

"Ride a roller coaster. A big one." It's the first thing that comes to mind, and the moment the words leave my mouth, the rest follows in rapid succession. "Experience a day in the life of normal people my age. Vacation in a big city and do the most touristy things possible. Meet the girl of my dreams. Start a family."

The last one is hard to say, because I don't know if it will ever happen. Can I allow myself to fall in love enough with a woman that I would ask her to be mine forever and bear my children when she could never know my past and who I truly am? Is that fair to do to someone I love?

In the silence that follows, I look up to see Lily frantically scribbling with the marker on the whiteboard. As she finishes the last line, she smiles and places the whiteboard back on the fridge for me to see.

It's scary to see these hidden parts of myself represented on that whiteboard, placed out there for the world to see. Lily reattaches the marker to the whiteboard and walks over to me, grasping my hand in hers and rubbing my skin with the lightest touch.

"It's a good start," she says encouragingly, her voice soft and her presence calming my residual nerves from having admitted all those things just now.

I want nothing more than to stay like this with her, perhaps take her in my arms the way she held me and return the gentle kisses of affection that showed her true kindness toward me, but I don't want to ruin this moment by starting something that we may not be able to stop. Instead I keep my response simple and bring the top of her hand close to my lips. "Thank you."

I touch my lips to her skin and squeeze her hand slightly before letting go. She looks a little breathless as she steps back from me, avoiding my gaze. She glances at the oven and clears her throat. "I guess we should check on dinner."

"Dinner. Right." In the unexpected direction of our conversation, I completely forgot about the pizza still cooking in the oven. I open the oven door just enough to see the perfectly browned crust and bubbling cheese. Lily hands me an oven mitt before I can even ask for it, and I put it on and pull our dinner out of the oven.

"I'm impressed," she compliments as I set the pizza down on the counter.

"I can't let down my Italian heritage."

Lily laughs. "Never." She looks at my thoughtfully for a moment before grabbing plates from the upper cabinet. "Now let's eat your beautiful creation. I'm starving."

As hungry as I am after working all day, fulfilling my stomach's need for sustenance suddenly seems secondary to my new desire to fill in the other parts of my life. It's scary to think that Lily has offered to take me on this journey, to encourage me to do the things I've dreamed of for years that always seemed out of reach. Perhaps they are actually within my grasp. I think I can do this, and Lily wants to be at my side every step of the way.

This is what it feels like to not be alone.

14

"What's on the agenda for today?" Mom asks as she fills her coffee mug for the second time this morning. I'm wearing some of my better quality clothes today–a white and light gray striped T-shirt and khaki shorts–so she knows something's up.

I push the remainder of the cereal around in the bowl with my spoon, unsure if I can stomach eating the rest of it with the anxiety pulsing through me. "Lily and I are going out today."

The past few mornings I've been working at Lily's house, trying to get the renovations moved along in the hours before she leaves for work as she refuses to waste another one of her only days off during the week working on the house when we could be out all day working on my bucket list we created a week ago.

Mom sits down at the table across from me, cupping her coffee between her hands and looking at me expectantly. "I'm not trying to be nosy," she finally says, then seems to think about her words for a moment. "Well, I guess this is me being nosy. I'm just more curious than anything."

I can't help laughing at my mom's interest in my plans. This must be what it feels like for kids who try to date in high school. "We're going to an amusement park. Lily insists I can't go through another day of my life without experiencing what it's like to go on a roller coaster."

Mom smiles in response, but it's almost a sad smile. I don't know what I've said to upset her, but I hate to see her this way, so I stand up and move around the table to hug her shoulders from behind.

"What's wrong, Mom? I don't have to go if you're worried about me."

"No, no." She shakes her head, and I'm forced to release my hold of her as turns around to face me. "Just wishing I could be there to see this all unfold and maybe experience it for myself. Your father and I never really had the chance to do couple things like going to amusement parks."

A pang of guilt zaps my heart knowing that I am partially to blame for that. Even in the years after the press coverage of my family died down and it would have been safer for my parents to be in public places for reasons other than buying food and supplies, they could never go out on dates together or have time to themselves in the outside world. They had me to care for at home and no one else in the world to help them.

"Stop," Mom insists, pulling me out of my temporary stupor. "I know what you're thinking, Dante, but I never want you to think that way. We're lucky to have you, and I can't think of anything else I would have rather been doing the last twenty-one years than raising you." She pauses a moment, the corners of her lips tipping up in a slight grin. "Except maybe during the terrible twos, or when you were potty training. I could think of a few things I would have rather been doing during those times in your life."

I roll my eyes at her and laugh as I take my seat at the other end of the table, her loving tease removing some of the weight off my shoulders and calming my nervous stomach. She laughs at me as I shake my head and finish the last few bites of cereal as quickly as possible, ready for my day to begin.

My nerves are back in full force by the time I make it to Lily's house and see her leaning against the wall just outside her front door, but the moment her face lights up in a smile, I feel all the worry drift away. The closer she gets to the car as I pull up, the more I feel her energy transfer itself to me.

I barely get the car in park before Lily's opening the passenger-side door and jumping in next to me. It's impossible not to notice her long, lean legs under her jean shorts as she settles into the seat.

"You ready to mark one off the list?" she asks with excitement, though I'm a little distracted by her brown hair dancing around her shoulders in that light blue top she's wearing to even remember what item on the list she's talking about.

I pull it together just in time to avoid her watching me openly gawk at her beautiful appearance, but I can't keep myself from commenting on what I'm seeing. "You look incredible today."

Lily gives me a shy smile before looking me up and down. "Thank you, sir. You look quite dashing yourself."

When she's buckled in, I pull out of the driveway and get us on the road. We drive to our typical soundtrack of classic rock blaring from the radio and Lily belting out the lyrics to most of the songs. Watching something so simple make her so completely happy next to me is absolutely mesmerizing. I've spent a lot of time with Lily in the last week, and the more I'm with her, the more I appreciate how much she really lives every moment of every day like it may be her last, leaving nothing to waste.

I can't deny the intimidation I feel at pulling up to the amusement park and seeing a sea of cars filling the seemingly endless parking lot. After paying the parking attendant and finding a place to park, I take in the distance between us and the front gate. It looks like it may be miles away from here.

"You look a little pale," Lily observes from the seat next to me. I both love and hate that she can read me that well.

"This place is huge."

Lily scoffs at my remark. "This is nothing. You should see Six Flags, or Disney World for that matter."

I try not to be bothered by the thought that I'll likely never see either of those places as I turn to face Lily, giving her as much of a smile as I can manage in my current uncomfortable state. "Well, this will be a good start for me, then. Shall we?"

She nods. "Let's go."

We aren't more than five steps away from the car when I feel something completely unexpected. Lily sneaks her hand into mine, entwining our fingers together and holding on to me as we trek through the parking lot.

I look to our connected hands then up to Lily's beaming face before glancing around at the other couples and families making their way toward the front gate, the people who would instantly peg us as a couple if they saw us right now. I'm about to question what Lily's doing, but she answers before I even get a chance to ask.

"Just relax. I want you to have fun. Enjoy this." With a reassuring squeeze of my hand, she quickens her step and pulls me a little faster in front of her.

It's then that I realize how ridiculous I'm being right now. I'm going into a harmless amusement park. I'm with a woman who's encouraging me to live my life, to do things I wouldn't have even considered otherwise. I'm getting a chance to be part of the normal world where everyday worries don't involve basic survival from one day to the next and living in constant fear of being discovered.

My family and I made it through the worst of our lives. We've earned something better. It's time to let go of some worry and enjoy what we have, otherwise what was the point of fighting for it in the first place?

"Hey." I stop moving and pull Lily around by our connected hands until she's directly in front of me. There's a lot I want to say to her both with my actions and words, but I stick with something simple to avoid complicating things between us any more than they already are. "Thank you for taking me here today."

Lily beams a smile before pulling me to her in a tight embrace. "There's nowhere I'd rather be right now. I'm with you every step of the way."

I can still feel the smile on her face as she says the words over my shoulder. I'm tempted to stay like this, never letting her go, but I have a feeling she'll bounce right out of my arms away from me if I don't let her continue to take us toward the park in the next few seconds.

I reluctantly pull back but manage to slip my hand back into hers, squeezing it slightly. I motion with my free hand toward the front gate which still seems miles away in the distance. "Lead the way."

Lily seems a little surprised by my gesture as she takes in our connected hands, but she quickly obliges and pulls me forward again, marching me toward marking off the first item on my impromptu bucket list.

We finally make it to the gate, and despite Lily's attempts to protest otherwise, I manage to pay for both of our tickets into the park. That's about as long as Lily lets me be in control, though. The moment we're through the turnstile and free to roam around the park, she's practically dragging me behind her as she leads us toward the best rides, telling me all about them on the way.

It's hard to match her level of excitement when I'm trying to pay attention to what's she's saying and take in everything around me at the same time. It's overwhelming to be this exposed in such a public place with what feels like millions of sets of eyes all around me.

Everywhere I look there are swarms of people going in every direction, all individually moving with purpose toward a specific destination while collectively making for a chaotic scene. I don't know that I've ever been in the middle of such an extensive crowd of people. It's slightly disconcerting.

I'm jerked back by the arm as I realize my body was still moving forward but my hand connected to Lily stopped a couple feet back. She looks a little worried as she takes in my face, her scrutiny causing me to immediately look away. I must look scared out of my mind right now and it would appear for no good reason to any sane person out there, including Lily.

With a subtle deep breath, I pull myself together and return my gaze back to where it should be, focusing on Lily's beautiful face and concerned eyes. "Sorry. Got a little lost in thought there."

"It's too much, isn't it?" The brightness dissipates from Lily's face and is replaced with disappointment. "Jesus. You've been kept in seclusion so long it's given you social anxiety."

I don't want her to diagnose me or judge me. I don't like the idea of standing here looking weak. If the point of all this is to get me to face the world and actually live in my lifetime, I'm going to fucking do it.

With a tug on Lily's hand, I encourage her the few feet off the main sidewalk in between two buildings filled with arcade games on one side and a gift shop on the other. Despite the constant flow of people continuing along the path just feet away from us, I feel like we have some privacy here, at least enough that I can get out what I want to say.

"It's not too much. It's just what I need." I hold our connected hands between us and encircle her hand with both of my palms. The worry on Lily's face seems replaced by shock at the turnaround I've gone through in the last ten seconds, or maybe it has more to do with how I'm looking at her like I want to kiss her.

I *really* want to kiss her.

Her lips look overly enticing, but I don't want to rush into that again. As much as I'd love to taste her right now, I opt for a safer route, placing the softest kiss I can manage at the corner of each of her eyes. When I pull away, she is back to smiling, her eyes lighting up at my gesture.

I'm a bit afraid of what she has to say, so I preempt her next move by pulling her out from between the buildings and dragging her along behind me like she was doing to me earlier.

She laughs and jogs to catch up so that we are both walking side by side at a quickened pace ready to take on these crowds and this amusement park and anything else life has to throw at us today.

Despite my attempts to steer us immediately toward the tall wooden roller coaster in the distance that I know is our ultimate reason for being here today, Lily insists on starting out small, and I mean really small. She drags me onto the carousel first and forces me to sit on one of the horses that moves up and down. I feel like a complete idiot the entire length of the ride, but each time I look over at Lily next to me and see her carefree smile and attitude, I start to care less about how ridiculous we must look.

Lily praises me for being a good sport and proceeds to take me on spinning rides and bumper boats and an antique car course. She finds ways to make me laugh and smile even when we're just waiting in line for the next ride. We're having such a great time together that I'm not even paying attention to the crowds anymore. I'm so consumed by the feelings Lily creates within me that the rest of the world seems to fade away. All the worry and pain and heartache and everything that's happened in the past vanish from my thoughts, and all that's left is Lily.

15

By the time we make it to the log flume ride–Lily's self-proclaimed favorite in any amusement park–I find myself studying her more closely, contemplating whether she would truly fit into my life and if I could fit into hers.

I seem to be doing a poor job at hiding my thoughts, though, because Lily's quick to call me out on them.

"You've been doing so well at letting loose, but I see those wheels turning in your head now." She gives me a mock look of disapproval from where she's leaning against the wooden railing as we wait for our log boat to arrive.

I shrug with my response. "Just thinking."

"Uh huh. Nice and vague there, Dante."

Something makes a clunking sound next to us, and I turn to see our log boat is ready for us to board. Lily leads the way in, sitting down in between the backrests for the front and back seats. I'm a little perplexed as I try to figure out where I'm supposed to sit given where she's put herself.

"Come on. Sit behind me." She motions to the far back of the seat, and I immediately realize where this is going.

She's going to sit right up against me, right between my legs.

Jesus Christ.

I somewhat reluctantly take the offered seat, and Lily scoots back to position herself directly between my open legs. Despite the layers of clothing still between us, we might as well be skin to skin in how intimate this position feels with her. It doesn't help matters when she pulls my arms around to encircle her stomach as she leans back against my chest.

The ride attendant lets our log boat go free to drift down with the river of water. As much of a relief as it is to get away from the eyes of everyone still waiting in line watching us, I find a new dilemma in that each bump of the log boat against the cement walls as we float along the river makes my entire body rub up against Lily even more.

In the rising heat of my body and the sudden stiffening of my cock, I seem to lose all willpower and control. One arm tightens around Lily's stomach while the other ventures higher, my fingers splaying out until they've just grazed the bottom of Lily's bra through her shirt. I dip my head forward, leaning into her soft hair and rubbing my head against hers as some primal need takes over me. My hand finds her entire breast this time, and the moment I squeeze it, a soft moan escapes her lips.

Lily quickly turns around in the seat and straddles me as our lips collide. I grasp her back and hold her steady as she dives in for kiss after kiss and grinds her lower body against me. One of my hands falls lower until I'm holding her ass, encouraging her to move even harder against me. I feel her hands in my hair and her chest pressing against mine as our tongues mingle and we taste each other all over again.

It feels like we've both just entered this beautiful state of connection when we're ripped right out of it as the log boat we're in hits something firm and begins its slow ascent up the conveyor belt to the ride's highest point. Lily pulls back from me the moment we hear the ride attendant at the top yelling at us, telling Lily she needs to turn around.

I'm sure the look of disappointment in Lily's expression is mirrored on my own face as she reluctantly turns back around and settles in between my legs. I know she can feel how hard I am for her, but I'm not uncomfortable with it at all. I like that she can feel it.

The ride attendant at the top of the incline scowls at us as we approach him. I try and fail to hold back my laughter as Lily blows him a kiss just as our log boat leaves the conveyor belt and is handed off to gravity to finish the ride for us.

I tighten my grip around Lily's stomach as we both yell out and plummet down the hill into the pool of water below. Our log boat splashes huge walls of water out to our sides as droplets and mist rain down on us. We're laughing hysterically, though I'm not sure it's even from the rush of going down that final drop. Everything that happened between us in this log boat up until that point is where the real excitement was.

Lily peers over her shoulder at me with a knowing look before belting out in laughter again. We both seem to have a hard time calming down from it all even as our log boat pulls into the unloading area to an annoyed-looking ride attendant waiting to help us get off the ride.

"You two need to wait here," she says sternly with way more authority than her sixteen-year-old appearance should have. "They want to talk to you."

As I hold on to Lily's waist to help her out of the log boat before getting myself out, my eyes follow to where the teenage girl is pointing. I'm not overly concerned by the two men in black pants and white button-up shirts approaching the door to the unloading area until the sun catches the light on the shiny gold badges pinned to their shirts.

Lily steps away from my grasp just as I realize this, and I'm temporarily frozen in place. I can't help what I know is an absolutely terrified look on my face, because except for encountering the prison guard who wanted to chat when I was driving Cindy away from the women's prison, this is the closest I've ever been to someone with a badge.

My mind immediately and inevitably turns to the worst case scenario. The instinct my parents engrained in me from birth triggers in my brain, and I do the first thing that comes to mind.

It's time to run.

I grab Lily's hand and bolt to a side door marked for employees only, bursting out into the sunlight and taking an immediate left turn down the sidewalk that is furthest away from where the cops were about to get us. I hear people yelling in the distance behind us. I feel Lily struggling to keep up as I pull her along, but I can't let us slow down. We have to keep moving. It's imperative we get away from them.

Internally I'm fuming at myself for so many things. I should have studied a map of this park to memorize the routes and find hiding places and exit points before I ever stepped foot in this place. I shouldn't even be at this park to begin with, all these people and eyes watching me, all with the potential to ruin me and my family if they discovered even a hint of who I really am. I shouldn't be involved with Lily at all, letting someone into my life who can never truly be a part of it. Everything about this situation is bad and wrong, and I feel stupid for falling for the idea that I could have a normal life when my existence is anything but normal.

We turn the corner at a catering area, and I see a spot where a wooden fence blocks off a small area from view of the sidewalk. I pull Lily with me until we're safely behind the fence and out of sight. I've been breathing hard this whole time, but it feels like only now my lungs are actually getting oxygen.

I continue to take a few moments to breathe before I dare to look at Lily's face, and the expression I see there is not at all what I was expecting. She's silently trying to hold in her reaction, her face about ready to burst into laughter until she seems to really take in my expression. I know without seeing myself that my skin is completely pale. I look scared and pathetic, not at all the way I want Lily to see me.

"Dante," she half-speaks, half-giggles, but the grin on her face quickly begins to fade. "Dante? Hey." She grasps my cheeks with her hands, forcing me to look in her eyes. "It's okay. It was just park security, probably pissed off about our public display of affection on the ride. They weren't going to arrest you."

Somewhere in my brain I knew there wouldn't be real cops here, but that didn't lessen my mind and body's reactions. That didn't change my inherent programming to run from the people who protect society from criminals and the dangerous people of this Earth.

I shake my head and try to look away, unable to face Lily or the realization that I can't just forget my past. I can't ignore who I am and what I have to hide from for the rest of my life.

Lily's too damn insistent, though. She still has her hands on my cheek and uses them to coax me to look at her again, but nothing works until her lips find mine. She kisses me gently, once, twice, three times. She runs one hand slowly through my hair as the other sneaks around the back of my neck. She stares into my eyes, willing me to calm down until my body finally responds. I take a deep breath and let out all the tension coursing through me.

"I have issues," I admit to her quietly, unable to hold back my honesty at this point, because I care enough about her to want to be as up front about this as possible so she can get the hell away from me now if she chooses. "There are things about me and my past that haunt me, that make me the way I am and affect how I live my life. As much as I wish I could talk about them, I just can't. You can never know these things, and if that means you never want to see me again, I won't hold it against you."

Lily's eyes are like tiny mirrors, her dark brown orbs glimmering back to me the same sadness and pain erupting from my heart. She pulls me against her and runs her fingers through my hair and rubs her cheek against my shoulder. She's quiet, and I fear that she's plotting out the words she wants to say to break off whatever this friendship or relationship is that's developing between us.

"If you're trying to scare me away, you'll have to do a lot better job than that."

I'm taken aback by her words. I have to pull back from her to read her face to understand what she's trying to say even though the words she spoke are completely clear.

"We all have issues, Dante. We all have secrets." She holds my gaze despite looking slightly uncomfortable at her own words. "Though I pegged you for potentially being a dangerous guy the night you offered to drive me home from work, I've since determined that you're completely harmless. I don't know why you reacted the way you did just now, and you don't have to tell me, but nothing changes my belief that you're a good person. I'm not going to run away from you."

My face remains even as I try to fully comprehend Lily's words. She's okay with me just as I am. She doesn't expect me to spill my life's secrets to her. She's understanding without having a clue about the history and context of all the strange things in my life.

She is true perfection.

"Thank you." I can't manage to say a word more than that as I take her hands in mine, willing her to understand just how grateful I am.

A smile returns to Lily's face just before she eyes me up curiously. "You didn't just pull that stunt to get out of going on the roller coaster, did you?"

"Hell no." Though I'm not thrilled about the idea of spending another minute in this park even though I know there is no real threat from the authorities inside it, we came here with one goal in mind, and I have no intention of leaving without completing that goal. "Let's go find that damn roller coaster."

"There he is," Lily comments with a relieved grin. "My Dante's back."

My Dante. I think I like the sound of that.

With a deep breath, I entwine my fingers with Lily's again and we emerge from our place of hiding. We weave through the crowds until we're in line at the large wooden roller coaster. We wait quietly in line, allowing our bodies and actions do the talking for us as we study each other in ways that aren't as easy during normal conversation. We sit next to each other in the front seat, hand in hand, as the roller coaster climbs toward the sky, reaching for the clouds and beyond. We scream at the top of our lungs as we fall hopelessly back down, releasing the reins and giving in to let the roller coaster take us where it may on its winding journey, and no matter how many twists and turns we encounter along the way, at the end of the ride we're still exactly where we should be.

Together.

16

It's taken me two days to arrive at this conclusion–two long, painful days–but I've learned a lot from the experience. I've come to realizations that I never thought I would arrive at, dreamed of things that were barely a thought in my mind before. I've seen a potential life for myself outside the walls of our secluded house in the woods, possibilities that existed as nothing more than whispers of ideas taunting me but completely out of reach.

I'm falling for Lily, and two days away from her is about all I can take.

After being spoiled with an entire day in her presence when we went to the amusement park on her day off, Lily was asked to pull double shifts at the tavern. She hasn't had time for renovation projects in the morning. I barely got to talk to her for fifteen minutes each night before she started falling asleep on the phone. The exhaustion and stress that overpowered her normally happy and carefree demeanor during our phone calls put me on edge and only made me want to see her more. I've been tempted on more than one occasion to stop by and see her, but I've managed to hold off.

Until now.

I have a good excuse, and I'm going to use it. A pipe is leaking at my grandparents' house and we purposefully didn't leave them much for tools to fix anything. My parents and I wanted to make their lives as comfortable as possible after their twenty-year sentences in prison for protecting us. The least we can do is help maintain their house for them.

It was hard not to stop at CJ's Tavern on the way to my grandparents' house knowing that Lily was inside working. I had the perfect motivation for completing the pipe repairs at my grandparents' house, though. The entire time I couldn't stop thinking about how I'd get the chance to stop in to see Lily on the way home, maybe put a smile back on her face and help her relax after spending so much consecutive time working.

By the time I finished the repairs, I was eager to get going, but when Robert offered for me to stay and visit, I couldn't say no. He poured two glasses of sun-steeped iced tea and motioned me to the front porch.

We've been sitting here chatting quietly while Cindy naps inside the house. I thought this little extra visiting was completely innocent, a grandfather's way to learn more about the grandson he's never really known, but the further we get into our conversation, the more I realize something's up. I've skirted around the topic of Lily the few times that Robert has brought her up, but we seem to keep coming back to her. I'm starting to wonder if this conversation is more like an interrogation.

"I'm worried about this girl and her intentions," Robert admits flatly.

I look back at him, frozen in shock and completely dumbfounded. I get that he's been repressing his detective tendencies for decades at this point, but how can he give that assessment with no basis for making such a determination about Lily? "She's absolutely harmless. There's no way she has an ulterior motive."

"How can you be sure, though?" Robert's gaze is firm. "You've only known this girl for a couple weeks. You have no idea who she is, and she can never know who you truly are."

"I realize that," I respond with more bite than I intended. "She already knows there are parts of me I can't share with her. She doesn't give a damn."

Robert's expression doesn't change. He's holding his ground. "She's taken to you quickly. I can't help wondering if there's a reason behind it."

I throw back the rest of my iced tea, wishing desperately that it was some form of alcohol instead. The undercurrent of anger flowing within me suddenly sparks, and I find that I need to physically remove myself from this situation.

After setting down the empty glass on the small table in front of us, I stand up and try to keep a scowl off my face when I address Robert again. "Is it really that hard to believe that a girl could like me?"

I want to say more. I want to explode with the amount of frustration and fury coursing through me at what my own family member is implying about the woman I've come to care so much about, but instead I channel those feelings toward wanting to prove him wrong. Gathering my keys from my pocket, I turn away and head to my car without another word.

I'm going to see Lily. I'm going to experience all the beautiful things about her. I'm going to confirm that there's nothing to prevent us from being together.

I'm going to prove that I can have this life.

My foot is heavy against the gas pedal the entire way to the tavern. It's rare for me to speed and risk getting pulled over by the cops, but at this moment I don't really care. Between the anger pulsing through me and my desire to see Lily for the first time in over two days, I've become a man on a mission to get to my destination as quickly as possible.

The tires screech just a bit as I yank the car into a parking space in front of the tavern. I'm out of the car and inside the building within seconds, and the moment I see Lily serving drinks at a table across the room, I feel the effects of the pound of bricks on my chest and the gallon of adrenaline soaring through my veins start to subside. I breathe a sigh of relief just at the sight of her, my overall reaction confirming everything I tried to explain to Robert.

There is something between us more powerful than friendship. She is the other half of my forever. She makes me feel complete.

I feel this moment of realization directly in my heart. It's right there in my chest, a pulsing source of warmth that I think for the first time makes me genuinely happy to be alive and excited about what's to come.

I now know the difference between existing and living, and it's such a stark contrast. There is much more to life than having a beating heart. That heart needs to beat for something. It needs a future to reach toward and a person to spend it with.

My heart needs Lily.

While Lily's distracted taking orders from a pair of younger couples, I slip over to my usual quiet table in the corner. The tavern is only about a quarter full this afternoon, and I smile knowing that this will only mean more time that Lily can spend with me at my table.

My eyes remain fixed on her as she finishes taking orders. She keeps a smile on her face, but it's more subdued than normal. When she turns to walk away from their table, her eyes briefly meet mine. I can't help smiling as she notices me, though the expression is short-lived when there's barely a flash of recognition on Lily's face at our eye contact. As she continues on her way through the door into the kitchen, I feel a small seed of doubt burrowing its way into my head or my heart, or perhaps both.

I wait anxiously during the minutes that seem like hours until she finally reemerges from the kitchen carrying a tray of food to large round table of six guys that look to be in their twenties. As Lily sets each of their plates down in front of them, they all thank her by name, clearly more familiar with her than the average patron to walk in this tavern. Lily seems uneasy the entire time she's serving them and looks even more distressed by the time she's finished and approaching my table.

"Didn't know you were stopping in today," she says quietly with a forced smile on her face.

I wait a moment to respond to gauge her expression, which is difficult given that she can hardly look at me. "What's wrong? You seem off today."

Lily continues to look at the wall on either side of me but refuses to meet my gaze. "I'm fine. Just tired."

I've waited as long as I can but can no longer resist reaching out to touch her. I take her hand in mine before she has a chance to withdraw it. "You don't seem fine. This isn't my Lily I see in front of me."

Using her own words from the amusement park against her is enough to get her attention. She finally looks at me, but in a way, I wish she hadn't. Her eyes are almost pleading for me to leave. "I promise everything is okay. I'm just a little stressed at the moment." She squeezes my hand slightly before letting go of me. "You want your usual to drink?"

She shouldn't need to ask, but I nod anyway. When she turns around to head toward the bar, I can't help noticing her glance at the table of guys she served food to just before she came to talk to me. She's not just checking on her patrons; she's gauging whether they noticed her talking to me.

The seed of doubt inside me sprouts into something more. I don't like this. Nothing about this situation is sitting right with me.

When Lily returns with my bottle of Sam Adams, I thank her but don't otherwise try to keep her at my table. If she won't tell me what's going on, I need to observe her and the rest of the tavern to figure this out for myself.

I keep a close eye on the table of guys she looked concerned about earlier. They seem completely normal. They're just bullshitting with each other, a group of friends having a good time. In the few times Lily has stopped by to check on them or bring them new drinks, I've caught a couple of them checking out her ass, but who wouldn't when she's wearing those tiny jean shorts?

It's not until Lily brings their bill and one of the guys offers his credit card to her that I notice something concerning. The guy's free hand ventures to the small of Lily's back as he hands her the credit card, and I immediately see Lily's body tense at his touch. She snatches the card and glances at me briefly before walking quickly away from their table.

It was a simple and likely innocent touch, but inside I'm fuming at the sight of it. My mind races with thoughts of what could have happened to Lily to make her react that way. Is she afraid of that guy or someone at his table? Did a patron try to feel her up during her double shifts the last two days? Did something worse happen?

Lily makes her way from the cash register back to their table, politely wishing the guys a good afternoon. As she hands the card, receipts, and a pen to the guy who paid, she leans in closely to him, but I can't hear her and her back is turned to me so I have no idea what she's saying. The guy nods and smiles at her before she turns away and heads into the kitchen.

I don't try to hide the scowl on my face as I watch the guys at the table stand up to leave. When the guy who paid rises from his chair, I notice just how tall he is compared to the others, well over six feet high. His brown hair is long enough to give him a disheveled look, but the expression on his face and the way he carries himself give him a confident and almost cocky demeanor. As he moves to follow the other guys toward the exit, he catches my glance only briefly but doesn't react to it.

I'm ready to react, though. I'd love to punch his pretty little face in.

It's a relief to see the guys filter out of the tavern. I don't care how much Lily doesn't want to talk about it. I need her to tell me what's going on and why she reacted the way she did.

When Lily emerges from the kitchen a minute later, her eyes immediately look to the empty table where the guys were sitting, and I can see the relief spread across her face at the sight of it. She approaches me with a little more life to her step, a slow transition back to the Lily I'm used to seeing.

She surprises me when she sits down at my table, something I've never seen her do with a patron while she's on the clock. She leans in close to speak to me. "Sorry. I know I've been acting a little crazy, but I swear everything is fine. I don't want you to worry."

"What was with that guy?" I burst out, managing to keep my voice down despite my desire to yell out the question. "I saw you stiffen up when he touched you. Did something happen with him? Did someone else touch you? I need to know, Lily."

She shakes her head and takes my hand from across the table. "Nothing happened. It was a little uncomfortable, but he's completely harmless."

"You know him, then?"

She nods. "I went to college with him and most of the guys at that table."

I don't know if this information makes me feel better. It still doesn't answer the question of what happened in the two days since I've seen Lily to make her seem so off. "So, what is it then? Did someone else do something to you?"

"Always looking out for me," Lily replies with a smile on her face, and this one is genuine. She stares down at our connected hands on the table in front of us and rubs my skin slightly before returning to meet my gaze. "It really is just stress. Work has been busy this week, and it's not over yet. I'm going to be tied up until my next day off on Sunday."

Over three full days until she wants to see me again. Two days was hard enough. Three days sounds like torture.

I try to keep an even face as I respond. "Is there anything I can help you with? You do what you need to do, but if I can make any of it easier on you, just say the word and I'm there."

Lily ponders over what she's about to say for a moment. "You're sweet to offer, but I just need the time alone."

The seed of doubt inside me feels like it's grown into a full blown weed. I hate the thought of Lily being sketchy about what's keeping her tied up the next few days and why she needs to be alone, but I can't press her for more when I'm keeping as much if not more secrets from her about my own life.

I'm still worried about her, though. Something clearly has her on edge. She's a beautiful woman working her ass off in an ideal environment for someone to take advantage of her or treat her inappropriately. Hell, she even insists on walking back and forth to work, alone without anyone or anything to protect her.

It suddenly hits me. I'll give her the space she needs, but I'll also give her something that will make me feel better about leaving her alone like this. "Just do me this one favor." I reluctantly let go of her hand and lift myself from the chair just enough to reach in my back pocket. Lily's eyes go wide as I pull out the three-inch folding switchblade I keep tucked away there. "Please carry this with you. Have it on hand just in case."

Lily adjusts her position to block the blade from view of the rest of the room and whispers, "What are you doing with that thing?"

It's one of the rules I learned at too young of an age that most people never have to learn in their lifetimes: always have a means to defend yourself and your family. I can't explain the reasoning behind that rule to Lily, though. "I spend a lot of time in the woods. Never know when I might need a knife for something."

Lily observes the folded switchblade cautiously as if it might suddenly jump out and attack her. I offer it forward to her again, and she finally accepts it, although reluctantly. "It looks well worn. I don't want to take your trusty knife."

My lips involuntarily turn up in a grin at Lily's concern over taking my switchblade. She would never expect I have plenty more at home. Other than a hunting rifle, my parents keep no other weapons in the house besides a stockpile of switchblades and knives.

I put my hand over hers, forcing her fingers to curl the rest of the way around the closed switchblade. "It's not my only one. I'll feel a million times better knowing that you have that with you when I'm not around."

"I suppose." Lily still doesn't seem convinced, but she stands up and discreetly pockets the blade in her jean shorts. "Thank you… I think."

I pull her hand to my mouth and kiss her knuckles lightly. "If you change your mind the next few days and need some company, just give me a call. I'll be missing you in the meantime."

She squeezes my hand before letting go of me and holds back a laugh as she starts taking slow steps backward away from the table. "I'm missing you already."

I see just a glimpse of it, but it's definitely there. A tiny spark of that vibrant life appears in Lily's eyes, that quality she has that pulls me in every time I look at her. It's a relief to see it reemerge, even in this subdued form.

As she turns away from me, I'm left feeling better than I did when I first stepped in the tavern, but I can't completely get Robert's voice and doubts about Lily out of my head. Something's going on with her. She doesn't seem to be in any immediate danger, but it's impossible not to worry about her. I can only hope she'll find it in herself to trust me enough to open up about it.

I want to be there for her. I want to be all she ever needs.

17

"Dante!"

Mom's sudden appearance at the front door yelling my name startles me, my head jerking straight up into the metal protruding from under the open hood of the car. I don't know what she could possibly need from me so urgently when I'm this covered in grease and grime, but the moment I see my cell phone waving in her hand, I drop the wrench I was using and wipe my hands on my jeans to run over to get the phone from her.

"Thanks." I quickly grab the vibrating phone from her and answer the call, hoping I beat it to voicemail. "Hello?"

"Hey, you." Lily's excited but drawn out voice fills my ear, and though I should be relieved to hear from her after two days of complete radio silence since I dropped in on her at the tavern, I can tell something's not quite right. She's almost *too* happy.

I manage a meager smile to my mom, my subtle cue that I'd prefer to have this conversation in private, before turning to walk out into the driveway to focus on Lily's call. "Are you drunk?"

"I'm not drunk," she replies emphatically, though the last word trails off into a sort of giggle. "I may have had a little something to get me started tonight, but I'm not drunk. Not yet, at least."

"To get you started for what?"

"For tonight. Bucket list item number two, baby!"

It takes me a moment to remember that ridiculous list I came up with on a whim the night Lily suggested she help me learn to live a little. "A day in the life of normal people our age?"

"Yes! But it's not really daytime for much longer, is it?" she responds with a noticeable slur sporadically linking her words.

"Well, how about this. We'll split it up. We'll do the day part another time, but tonight we do the night part. Yes, that's it. That's exactly what we'll do."

I haven't been around drunk people enough to know whether this behavior is normal, but I try to keep my worry about Lily to a minimum. I'll do anything she wants if it means I'll get the chance to see her tonight and take care of her through this strange drunken state she's in. "Okay, it's a plan, then."

"When can you be here?" She sounds almost desperate for my presence. It makes me wish I could jump through the phone to be with her immediately.

I glance over at my car knowing I'll need some time to put everything back as it was before I started tinkering with car maintenance to keep myself busy. I also need to clean myself up, and it's over thirty minutes just to get to Lily's from here. "It will be at least an hour before I get there."

"An hour." The line goes quiet for a moment. "An hour's good. I need to shower. I stink and I want to look pretty for you."

I laugh at what I can only hope are Lily's honest feelings piercing through the alcohol. I'm absolutely in love with the idea that she wants to make herself look nice for my arrival. "Okay, you go do that, but do me a favor, okay?"

Lily's voice turns sultry. "What kind of favor?"

I bite my lip, suddenly grateful I'm not with Lily at this moment because I'm not sure we'd be able to keep our hands off each other much longer if she were to keep talking like that. "No more drinking, okay? I don't want to carry you wherever we're going."

"What if I want you to carry me?" Lily counters, her voice turning even softer and more seductive. "What if I want you to do more than carry me, Dante?"

I can feel myself hardening beneath my jeans with each of Lily's tempting words. I'm going to need a damn cold shower to get over this phone call. "We'll talk when I get there."

"Dante." As Lily moans my name, I'm about ready to lose it completely right here on the driveway. I walk over to the side of my car and lean against it, doing everything I can to focus on anything but the continued sounds of pleasure humming across the phone line. "I want you, Dante. I wish this was you touching me, squeezing me and feeling me right there."

She gasps loudly, and I can only imagine what her hands are doing to her body on the other end of this call. I don't know if I should even be listening in on this. She's clearly had too much to drink and doing something any sober person would do in private, but I honestly can't help myself. It's a beautiful sound to hear her bathing in absolute pleasure, and with each moan she makes and frenzied breath she takes, I can imagine myself more and more as the hands and body prompting those sounds from within her.

"Dante?" she calls out to me breathlessly.

"I'm here," I whisper back.

"Oh, Dante." I hear her breathing quicken to a rapid pace amidst the delicate squeaks and moans that greet my ears. "Dante!"

By the time Lily screams my name and her sounds of ecstasy crescendo to their peak, I find myself breathing hard and desperate for my own release. While she's coming down from the height of it, I'm struggling to keep it together and calm myself down.

I need that cold shower. Now.

"Did you enjoy that?" Lily asks before her laughter trickles across the phone. "Because I did."

"I can tell," I respond with as even of a voice as I can muster after what just transpired during our call. "I think we both need to shower now."

"Yes, a shower," Lily agrees. "Will you be thinking about me during your shower?"

"I'm always thinking about you, Lily."

She sighs deeply. "You're too sweet to me."

"You deserve it. Every bit of it."

A long moment of silence fills the line, and for a moment I wonder if she fell asleep or if the call dropped until Lily whispers, "I hope you're right."

The call ends with a definitive click, and I'm left completely confused over what just happened. In the moments I stand here to calm myself down and put the pieces of my car back together, I come to realize both amazing and concerning things about Lily's current state of mind. I hate that someone or something caused her to get drunk like this, but I love that she thought to call me when it happened. It worries me that she doesn't think she deserves the treatment I give her, but to hear her blatantly admit her physical attraction toward me makes me only want to give her more.

My thoughts remain fixed on Lily the entire time I'm finishing up with my car and taking the coldest possible shower. As I'm making the drive to her house, I wonder what state of mind she'll be in when I get there. It's impossible not to be nervous about the thought of her realizing she made a mistake in calling me. I'd hate for our friendship to become awkward after she shared such an intimate personal experience with me over the phone.

I take a few deep, calming breaths as I pull into her driveway and continue that effort as I walk up to her door. My palms are sweaty with anticipation as I knock a few times. When there's no sign of movement or sound from inside the house, I try the doorbell instead. I give it one more try, and with the continued lack of response, I start to get worried. Adrenaline shoots through me as I grasp the doorknob, fear racing through me at the thought that the door is locked and Lily's trapped inside unconscious or injured, but the metal knob surprisingly moves when I turn it. The door is unlocked, and I quickly make my way inside.

"Lily!" I call out to the seemingly empty house. My voice echoes down the dining room into the living room only to be greeted by silence and stillness. I move further in and am about to bolt up the stairs when I hear the slightest sound of breathing nearby.

I peek over the couch to find Lily fast asleep, her brown hair a tangled mess all around her peaceful face. The loose-fitting T-shirt she's wearing is riding up her stomach on one side to the point that the bottom of her breast peeks out from underneath it. Her jean shorts are unzipped, revealing the top of the pink striped panties she's wearing. One of her hands rests innocently on her bare belly.

I know exactly where that hand has been.

I find myself in the now familiar situation of needing to calm my body down as I do what I can to cover up Lily while she sleeps. I tug her shirt down over her belly and pull a nearby blanket over the rest of her. She doesn't move an inch the entire time, her body probably too busy trying to sleep off the alcohol she drank to even notice she had a visitor at the door who is watching over her now.

My experience with drunk people being essentially non-existent, I opt to take a seat in the chair across from the couch and let Lily sleep. It's fascinating that even in her unconscious state she manages to keep the slightest hint of a smile on her face. Though she appears a mess with her hair all over the place, it does nothing to detract from her beauty underneath.

After a while I let my eyes close as I try to relax and sleep. It feels like only minutes have passed when I open my eyes at the sound of a sudden gasp in front of me.

"Oh my God," Lily exclaims. She looks terrified as she looks at me then takes in her sprawled out state on the couch. "What are you doing here?"

This is what I feared. She may not remember anything about our phone call, and I'm not sure how she'll react when I tell her everything that happened. "You called me."

Lily stares at me in confusion. "I called you…" She thinks long and hard for a moment before recognition lights up her face. "I did call you. I told you to come here?"

I nod. "You said we were hitting bucket list item number two and going out tonight."

"Well, that was ambitious of me," Lily replies in disbelief. "Given how I feel right now, I don't think we'll be marking that one of the list tonight."

Lily's hand moves to her stomach just as her face twists in an uneasy grimace. I know what's coming, and I bolt up from the chair to do what I can to help her. "Let me get you to the bathroom."

She nods her head and holds a hand to her mouth as I scoop her up in my arms and carry her the short distance to the first floor bathroom. I set her down gently but just in time for her to fling the toilet seat up and start heaving the contents of her stomach into the porcelain bowl. I sit against the wall behind her and keep a hand firmly on her back for support as she holds her hair back and expunges the alcohol from her system.

The heaving eventually stops, and Lily remains still except for the rapid rise and fall of her chest. I rub her back softly but don't dare say a word as she recovers.

"This is why I usually serve the drinks instead of ingesting them," she finally says after a few minutes. She reaches up to flush the toilet and starts to push herself up from the floor, but I'm there to help bring her to her feet in front of the sink before she can get very far.

What I didn't plan for was the subsequent falling of her shorts to her ankles when she finally found vertical.

We both remain completely still for a moment as I stand behind Lily, observing both our shocked expressions in the mirror above the vanity.

"What just happened?" she asks in a bit of panic.

Internally I'm struggling between bursting into laughter and pleading for her understanding of why her shorts are around her ankles for no apparent reason. "Do you remember what else happened during our phone call?"

Lily stares at me blankly through our reflection in the mirror. *Please, dear God, let her remember so I don't have to explain this to her.*

I'm about to open my mouth to speak when I see the look of horror emerge on her face that lets me know no explanation will be necessary.

"Shit." Lily closes her eyes and braces herself with both hands against the vanity. "Oh my God. This is embarrassing."

I'm not sure how to react. The easiest thing would be to make light of the situation and play it off to make her feel better, but I don't want to come off as insensitive to how she must be feeling at this moment. I opt to play it safe and be as helpful and comforting as possible.

With Lily holding herself against the vanity, I take the opportunity to release my grasp of her to help pull her shorts back up. When she realizes what I'm doing, she opens her eyes and takes over in time to secure the zipper and button.

"I can't even imagine what you think of me now," Lily says with disappointment before diverting her gaze from the mirror. "First I jump you in your car after barely learning your name. Now I'm having drunken one-sided phone sex with you." She turns the sink on and washes her hands roughly with soap, as if to scrub away more than just what's on the surface of her skin. "I swear I'm not some sex-crazed animal."

She promptly leans down to splash water on her face and rinse out her mouth. She does this repeatedly until she cups her hands together one last time and presses the water against her skin, but her hands never leave her face. I don't realize there's something wrong until I see her chest heaving with heavy silent sobs as she continues to hold her head in her hands over the sink.

"Hey." I turn off the water and quickly wrap my arms around the front of Lily's shoulders, forcing her away from the sink. Her reflection greets me in the mirror, and I can see her face dripping with what I'm sure is a mix of water and tears. I turn her around and envelop her completely, pulling her to my chest and wrapping my arms around her.

We remain connected like this until I feel Lily's sobs begin to ease. With each deep, deliberate breath she takes, I feel the heat of her exhaling through my dampened shirt. She eventually pulls back from me but can't even look me in the eyes.

I can't stand to see the blank expression on her face for a moment longer. I need to do more for her. I need to bring back that signature smile.

"I enjoyed it," I whisper softly in her ear. "Every second of it. You were beautiful, and I couldn't even see you."

"I bet it was torture for you," she replies with the tiniest hint of a grin.

I nod in agreement. "Painful torture. You can't imagine how cold of a shower I took after that phone call."

Lily's grin blossoms into a steady bout of laughter. "So maybe it wasn't all that bad, then."

"Not at all. I'm glad you called."

We're standing in front of each other in this strange but perfect moment. Lily looks infinitely better than earlier. After everything that happened today, she's not running away from me or kicking me out. She looks content despite the ordeal she just put herself through.

I still don't know what caused her to turn to booze, though. I'm desperate to ask her about it, but the last thing I want to do is upset her again.

The doorbell sounds from the dining room, instantly drawing our attention.

"Are you expecting someone?"

Lily shakes her head, clearly just as confused as I am.

"Why don't you go lie down," I offer. "I'll tell your visitor you're not feeling well."

"No, it's okay." The doorbell rings again as Lily quickly runs her fingers through her messy hair. "I'm feeling better. I'll take care of it."

My first instinct is to push back and make her to get some rest, but by the way she's forcing her way out of the bathroom toward the front door, I know it's a battle I won't win. I watch from the living room as Lily opens the door to her visitor.

It's a good thing I didn't open the door. I might have bashed this visitor's face in.

The guy with the brown hair and smug expression and touchy grasp from the tavern the other day is standing in the porch light at Lily's doorstep.

"Derek? What the hell are you doing here?" She holds out her finger to him, motioning for him to hold his response as she looks back at me. "Do you mind if I speak with Derek outside a moment?"

That's all the time it takes for Derek's gaze to meet my own. I'm sure he's already familiar with the scowl I'm giving him.

"Hey, I know you," he says, nodding over at me. "You're that guy from the bar."

"I could say the same about you," I counter, taking definitive steps toward Lily.

"Derek, come on. Outside," Lily insists, but Derek is having nothing of it. He takes his own warning steps toward me, and I wonder how close we are to this situation escalating even further.

Derek looks over at Lily and only now seems to realize she's recently been upset. "Have you been crying? What did this asshole do to you?"

I'm about at my breaking point. If this guy doesn't shut his mouth, I'll gladly introduce my fists to his face to do it for him.

Lily physically moves herself in between me and Derek. "I had a rough day and Dante came over the help me out. I'm fine, Derek."

Derek looks just as angry but even more confused after Lily's explanation. "What? Are you two dating? Or is this guy your latest target or something?"

"Derek!" Lily yells before she pushes him by the shoulders toward the front door. "Let's talk outside. Now." Lily continues to nudge Derek out the door, giving me the slightest apologetic glance as she pulls the door closed behind her.

I'm left alone in the silence of the house, fuming at Derek's sudden appearance at Lily's door and threatening gestures toward me. I hate that Lily apparently knows this guy a lot better than she knows me. I think about what he said and how she reacted, and I can't deny the worry that bubbles up within me that maybe Lily's intentions toward me aren't as pure and innocent as I made them out to be. Why would he call me her latest target?

I take a seat on the couch in the living room and wait anxiously for Lily to come back in the house. It takes all the willpower I have not to get up and peek out the window by the door to see them talking. Images of Derek holding Lily or kissing her or touching her inevitably fill my mind for the eternity of the time it takes for their conversation to end even though not more than ten minutes have passed.

The moment I hear the doorknob turn, I stand up and make my way into the dining room to meet Lily. She looks a little paler than she did before stepping outside. "Are you feeling okay?"

She nods. "I'm fine. Let's go sit down." I follow Lily into the living room where she takes a seat on the couch and pats the cushion next to her. "I'm sorry about Derek. He can be like a big brother sometimes."

Big brother. I'd much rather think of him like that than as an ex-boyfriend, which I what I fear he could be. It's worrisome enough that I have to ask the question. "Did you two used to date?"

"No. We've only ever been friends. We tried kissing once and it was completely awkward. In some ways I wonder if that ruined the friendship we had."

My racing pulse begins to quiet just a little at the relief of knowing she never dated the guy. "What did he want, then?"

Lily shifts uncomfortably in her seat. "He needed to talk to me about something. You don't need to worry about it."

I hate to ask the question, but I need to get it out there. I want to dispel this growing doubt in my mind before it overwhelms me. "What did he mean, though? About me being your latest target?"

"He's just jealous," Lily replies, her answer almost too automatic. "He's always wanted more than just friendship between us, and I've never been ready to give it to him. We even tried it briefly and it didn't work. I've dated a few guys since then, and each time he reacted the same way."

"Then why does he keep showing up around you? Why stay friends with him?"

Lily sighs, and I immediately know I've asked too many questions at this point. "That's something I don't really want to talk about today, or ever really. Can we just call it a night for now? I'd really like to get some rest."

I hate the thought of leaving her like this, but I can understand why she needs some space. She seems to have had a traumatic day. "You're right. You should rest." I wrap my arm around her shoulder give her a squeeze. It's difficult to keep my contact with her to just that as I'd love nothing more than to kiss her goodnight, but I know that's not in the cards right now.

When I pull away from Lily and stand up to leave, she stands up right behind me and grabs my hand before I can make it a single step. "I'll see you tomorrow, right?" she asks, her eyes pleading with me. "I'd still like to spend my day off with you. We have more to mark off your bucket list."

That damn list is about the last thing on my mind at this moment, but there's no way I'm missing out on a day with Lily. An idea sparks to life inside my brain, something I've wanted to do for years but never had someone to do it with. It's something from my own secret bucket list. "I'm all yours tomorrow but under one condition: we get to do what I want to do. Let me call the shots this time."

Lily seems skeptical at first but she ultimately shakes my hand, solidifying our agreement. "Deal. I'll see you tomorrow, then."

"Until tomorrow." I nod to her with a smile before we both make our way to the front door.

With every ounce of willpower I have left, I manage to leave without kissing Lily goodbye. She watches me from the glowing light of the open doorway as I walk in the darkness toward my car.

"Hey, don't forget to lock your door this time," I call out to her as I reach the driver's side.

Lily rolls her eyes at me with a sarcastic grin before stepping back inside the house and closing the door behind her.

18

It's my day with Lily. We're in my car together with the windows down and the radio blasting classic rock.

There is absolutely nowhere else in the world I'd rather be.

I keep looking over at Lily next to me, a little stuck in disbelief at her turnaround since yesterday. Her smile and energy are back in full force. It's like the stress of the last few days and the events of yesterday never even happened, and honestly I'm content to keep it that way. I don't want either of us to dwell on those thoughts today. This is my day for Lily–a thank you, in a way, for the simple things she's done to make me feel like my beating heart has a purpose in this life. I don't have much to offer her, but I can give her a piece of my serenity, a place where the rest of the world fades away. I want her to experience that with me.

It's dangerous to bring Lily to my favorite place in the woods, but I want her to experience it with me. It's far enough from my house that I'm comfortable taking her there, though if my parents knew what I was doing, they'd be absolutely furious. At least we're approaching it from the opposite side, far away from my family's place of hiding in the world.

We've been off the main road for a while now, and the more turns I take down these dirt roads, the more confused Lily's expression becomes next to me.

"It's a good thing I brought that knife with me," Lily pipes up next to me, practically yelling over the loud radio.

I turn the music down and give her a confused glance. "What do you mean?"

"I'll need it to survive out here in the woods or defend myself if you're planning to kill me and bury me here." She grins, and I'm immediately relieved to see she's only kidding. "I know pretty much anywhere in Maine is the middle of nowhere, but this place really brings out the nowhere part."

"That's the beauty of it," I respond. "The rest of the world doesn't matter out here. Nothing else matters. Where else can you escape it all like that?"

Lily nods as she takes in the view outside her window. "Point taken. You come here a lot, then?"

"I've spent my fair share of time here," I reply as I pull the car over at a small widening in the old dirt road. To anyone else there wouldn't appear to be anything of note here, but I've explored this area enough to know there's a worn path that begins just off this part of the road that will take us to our destination. "This is where our drive ends. We have to walk the rest of the way."

"Hence the tennis shoes," Lily says, clicking her heels together. "I'm glad you convinced me to ditch the sandals today."

I beam a smile at her, loving that I've planned this day just for us.

Lily's eyes suddenly brighten. "And you had me wear a bathing suit. Does that mean what I think it means?"

I turn off the car and take a moment to soak in Lily's excitement before I reply. "Perhaps. You'll just have to wait and see."

She bites her lip in anticipation and leans across the center console to kiss me briefly on the cheek. "Show me. I want to see this place of yours."

Excitement and nerves pulse through me as we get out of the car and collect our things. It's a beautiful day, the sun's warmth blanketing the Earth's surface through perfectly blue sky. I hear nothing but the sounds of nature around us as I throw on my hiking backpack and sling Lily's duffel bag over my shoulder.

When I come around to the front of the car, I see Lily digging in her purse and slipping her hand in her back pocket. "I wasn't kidding about the knife," she says with a laugh when she notices me watching her. She grabs her phone and drops the rest of her purse on the floor of the car before nudging the door shut with her hip. "Okay, I'm ready."

"This way." I motion Lily toward a small break between two trees that mark the beginning of the hidden trail. She hesitates and gives me a slightly skeptical look when she sees the path before us. "I'll be right behind you all the way," I reassure her.

"Promise you won't stab me in the back," she responds with a deathly serious expression that she can only hold for about a second before her face morphs into a grin.

I hold up my hand to her. "Pinky swear."

She links her pinky with mine. "Good."

We make our way into the forest, and despite Lily's initial reservations about the worn path we're taking, she quickly warms up to it. I can tell she's enjoying this just by the amount of energy in each step she takes. Seeing that she's this excited to experience my favorite place in the world only makes me fall for her more.

By the time we reach our destination and I see the look of amazement on her face, I know for certain that bringing her here was completely worth it. I've dreamed of showing this place to someone other than my parents. Today that dream becomes a reality.

"Wow." Lily steps forward toward the water as if the few feet she's moved will give her a better view of the fifty-foot-high waterfall in front of us. "This is beautiful."

The water rushes from the stream above into a wide open pool below, its surface relatively calm and its bottom deeper in the middle than it looks from land.

"This is only the beginning," I explain as I step up next to Lily and take her hand in mine, "but this is primarily where we'll be today. It's the highlight of what I wanted to show you."

Lily pulls me by our connected hands so that I'm facing her. "Thank you for bringing me here."

"Thank you for coming with me. I've always wanted to bring someone here. I'm glad that person is you."

"You've never shown this place to anyone?"

I shake my head. "My parents have seen it before, but that's it. I've never shown it to anyone else or even seen someone else here."

A sly look crosses Lily's face as she glances to the side at the waterfall. "I've had something on my bucket list…" she begins to say, but her words quickly turn into unexpected actions as she lets go of my hand and slips off her shoes and socks. Her jean shorts and T-shirt quickly follow, revealing the incredibly sexy black bikini she's wearing underneath.

The moment she starts pulling at the strings of the bikini top, I immediately put my hand on top of hers to stop her.

"What are you doing?" I ask incredulously.

"We're going skinny dipping," she declares, and I'm quite sure my jaw has hit the ground. "Or at least I'm going skinny dipping, but I hope you'll decide to join me." She glances down my body until her eyes narrow in on the black swimming trunks I'm already wearing, and I'm immediately grateful they're black to hide the twitch she just caused in my cock.

I quickly set down our bags and stand here in disbelief as Lily turns away from me and unties the bikini top, tossing it to the ground just before slipping the bikini bottoms down her slender legs.

The moment I see the perfect lines of her bare ass, my decision is made. I yank my shirt over my head and pull off my shoes and socks before letting my shorts fall to the dirt.

Lily doesn't look back at me as she takes slow but steady steps toward the water. She doesn't jerk back or otherwise react when her feet enter the pool even though the water has to be cold. Her legs begin to disappear below the surface with each step she takes, and I know this is my cue to join her if I have any shot of getting in the water before she turns around to see me.

I quickly walk to the edge of the water and take even steps forward, pressing through the water quietly and without splashing so as not to ruin the pristine picture in front of me of Lily's bare backside disappearing beneath the surface. By the time the water is to her shoulders and she's clearly lost the bottom of the pool to walk on, my lower half is safely hidden beneath the surface.

Lily glances back at the shoreline, no doubt noticing my pile of clothes discarded on the dirt, and she smiles broadly as I swim out to her. "Glad you decided to join me."

I'm glad this water is so damn cold, because this is definitely the most exciting and stimulating thing I've ever done in my life. "How could I miss an opportunity to mark something off your bucket list?"

"Uh huh. I'm sure that was your only motivation," she teases before splashing my face with water as she turns away from me.

I watch in awe as her bare back and ass skim just beneath the surface of the water with each stroke of her arms to swim away. This is completely unexpected and new to me. I have no idea what to do or how to react, so I follow Lily's lead and swim quietly behind her.

We're getting closer to the waterfall when Lily stops and turns to face me. "Have you been behind there before? Is it safe?"

I nod to her. "The water's rough where it drops down into the pool, so I'd stay away from there, but the cliff dips in a bit behind the waterfall. We can go back there." I pick up my pace so that I'm swimming a little ahead of Lily now. "Let me lead the way."

When I made the move to get in this position, I didn't realize that I'd be giving her a view of my bare backside in the same way I was just enjoying watching her, but I find that I don't really care. This is exhilarating and amazing on so many levels. I just need to roll with it.

I swim ahead with an occasional glance toward Lily behind me to make sure she's still okay. She looks more than okay. By the mischievous grin on her face, I can tell she's enjoying every second of the view she's getting right now.

The sound of the water crashing down into the pool gets louder the closer we get to the waterfall. I lead us along the shallow edge of the rocks, avoiding the area where the waterfall meets the pool by a few feet. The space between the rocks and the waterfall widens just a bit more until we're well into the small cave-like area behind the rushing water.

"This is amazing," Lily yells over the echoing sound of the waterfall. To see her excitement in experiencing this for the first time is incredible, almost like I'm experiencing it for my first time, too.

As she inches away from the rocks and reaches toward the falling water, I find myself instinctively grabbing for her arm to pull her back toward me. "What are you doing?"

Lily's bare chest comes crashing into mine, an unintended side effect of my effort to keep her safe from the rushing water, and that's all the connection it takes for something to spark between us. By the time we both look up from her breasts pressed firmly against my chest, our lips are colliding, our tongues entwining. My hands are all over her back and in her hair as she slowly rocks her body against me and doesn't let our lips part for more than a second.

    The temperature of the water no longer matters. Nothing can stop the hardening of my cock as Lily's leg rubs against it with each movement of her body against mine. My hand finds her firm ass, and it only encourages her to rub against me harder and faster until I feel like I might explode from the sexual energy igniting between us.

    I need to feel her. I need her to experience this pleasure she's giving me in every way possible, so I let my hand travel from her backside to the front, my fingers immediately finding the hidden warmth between her legs. She gasps out as I touch her, and I immediately stop what I'm doing.

    "No," she breathes out next to my ear as she links her hands behind my neck. "Don't stop. Please don't ever stop."

    That permission is all I need for my fingers to resume their work as Lily clings on to me. I rub her in circles that make her moan into my ear. I can't help myself as I go a step further, inserting two fingers inside her that cause her to cry out in pleasure.

    "Dante." She says my name in bliss as I move my fingers in and out of her, savoring the warmth of feeling inside her. I want to hear her moan my name again. I want her to scream it to the fucking world when I make her come.

    As I quicken my pace, Lily's hips begin to move with me, meeting my fingers with each thrust into her until she's practically gasping for breath. My name bursts from her lips the moment I feel her tighten around my fingers as she rocks her hips against me, riding out her rush of pleasure while I continue to feel inside her until her movements slow and she collapses her head against my shoulder. I reluctantly remove my fingers and encircle her back with my hands, pulling her completely against me as she takes some time to catch her breath.

"I'm not done with you," she finally whispers in my ear.

Lily pulls back from me and grabs on to a large rock against the solid wall at the back of the waterfall. She hoists herself onto the rock and stands up. Before I can even process the beauty of her wet naked body standing above me, she does something completely unexpected.

She dives toward the waterfall.

My heart rate seems to double the moment I see her body moving directly through the cascading water and disappearing beneath the surface on the other side. I'm holding my breath in the two seconds it takes for her head to reemerge. I can barely see through the breaks in the falling water between us, but by the look of elation on her face, she seems to be okay.

"Your turn!" she yells at me over the cacophony of rushing water between us.

"You're crazy!" I yell back, but I find myself climbing onto the same rock as Lily just did a moment ago anyway. I don't know how much of my naked body she can see through the waterfall, and I honestly couldn't care less at this moment. Without hesitation I push off from the rock and dive forward into the falling stream of water. It hits me hard as I move through it, but I feel the rush of what I'm doing more than any pain.

My body plunges into the tumultuous water on the other side, and when I come back up for air only a couple feet from Lily's grinning face, I match my expression to hers, knowing exactly how she's feeling at this moment.

"Incredible, right?"

"You are incredible," I reply.

Lily closes the distance between us and pulls me by the shoulders until our lips are connected once again. She gives me only a tease with her tongue before pressing off from my shoulders and sliding her hand all the way down my arm until her fingers connect with mine. "Come on. I told you I wasn't done with you yet."

I let Lily drag me along through the pool while my thoughts race with what could possibly happen next. All I know is my heart is pulsing with anticipation and excitement. I feel more alive in this moment that I ever have before.

When we get into the shallower water and our feet easily touch the ground, Lily stops our advance and turns me. As she stands up completely, her chest rises up just enough from the water to expose her breasts. It's impossible to keep my eyes from their perfectly round shape and their pebbled nipples eagerly poking out toward me.

"Touch me," Lily commands as she directs my hand to her breast. "I want you to feel me, Dante."

I'm speechless as my hand immediately responds to encompass her breast. The moment I squeeze it in my grasp, I feel Lily's hand enclose itself around the length of my cock, and it only causes the fire to flare up within me. Any control I had completely disappears as my free hand finds Lily's other breast, kneading it with urgency and desire as her hand slowly strokes me.

Within seconds my mouth is devouring her nipple, my lips hungry to draw it out and my tongue desperate to tease it to stay. Lily gasps as she pulls away from me, and I'm immediately concerned that I've done something wrong or gone too far.

"What is it?" I ask with concern.

She doesn't say a word but grabs my hand and pulls me toward the shoreline. The closer we get to it, the more I realize we're about to be naked out of the water together and I have no idea where Lily's mind is at. The combination of the two is both terrifying and exhilarating.

Lily takes the first steps onto the dirt, still pulling me behind her until we've both emerged completely from the water.

We pass by our discarded clothes, and with just a few more steps, we reach a small grassy area.

When Lily turns around to face me, I should be distracted by her dripping naked body, but I find myself completely lost in her dark brown eyes. I can't take my eyes off them as she takes my other hand and encourages me downward onto the grass with her. Her hands move to my shoulders as she helps lower me until I'm lying completely flat on the ground.

I expect Lily to lie down next to me, but instead her lips find the bare skin of my chest. She places delicate kisses there, trailing them slowly down my body.

"I lied," she murmurs between kisses as she approaches the lower part of my abs. "I am a sex-crazed animal, but only around you." Her lips continue to move lower, and my entire body involuntarily jumps as her lips enclose around the head of my cock.

"Lily." I practically groan her name as she takes me in fully, encompassing me with the wetness and warmth of her mouth. It's the most incredible feeling I've ever experienced, and it only gets better as her tongue starts massaging my shaft as she devours me.

She's too good. Everything about this is too damn good. I don't know how much more I can take.

"Lily," I breathe out, and she instantly looks up at me. With one final kiss, her mouth releases my cock. She climbs up the length of my body until she's directly over me, holding my gaze for a moment before rolling onto the grass beside me.

As I watch her stand up and walk toward her clothes, I fear I've just insulted her and ruined this incredible moment we were sharing. She grabs her shorts, but instead of putting them on, she fishes something out of the back pocket and drops them back to the ground.

She's mesmerizing to watch as her breasts bounce and her hips sway with each step she takes toward me. In the moment it takes her to kneel in the grass and then straddle my waist, I realize exactly what she has in her hand and what's in her mind to do next.

With a quick rip she opens the condom package, and in that moment I don't know whether to rejoice to the heavens or run like hell.

"What are you doing?" It's the first thing that comes to mind to say in my shocked and confused state and the only way I can think of to stall her.

Lily leans in close to my ear, so close that her breasts are pressed firmly against my chest. "I'm checking something else off my bucket list." She sits back on her knees and begins to work the condom down my cock.

My heart is absolutely racing while my mind is at a standstill. Do I let her continue? Are we really going to do this? Do I tell her I'm a virgin first?

"Lily, wait," I interject, my body instantly wanting to kick my own ass for interrupting this.

"It's okay, Dante. I want this." She looks at me curiously for a moment, confusion overtaking her expression. "Unless this isn't something you want?"

"I want this. I want you. God, that's not the issue here at all." Fuck. How do I say this without making this any more embarrassing than it already is? "I've just never done this before."

Lily's eyes widen. "Oh my God. I should have realized..." Her voice trails off as her eyes skim my naked body underneath her. She bites her lip as her eyes meet my gaze. "The female population has been missing out, honestly."

A laugh bubbles up from inside my chest, and I'm grateful that Lily has made light of the situation to ease my embarrassment. The moment of humor quickly fades as I take in the beautiful naked woman perched on top of me. "I just thought you should know before–"

"Before I steal your virginity," Lily interjects with a playful grin. "I've never been a guy's first before, but I'll be your first if you want me to be."

I feel like Lily is my first for everything: my first friend, my first kiss, my first something more. She's the first step toward the rest of my life, and I want to walk that path with her. We're well on our way down it at this point, making me more than ready to give her this first.

I grasp Lily's hips and reaffirm her position straddling my waist. "I want you to be my first."

Lily grabs the base of my pulsing cock and lifts herself just above me. "I'll take good care of you."

Before the final word even rolls off Lily's tongue, her body slides down easily onto my cock, letting me fill her completely and connecting us in this intimate way. Her hips rise up again before she falls back down on me, taking me deeper inside her, leaving no space between us in our connection. Her thrusts steadily increase, becoming smooth movements on top of me as she finds her rhythm, and I'm mesmerized by the sight of her.

The movement of every wild strand of her wet hair and bounce of her breasts and roll of her hips brings something to life inside me. The dormant beast that's finally been awakened takes over, and within seconds I'm pulling Lily to my chest and rolling us so that she's underneath me and I'm in control.

Except I'm not in control. My instincts are taking over. I have no idea what the hell I'm doing, yet my body is moving like I've done this a million times before. All logic and reasoning are tossed aside as I pump myself inside Lily and take her nipple within my mouth. When she moans out my name, my pace immediately quickens. By the time she's gasping for breath, I'm so close I don't know if I can hold out much longer.

The moment I feel her tightening around me, there's no holding back my release. I continue to thrust into her, and in that moment I realize that this is what true serenity feels like. There's nothing but me and Lily together, temporarily transcending the rest of the world to a place where our pasts and our worries are left behind and nothing else matters.

"Jesus, Dante," Lily says in exasperation as my movements slow to a complete stop. "You've been holding out on me and the rest of the women in this world."

I can't help the victorious smile on my face at Lily's compliment. "I was lucky to have you as my first."

"I was lucky, too," Lily replies, still trying to catch her breath. "You wouldn't believe how hard it is to get a guy to have sex with a reporter."

My entire body tenses. I try to replay the last few seconds in my mind just to be sure of what I heard. "What did you say?"

Lily's hand flies to her mouth as her eyes bulge in terror. It's all the confirmation I need to bring my new world crashing down on me.

I immediately roll away from Lily and get up to move as quickly as possible back to my clothes. The reality of what I've done hits me square in the chest as I remove the condom and pull on my swimming shorts.

I've fallen for someone who spreads news like wildfire.

I've given my virginity to a woman who could take everything away from me.

I've betrayed my family, taking advantage of their trust to follow this reckless dream that in the end will never be more than a haunting nightmare.

Instead of finding purpose, I've only found failure, and I'll have the punishment of living the rest of my life with the knowledge of what it's like to be happy and free and alive with Lily even though I can never have her.

"Dante." Lily grasps my shoulder, demanding my attention. She's still completely naked, and it physically hurts inside my chest to know that I'll have this image of her in my head for the rest of my life but will never actually see her like this again. "I'm sorry. I should have told you sooner, but this is exactly why I didn't. People freak out when they find out about it."

I can't listen to this. I can hardly even look at her. *A reporter*. How the hell could this have happened?

"I just don't understand," I barely manage to say, my voice pained with an unavoidable tremor. "How can you be a reporter?" My throat clenches at the word. God, of all the fucking career paths she could have taken, she had to be a goddamn reporter?

"Investigative journalist. That's technically what I am, and it's only part-time."

I laugh at the irony of her explanation that's somehow meant to make me feel better. She's not just reporting the news to the world, she's investigating stories that otherwise would remain unexplored so she can expose them to the world.

I'm so fucked.

"I don't know what to say." I honestly don't. There aren't words for how confused and angry and disappointed I am with the world right now.

Lily's hands find each side of my face, forcing me to look at her. "Please let me explain. Give me a chance to make this up to you."

The Dante my parents raised is screaming at me from within, reminding me how much my family has to lose and how easily our lives could be stripped away from us. The Dante Lily brings out in me is begging me to give her a chance, to hear her side of the story and hold judgment on just how bad this situation really is.

When I see the tears forming in Lily's eyes, my answer is clear. I need to hear her out. I'm lost and confused and feeling betrayed right now, but I owe her a chance to explain. It's only fair given that my secrets are drastically worse than hers.

With a deep sigh, I nod my head. "I have somewhere we can talk."

Relief instantly floods Lily's face as she kisses me softly on the lips. "Thank you for understanding."

I can barely manage a smile back as Lily busies herself with getting dressed. What she doesn't realize is regardless of her explanation, I already understand too well. There is no place for a reporter in my life. There's barely a place for a normal twenty-six-year-old lively and vibrant waitress in my life.

Ignorance truly is fucking bliss.

19

It's not far from the waterfall to my rock bench along the creek, but it feels like miles to get there as Lily and I walk in silence through the forest. The sun is still shining brilliantly in the sky and the soundtrack of nature's serenity plays softly in the wind blowing through the leaves and the birds chirping in the trees. It's all so damn beautiful and peaceful around us, but it feels like nothing more than a mirage at this point. Deep down I know life isn't that simple or serene.

Life's a fucking pain in the ass.

As our destination appears a little further up the path, I find myself already regretting bringing Lily here. This practically sacred place for me has already been tainted enough lately, and I'm about to leave the stain of the end of my relationship with Lily here, splattered all over that damn rock.

When we're within a few feet of the rock bench, I motion Lily toward it and extend my hand to help her up. "We can talk here."

Her skin feels warm and inviting. God, why does she have to be so perfect yet so completely untouchable for me?

I help Lily up onto the flat surface atop the rock before hoisting myself up to sit next to her. The subtle hum of the running creek below fills the awkward silence between us. I don't have a clue where to begin this conversation, so I wait for Lily to speak up first.

She sighs deeply next to me. "I'm an awful person."

"No, you're not," I reply automatically. Nothing Lily says in this conversation will make me believe any differently. Though I clearly don't know everything about her, I've seen enough to know she has a good heart.

"Derek was right," Lily continues, staring into the creek ahead of us. "From the moment I first saw you in the tavern, I thought you were intriguing. I wondered what circumstances could have brought you into my world that day, and I wanted to learn more, but you left so suddenly I never got the chance."

The prickling of nervousness starts tingling throughout my body. I don't like where this explanation is going.

"When you came back those months later, I was even more intrigued. Don't get me wrong, I was absolutely attracted to you with your looks and personality, but in the back of my mind, I was looking for a story. I'm always looking for a fucking story."

Lily's head falls into her hands as she takes two deep breaths. I want to reach out and comfort her. I want to make her feel better about all this, but I don't know how to react. She's just blown my world completely to pieces, and I don't know where that leaves us.

She leans her head back and laughs sarcastically. "That's the beauty of being a waitress. I overhear all sorts of things on the job. Scandals and drama and dirty politics you'd never dare hear spoken in any other public place. It's the perfect source of information for my monthly column."

This catches my attention immediately as I look at her. "You write for a newspaper?"

Lily meets my gaze and nods at me. "The Bangor Daily News. When I was a young girl I dreamed of becoming a news anchor on TV, but by the time I got to high school, I realized public speaking wasn't for me. It's much easier to talk to the world from behind the text on a page."

Strangely this makes me feel just the tiniest bit better. My parents know too well how quickly information can spread in television media. Newspapers are at least slower and more likely to remain contained to a region.

"Creative writing was only my minor in college," Lily continues. "I actually majored in journalism. The rest of that story is still the same, though. I haven't made a career out of it yet. The part-time gig was the best Derek could do for me."

I groan internally at the mention of Derek's name. He's the last person in this world I want to be talking about right now. "What the hell does Derek have to do with this?"

"That's how we know each other. He also studied journalism. We were good friends in college and both applied to the same local paper for work after graduation thinking we'd have a better shot at landing a job in the same town as our college." A defeated laugh escapes her. "Turns out there's not much for work in the declining newspaper industry. Derek was the lucky pick at the paper."

"So you became a waitress instead?" I conclude.

"I had to pay the bills until something else came up, except nothing else ever came up. Derek felt bad for getting the job at the paper instead of me and begged the editor to give me anything to do. He was intrigued by some of the stories I told Derek I'd overheard at the bar, and that's how I landed the monthly column."

I nod my understanding while internally wishing I wasn't hearing any of this. I'd love to be back at the waterfall right now swimming with Lily or lying with her in the sun. Instead I'm stuck on this damn rock hearing all about her past with Derek and all the reasons why Lily and I can never be together.

"What did you call yourself?" I ask, trying once again to fully wrap my head around this situation.

"A horrible person?" Lily laughs at her own response, but my expression remains firm as I shake my head. Her smile fades slightly. "An investigative journalist."

"You wanted to find some story about me, then? That's what Derek really meant when he asked if I was your next target."

"It's just as I told you. He's jealous. He thinks every guy I show interest in is just another story because he can't accept that I don't want to be more than friends with him. He's holding out hope where there is none." She pauses and sighs. "The only truths in what he said are that yes, I do go fishing for stories in some of the people I meet, and yes, I was curious about you when I first saw you. What he doesn't realize–and what I'm trying to help you understand–is that I learned quickly that I care too much about you to dig into your story. That day at the amusement park solidified the decision for me. It's your tale to tell, not mine."

Tiny sparks of hope flicker within me, and for a moment Lily's explanation makes me believe that being with her can still work.

Then I think of my parents and what they would think of me dating an investigative journalist, and that hope comes crashing down.

Desperate for anything else to help justify me being together with Lily, I ask, "Is this why you were upset this week? I've been worried about you since the day Derek and his buddies were at the tavern."

Lily eyes me uneasily. "Seeing you and Derek in the same room was like seeing my two separate worlds collide. It was a huge wakeup call. I didn't want you to know about my part-time gig or my history with Derek because I was afraid of how that would change your opinion of me. It was only then that I realized I didn't necessarily like who I was as a journalist, surreptitiously extracting information from people to further stories I don't even stand behind with my real name."

"What do you mean?"

"I write my monthly column under the penname L.A. Woods. Few people in my daily life know about the work I do on the side."

It's nice to know we have this in common, both putting ourselves out to the world with names that aren't our own.

"I just have one more question," I say with my eyes trained on our feet dangling off the rock. "Why did Derek show up at your place last night?"

"I owed him my next column for the paper," she replies. "The last few days I spent all my free time writing it, except I couldn't finish it. I kept imagining you being the subject of the story, and the more I wrote, the more wrong it felt. My draft was due to the editor yesterday afternoon, and when I blew the deadline off completely and turned to drinking the rest of the afternoon instead, Derek eventually came by to check on me."

I nod my understanding, relieved to hear even more evidence that Lily and Derek are only friends and work colleagues and that he's not some ex-boyfriend I need to worry about.

I still don't know where this all leaves us, though.

My gaze turns to Lily just as she looks up at me. "I don't know what to say."

"I hope you'll say you'll stay with me," she responds. I can hear the hope and pleading in her voice. "Give me a chance to prove that I want to be with you because of you and nothing else."

"I don't want to lose you." I grasp Lily's hand with mine, entwining our fingers between us. "I've only just found you."

A smile brightens across Lily's face. "And you've only just discovered how great we can be in bed together."

I laugh. "About that, I have to ask… do women normally carry their own protection around with them? I thought that was a guy thing."

Lily's face instantly reddens. "Call it wishful thinking?" she says sheepishly. "I know that was a bit presumptuous on my part."

I shrug. "Hey, you're allowed to be attracted to me." When Lily sees my smug grin, she instantly responds by jabbing my shoulder playfully. I'm grateful for the lightening of mood after the difficult conversation we just had.

We sit in silence for a few minutes, though we seem to be continuing our communication through the touch of our connected hands as I rub my thumb back and forth lightly over Lily's soft skin and she squeezes my hand supportively.

"I'd like to be with you," Lily says quietly, "like in a couple sort of way."

When I look over at Lily, I see the hopefulness there, but her eyes are laced with worry. My heart is screaming at me to say yes, to test these uncharted waters and be with her to see what this relationship could be, but my mind knows better, fighting back with logic and reason and reminding me of all the justifications for why we shouldn't be together.

"If I've scared you away with all this or if you need time to think, that's okay," Lily continues when I don't immediately respond. "I completely understand. I don't want you to feel–"

"No." The word erupts from my mouth with decisiveness as I reinforce my grip on Lily's hand. The debate is over. "I'm not going anywhere. I want to be with you. There is absolutely nothing in this world I want more."

I can barely get the last word out when Lily's lips are on mine and her hands are in my hair. She kisses me so fiercely that I'm afraid we're both going to tumble right off this rock. By the time she pulls away, I'm having a hard time controlling my laughter. "I take it you're happy about this, then."

Lily readjusts her frazzled hair behind her ears with an innocent look on her face. "Maybe a little." Her lips turn up into a subdued but genuine smile. "You make me feel like so much more than a waitress and wannabe journalist. I'm really grateful for that."

"You make me feel like a normal human being," I respond automatically, *not the son of wanted criminals hiding from the world*, I wish I could add.

"I think you're anything but normal," Lily says defiantly as she looks me over from head to toe, "and that's just the way I want you. There's too much normal in the world."

I open my mouth to speak but quickly think better of it. She's right. I can pretend to be normal and dream of suburbs and white picket fences, but that will never be my life. We are who we are, and that's how it's going to be.

Leaning forward, I press my lips softly to Lily's before letting our foreheads touch. A sigh escapes me as I savor the moment, truly letting myself relax and enjoy this time with Lily in the place that used to be my sanctuary from the world.

I wonder now if this has changed, if perhaps my source of comfort and serenity is no longer at a physical location but in an actual person instead.

I'm walking a fine line. I'm not afraid to admit that. It's dangerous to be romantically involved with someone who could discover who I am and expose my family to the world. She could end me just as easily as she could make me the happiest I've ever been.

But how can I not give in to this? How can I resist being with the person who makes me feel whole?

20

Life really screwed me and my family over for a long time, but it's been slowly making up for it lately.

I've never seen my parents this happy before. Having my grandparents out of prison and living nearby with no apparent threat of intervention by the media or the authorities has done a lot to change my parents' perspective. Though they still disguise their appearance in public, they're venturing out of their protective bubble in the woods more often, even going on an official date together complete with a movie and formal dinner. For the first time ever there is more happiness than worry in our house, and I couldn't be more grateful for that.

My parents and even my grandparents were ecstatic when I told them Lily and I were officially together as a couple. As my family hugged me and congratulated me, I felt guilty for not telling them the whole truth about Lily and her gig with the newspaper, but I couldn't bring myself to do it. I won't deny that I felt like a coward keeping that from my family, but the thought of them freaking out and making me choose between my family and my girlfriend was too much. I trust Lily and her commitment to leaving my untold story alone. I don't want to risk ruining what we have over a part of Lily's life that could be completely harmless.

Lily and I have been officially dating for over a month now. We don't need excuses like renovations or bucket lists to spend time together. I'm over at her place almost every day of the week, regardless of whether Lily needs time to work on her column for the paper. Since inadvertently spilling the beans to me about her side job, Lily doesn't hide her writing time from me anymore. She's even let me read some of her past works that are stacked away in disorderly piles in her office. I've tried to balance giving her the space she needs and being there to support her when she's facing a deadline.

Today is a particularly special day that I'm spending with Lily. For the first time in my life, I'm celebrating the birthday of someone outside of my family. I'm used to these celebrations being happy but subdued. My parents' frugality in stretching out their money as much as possible made for simple birthdays. A big cake was a must, but gifts were small and few in number. We celebrated at home, just the three of us like it always was. When I was a kid, it was more than enough, but as I got older and more rebellious, I selfishly wanted more. It wasn't until my parents told me the full truth of our family's history when I was a teenager that my attitude completely changed. I insisted on no gifts after that. I even resisted the idea of birthday cake, though I never won that battle against my mom.

For my twenty-second birthday a week ago, Lily insisted on making a big deal of it. We marked another event off my bucket list that day, spending our time doing social things that are completely normal for people our age but way outside of anything I've ever done before. Lily started out small, reserving half the day for us to do couple things like catching a movie and getting some bowling in before the real madness of the day began. She made an event out of it, inviting her friends from college to go bar hopping with us before dancing the night away at a local nightclub. It was a completely overwhelming experience for me, but by the end of the night, I realized it was easily the best birthday I ever had.

This is my opportunity to make up for a lifetime of simple birthdays and reciprocate Lily's incredible birthday celebration for me with something equally as amazing for her birthday. I want nothing more than to take Lily out and do something spectacular for her, but of course what does she want to do?

Spend a quiet evening at home with me.

Overall I can't complain. We're completely comfortable together within the walls of her house. Any lingering worries I have about the outside world fade away here. We can be ourselves and get completely wrapped up in each other. If I wasn't still sleeping at home each night, one would think I had moved in with Lily given how much time I spend here with her.

Of course that's all about to change tonight. When Lily insisted on spending her birthday at home with me, she also insisted I stay the night for the first time. I jumped at the opportunity, though explaining to my parents that I wouldn't be home tonight was a bit awkward. They instantly gave me wide-eyed looks that pretty much said without saying that they knew Lily and I were sleeping together.

Sex with Lily has been life-changing. It's not just the incredible experience of the intense physical feelings that come with sex, but being connected with her and sharing such intimate experiences with her remind me I'm not alone. When we're stripped down to our most basic level to let human nature take over and express our feelings and desires through the connection of our bodies, the feelings of isolation and solitude that have plagued me for years are instantly brushed away.

Just thinking about Lily naked in bed is enough to give me a raging hard on, which is not ideal when trying to teach one's girlfriend how to make marinara sauce from scratch.

"You really should go sit down and relax," I insist, secretly hoping to get Lily out of the kitchen so she doesn't notice the bulge I'm trying to calm in my shorts. "You've already had to work half a shift on your birthday. You don't need to work on honing your culinary skills today, too."

Lily puts her hands on her hips defiantly. "This is your parents' famous sauce, though. I've only ever seen pasta sauce come out of a jar. This is fascinating to see it come together from fresh tomatoes and herbs."

It's hard not to smile at Lily's interest in something that has been part of my family's lives since we moved to Maine. My parents' vegetable garden got larger from year to year as they learned how better to grow their own food, all part of their efforts to save money and avoid trips into town for supplies.

"Okay, you can stay and watch," I concede as I add some salt and pepper to the ingredients in the sauté pan, "but the hard part is over. We're just–" The doorbell rings, cutting me off, and I look over at the front door with concern. "You expecting someone?"

Lily looks about as confused as I am as she moves toward the front door and shakes her head. "Wasn't planning on any other company."

I remain in the kitchen while Lily unlocks the front door to greet our unexpected visitor. The moment I hear Derek's name come out of her mouth, my heart rate seems to double. I try to relax as I give the sauce mixture a final stir before setting down the wooden spoon and reducing the heat on the stove to a low simmer.

When I turn the corner to see Derek standing in the doorway, his gaze latches on to mine, his grinning expression immediately faltering as he takes in my presence in the room. He's holding a bottle of wine in his hand with a white ribbon tied in a fancy bow around the neck of the bottle.

I take a few steps closer to the front door and notice that the bottle has condensation on it. He didn't just bring the wine as a birthday gift for Lily. He brought a cold bottle, clearly expecting to crack it open with her during his impromptu visit.

"Hi, Derek," I say with a forced smile as I slip my arm around Lily's waist, making it abundantly clear that he will not be partaking in any wine with my girlfriend tonight.

Derek's eyebrows rise slightly as he looks from me to Lily.

"This is Dante Martes," Lily says casually as she glances to the side at me. "My boyfriend."

"Boyfriend?" Derek questions as if Lily's speaking a different language. "I thought he was your contractor, helping you out with renovations or something?"

"He is," Lily confirms as she glances behind her to the newly stained white cabinets with tan-tiled backsplash in the kitchen, "but he's also my boyfriend."

"I see." Derek shifts uncomfortably where he stands before extending the bottle of wine in front of him. "Well, this is for you. Maybe we can catch up another time."

Lily accepts the bottle from him with a meager smile, and in a way it pains me to see the torn look in her eyes. The civil thing to do would be to invite Derek in to join us for dinner, but given that I can barely stand him being in the doorway, I know an extended stay would be disastrous for the rest of Lily's birthday.

"Thanks, Derek. I'll give you a call this weekend, and I promise we'll talk about more than just work stuff this time."

Derek nods, looking slightly more satisfied but still disappointed. "Happy birthday, Lily."

There's this awkward moment when it looks like he's going to lean forward to hug her, but he seems to think better of the move and turns around instead. We watch as he strolls back to his shiny black truck. I feel even better with each step he takes away from us. By the time he's pulling out of the driveway, I find myself breathing a sigh of relief.

"Well, that was interesting," Lily comments as she closes the front door. "Sorry about that."

I shake my head at her. "I should be the one apologizing. I don't mean to turn into an overprotective bear like that, but something about him just rubs me the wrong way."

"It's okay. It's good that he saw us together."

I glance at Lily curiously before making my way back toward the kitchen. "You really want to feed his raging jealously more?"

Lily scowls at me playfully and shakes her head. "He needs to see me with someone else. He needs to know I'm serious about this."

I'm about to grab the wooden spoon to start stirring the sauce on the stove again, but I freeze at Lily's words. When she gives me a questioning look, I abandon the stove and slowly wrap my arms around her waist. "We're getting serious, are we?"

I see the change in Lily's eyes like a switch being flipped. It takes less than a second for her to grasp my face between her hands and crash her lips to mine. I meet her advance with equal vigor as my hands snake up her back and into her hair. Before I even realize what I'm doing, I have her pressed against the counter while I'm working the button and zipper on her shorts.

So much for dinner.

By the time I have Lily's shorts and panties to her ankles, she's already removed her shirt, revealing her black lace bra that she knows is my favorite. I glance up her practically naked body with hungry eyes before lifting her so that she's sitting on the edge of the counter.

"Dante!" She cries my name I swiftly separate her legs and dive in between them with my mouth. My eager tongue finds her tantalizing clit and teases it with soft flicks and nibbles before licking the entire length of her wet pussy over and over.

"Oh my God," Lily breathes out in barely a whisper before she gasps the moment my tongue probes her opening. "It's too good, Dante. It's too fucking good."

Her hands are in my hair, only encouraging me to lick her harder and faster. When her moans fill the room, I find myself overwhelmed with the need to feel more of her. Two of my fingers enter her and slowly work their way in and out, savoring in the warmth and wetness of feeling inside her.

When I enclose my lips around her clit and tug it firmly with my mouth, I know she's getting close. Her hips buck slightly with each movement I make. Her heavy breathing escalates into a cry of pleasure at the same time I feel her clench around my fingers. I don't stop or slow down. I keep pleasuring her until she has fully come back down from the height of her orgasm.

When my movements eventually slow to a stop, I grasp Lily's hips and step between her legs as I return to eye level with her, happy to find a look of utter satisfaction on her face.

"You're a beast," she declares as she struggles to get her breathing under control. She grasps my face between her palms and leans forward to kiss me, surprising me when her tongue sneaks into my mouth that was busy pleasuring her just moments before. After a few seconds, she pulls back with a curious grin on her face. "I can see why you like doing that. I don't taste half bad."

I laugh. "You taste incredible, but that's not why I do it."

A spark of spontaneity ignites within me, and suddenly I find myself ready to throw my well-planned romantic gesture for later out the window. I'm absolutely ready to do this now. Reaching in my pocket, I pull out a tiny white gift box and place it in Lily's hand. "I do all of this because I love you. Words and gifts and gestures only do so much to show this indescribable feeling I have inside, but I hope you feel it, too. I hope you know how much I care about you."

Lily is speechless as I grasp her hand from underneath to curl her fingers around the gift box. She stares down at it for a moment before looking back at me.

"Open it," I encourage her with a nod to the box.

She doesn't hesitate as she pulls the loose strand of the ribbon to untie it from the box. When she removes the lid and pulls apart the tissue paper to see my gift inside, her face lights up in an exquisite smile. "Dante, it's perfect."

She pulls the necklace by its delicate chain out of the box until the silver symbol of my love for her is dangling at the bottom of the necklace between us.

The symbol of infinity.

Tears lace Lily's eyes as she looks up at me from the necklace. "It's so you," she says quietly.

I ease the necklace out of Lily's hand to help her put it on, but when I take it from her, she catches my hand with hers, turning it over and inspecting my tattoo carefully. She runs her finger along the black lines of the tattoo until she's traced the entire symbol of infinity.

"How long have you had this?" she asks cautiously. I've seen her curiosity about my tattoo before, but she's never asked me about it.

"Four years. I got it when I turned eighteen."

"It clearly has meaning to you."

Lily can never know the full story behind my tattoo, but I at least want her to understand how significant it is to me. "That symbol has a lot of meaning to my family."

When I don't elaborate any further, Lily nods her understanding. "Well, now it has a lot of meaning to me, too."

My heart swells within my chest to hear Lily say this, and it catches me off guard. It's strangely comforting to know that Lily draws meaning from this simple symbol that has been at the core of my family's love and commitment from the beginning. I wish I could tell her how much what she said just affected me.

Instead I kiss her softly on the lips, then on the cheek, then on her neck. I kiss her with reverence down her bare collarbone until my lips find the area of her heart, and I kiss her there, too.

"For you," Lily whispers softly above me. "It beats for you, Dante."

I glance up at her, tears burning behind my eyelids as I realize just how lucky I am.

I have never lived a normal life, and I never will, but I may have found everything I'll ever need right here in this beautiful woman before me. The hardships and solitude and years of hiding from the world all somehow led to this, and I couldn't be happier for it. Every single thing I've had to endure was completely worth it.

I've known my parents' story for years but never truly understood it until now. The physical and emotional pain and suffering they had to endure should have broken them, but they rose above it. In the end they had each other and they had me, and that was enough. It didn't matter how they got there or that they lost everything else along the way. It was all worth it in the end.

Now it's my turn. It's time to put my past behind me and focus on my own new beginning. It all starts right here with Lily in my arms.

I'm ready.

21

The reinvention of my life has begun.

I'm essentially living at Lily's house now, which started a month and a half ago after I spent the night with Lily on her birthday and we both realized how amazing it was to spend even our non-waking hours together. There's nothing quite like starting each day with the love of my life by my side, especially when she's lacking in clothing and hungry to show me just how happy she is to find me in bed next to her in the morning. The experience of having a partner to share each day with is completely new to me but absolutely welcome in my life. With each passing week it makes me think more to the future and the possibilities that await us.

In the meantime, I've slowly been working my way into society, stepping more outside the protective bubble I grew up in than I ever have before. I actually have a job now, and even though it doesn't pay anything, it's rewarding in other ways. I volunteer building houses with Habitat for Humanity, a way to integrate with the outside world and do something productive without bringing too much attention to myself. Applying my home construction and renovation experience toward making other people's lives better has given me a sense of purpose unlike I've ever felt before.

It also leaves me exhausted by the end of the day, but it's a good kind of exhaustion. Today has been a particularly long day trying to help finish out a project before the weekend is over, and while I know I should go back to Lily's and clean up before she gets off her shift, I decide to drop in at the tavern for a drink instead.

The tavern's parking lot is particularly full on this Saturday evening. I don't usually like coming here when it's packed because Lily can't spend as much time with me and I feel bad distracting her from her other patrons, but tonight I'm making an exception. It's been exactly six months since I first laid eyes on Lily the day I had a mental breakdown after bringing Cindy home when she was released from prison. Lily may not realize what this day means to me, and I don't really plan on telling her, but I'm going to celebrate it anyway. What better place to celebrate than having a drink right where it all started?

After I park and step inside the tavern, disappointment overwhelms me at the sight of my table being taken. Taking a quick look around, I realize every table in the place is taken except for a couple seats at the bar. I reluctantly settle into the nearest seat at the end of the bar.

"Hey, Dante," Jodi greets me from behind the counter as she fixes her long brown hair into a ponytail.

Ever since Lily and I became an official couple, I've been on a first name basis with almost everyone at the tavern. I smile back at Jodi. "Just a little busy in here tonight."

She shrugs off my comment. "Typical Saturday." She leans in over the counter close to me to overcome the steady hum of the room and whispers, "At least we have some good tippers tonight."

I'm about to respond to her when the words get caught in my throat at the sight of Lily emerging from the kitchen door on the opposite end of the bar. She looks a bit frazzled and doesn't even notice me as she makes her way into the sea of tables with a large tray of food in her hands.

Jodi follows my gaze to Lily and laughs. "I guess I won't be getting any tips from you tonight. I'll let your girl take care of you."

I nod gratefully at Jodi. "Thanks."

With a brief smile, Jodi gets back to helping the other guys seated at the bar. I turn in my seat to look for Lily among the packed tables and constant motion throughout the room. She's just finished setting down the last plate at a table of four middle-aged men when I spot her, and though her beauty and charisma should be demanding my attention, my eyes are drawn instead to the balding man at the table checking out her ass with a hungry look on his face.

I find myself struggling against the primal reaction inside me at the sight of another man mentally undressing my girlfriend. With a deep breath, I get my emotions back in check and train my gaze on Lily, finally catching her glance as she sees me on her way to check on another table. She speaks with the young couple for a moment before making her way over to me with the widest smile on her face.

"Dante Martes. My favorite patron," she comments as she leans her elbow on the counter on the end of the bar next to me.

"Lily Alistair. My favorite waitress," I reply with a smug grin, knowing that in these past six months she has become much more to me than just my preferred waitress.

"I didn't expect to see you here tonight." She sighs deeply and glances around the room. "I'll get your drink, but I won't have much time to stick around. My other adoring patrons need me."

I nod over my shoulder at the table she was serving earlier. "One of your patrons is being a little too adoring with you over there. Baldy was eyeing you up a little more than I'd like."

Lily looks over in that direction as she sneaks behind the counter of the bar. "Mitch? He's one of my regulars, and that behavior is pretty regular for him, too."

If Lily's trying to make me feel better about this guy, she's not succeeding. One of these days I'll persuade her to ditch this job. I don't know how much longer I can stand to have her work in a place where she's gawked at by strange men on a daily basis.

"I don't like it," I admit as she pops the top from my Sam Adams and sets the bottle down on the counter in front of me.

Lily's hand finds the side of my face as she considers me thoughtfully. "I appreciate the sentiment, but it's fine. I can handle these guys."

I shake my head with playful defeat, knowing this is a battle I'm not going to win. "Okay, okay. I'll stop being the overprotective boyfriend, just for tonight."

With a couple light slaps to my cheek and a satisfied grin, Lily lets go of me. "Good boy. Now enjoy your beer and try not to laugh at me waiting on half the population of this state for the rest of my shift."

As Lily steps out from behind the bar and walks past me, I have to will my body not to reach out to pull her against my chest. I just keep remembering that at the end of the day Lily and I will go home together and sleep in the same bed. Regardless of anything else, this woman is mine.

I try to focus on my beer to not constantly look over my shoulder for Lily, but she's a distraction my eyes and mind desperately want to pursue. Leaning my elbow forward on the bar, I bow my head and close my eyes, pleased to find that I can pick out Lily's cheerful voice from the strange soundtrack of conversation and noise that fills the tavern. I smile, wondering if this is what Lily secretly listens to when she's fishing for stories to pursue for the paper. All together the conversations are just white noise, but if I listen closely enough, I can actually gain context about what's being discussed in individual exchanges.

My few minutes of fun at eavesdropping are cut short when I hear something that instantly puts me on alert. It's the briefest sound of Lily crying out, "Hey!"

I instantly turn in my seat to find Lily at that guy Mitch's table again, except she isn't standing next to it taking plates away or serving them drinks. She's sitting in Mitch's lap trapped by his large hands around her waist.

Before I even know what I'm doing, my body is reacting. I'm out of my seat and pressing forward to their table, rage pumping inside me with each step. Lily's eyes widen as she sees me approach. She struggles to push against Mitch to escape his grasp, but he continues to hold her there.

With one swift movement, I forcibly remove Mitch's right hand from Lily's side and punch him hard across the face, sending his head flying sideways at the same time Lily scrambles away from his lap. My fist finds his face again and again until his chair is tipped over to the floor and I'm on top of him. His nose and lip are bleeding and he's crying out in pain by the time I feel hands grabbing at my shoulders to pull me away, but all I want is to make him bleed more.

My heart is beating so rapidly from the fury fueling my actions that I can't hear anything around me and hardly feel a thing when my head is pushed down roughly to the surface of a table. A firm grip holds me there, and it's only then that I realize someone is pulling my hands behind my back. Cool metal encloses itself around my wrists, the clinking sound it makes instantly bringing me back to reality.

A reality I've tried to avoid since the moment I was born. The worst possible reality I could find myself in.

I just possibly made the worst mistake of my life.

"What are you doing?" I croak out with a glance behind me to the man holding me to the table. He's dressed in jeans and a button-up shirt with a brown leather jacket. He sure as hell doesn't look like a police officer.

The man ignores my question completely, calling out to someone across the room, "Yes, call the police. I'll hold him until they get here."

"You don't need to call the police," Lily implores from somewhere nearby. I can't see her from my position, but I can hear the shock and nervousness in her voice. "He's my boyfriend. Mitch was getting handsy and he was just protecting me."

"It doesn't matter, miss. Your boyfriend just assaulted a man. I have to let them take him in."

"Jesus," Lily breathes out as I feel the vibrations of quick steps in my cheek pressed against the wooden table. Lily's face suddenly appears in front of me as she leans down to my eye level. "Dante, I'm so sorry. This is all my fault."

I shake my head, what little I can. "Not your fault. I fucked up." I take a deep breath and swallow the painful lump forming in my throat. "I just fucked it all up."

Lily presses her lips to my forehead and holds them there, and by the time she pulls away, her cheeks are stained with tears. I don't want to see her cry. I don't want what could potentially be my last memory of her to be of her face filled with sadness and pain.

"I need to see you smile," I whisper. "Please smile for me, Lily."

Her lips turn upward at my request, but the sorrow in her expression remains. She reaches for my face at the same moment I'm ripped by my cuffed hands away from the table, her skin coming within millimeters of mine by not actually touching me.

Just like I came so close to achieving true happiness and contentment and a life with Lily only to see it snatched away.

I'm pushed roughly toward the front door, my feet having difficulty finding their footing with all the adrenaline pulsing through my veins. Someone opens the door for me as the man who cuffed me keeps a tight grip on my shoulder and directs me outside.

The man frisks me and empties my pockets, removing my wallet, keys, and cell phone. I try to remain calm as I remember that I've never tested my ID with the authorities before. My parents' attorney friend did his best to get me the most authentic forged papers he could, but the reality is we have no idea how good or bad his resource was.

I guess I'm about to find out.

"Dante Martes," the man says as he sifts through my wallet and finds my ID. "You picked a bad day to pick a fight in a bar, my friend."

I remain completely silent as I take in the last remnants of daylight fading into the darkness around me. My body and mind feel numb. It's almost like I'm similarly fading away into the night. Though the sun will rise again tomorrow, the light in my life may be extinguished for good.

I'm gratefully pulled from those thoughts as I hear a struggle behind me coming from inside the tavern.

"Let go of me!" Lily screams as the front door flies open. Lily bursts into uncontrollable tears as she runs to me, throwing her arms around my neck and holding on to me as if we'll never see each other again.

Except that we may never see each other again. This could be it.

I fight back my own tears as she grips on to me, desperately wishing my hands were free so I could embrace her back and give her the comfort she needs. Instead I nuzzle my head against hers and whisper comforting words in her ear, wishing I could believe them. "I'll be fine. Please don't worry about me. Go home and relax, and I'll be back there with you before you know it."

In the movement over my shoulder, I can feel Lily shaking her head at my suggestion. "I got you into this mess. If it wasn't for me and this stupid job, this never—"

"Lily," I implore her, taking two deep breaths to try to calm both her and myself down. "Don't say that. This isn't your fault. This is all me. I'll handle it."

Lily pulls back from me with a sob just as I hear the beginnings of a siren echoing from somewhere nearby. She searches my face desperately for a moment before kissing me softly on the lips.

"I love you," she whispers as blue flashing lights approach from the road and illuminate her face.

The constriction in my throat makes it seem impossible to speak, but I somehow manage to find a way. "I love you forever."

"Forever," she repeats with a soft but brilliant smile.

Exactly the way I want to remember her.

22

With each fingerprint they take, I feel my freedom slipping further away. Despite the calm exterior I'm putting forth as they process me at the police station, I'm absolutely terrified inside. I've landed myself right in the middle of the fucking lion's den, completely vulnerable with the potential for my false identity to be exposed for what it is, and there is absolutely nothing I can do about it.

What's done is done. I made a stupid mistake, and in the end it may cost me everything.

The more I think about it as I stand here while officers take my picture and fill out my paperwork, the more I realize how much I truly failed. After spending my entire life hiding from the world as nothing but a shadow amidst the darkness or a whisper against the wind, it took just one moment of weakness to throw it all away. I became complacent with my new lifestyle. I conveniently forgot to give the proper attention to the rules that have kept my family safe for so long. While I was off having the time of my life, I became careless.

But at least I got to experience life. Lily showed me happiness and love and vitality unlike I ever could have dreamed just a few short years ago. I wouldn't change the last three months with Lily for anything. All I can do is hold on to hope that I'll get through this so I can spend more months and years and maybe even a lifetime with her.

I will hold on to hope, because that is the Marini family way.

"Mr. Martes, you get one phone call while we finish processing your paperwork, then we'll take you to a holding cell."

I take a seat and nod in response to the woman in uniform behind the desk in front of me as she turns a black office phone around so I can access it. It's awkward trying to pick up the handset with my hands cuffed together in front of me, but I manage to get it on my shoulder and dial the number of the only person I feel like I can handle talking to right now.

"Dante?" Robert answers worriedly after two rings. I can tell in the tone of his voice that he knows something's wrong. It's unusual for me to call him out of the blue like this.

"I need your help," I respond flatly, getting right to the point as I have no idea how long they'll let me stay on the phone. "I'm at the police station in town. I need–"

"Jesus Christ. What happened? Who's with you?" He sounds on the verge of panicking, and internally I hate myself for bringing this kind of stress and worry back into Robert's life after he's already been through so much for me and my family.

"I'm alone. I screwed up." My voice chokes slightly by the last word, and I have to take a deep breath to bring myself back to center.

"What are the charges?"

"Aggravated assault," I explain, quickly adding, "The guy had his grabby hands all over Lily. How the hell was I supposed to react?"

He sighs heavily. "What's bail set at?"

"I don't know." At his mention of bail, my first thought is getting out of this police station on bail and making a run for it. I could be states away before they realize my identity is a fraud.

Rustling sounds and clinking keys fill the line. "I'm on my way to you now. I'll see what I can do when I get there."

"Don't tell them yet, please," I quickly interject, hoping he'll understand who I'm talking about as I have no intention of bringing my parents into this even by mentioning them over the phone call. "I don't want them to worry."

"I won't say a word. We'll get this figured out. Hang in there."

"Thank you," I breathe out in relief, and the call disconnects.

I hang up the phone and sit back in the chair as the woman types vigorously at her computer, looking between the LCD monitor and the paperwork on her desk. My foot taps anxiously against the floor as I wait the few extra minutes for her to finish what she's doing before she takes me to a holding cell deeper inside the building.

The moment the lock of the barred door clicks shut, a sickening feeling washes over me at the realization of where I am. I know the whole story of the harrowing circumstances that brought my parents together. As I stand here in this tiny room surrounded by concrete walls and barred doors, it's impossible not to wonder if this suffocating space is similar to the cell my mom was kept in when she was kidnapped and held for ransom. It was a room like this where my parents first spent time together and began to fall in love.

It was also a place where they were physically and mentally tortured by a madman.

I take a seat on the small cot attached to the wall and lean forward with my head in my hands, trying desperately to control my emotions and not become overwhelmed at the thoughts racing through my head about my family's past and what lies ahead for my future.

Regardless of the possible outcomes for me, I can't let my mistakes destroy the rest of my family's lives. My parents deserve to be happy and safe after everything they've been through just to survive and be together, let alone for all they've done to raise me. My grandparents sacrificed everything to keep my family safe, being uncooperative in every aspect of the authorities' investigation and not giving a single detail about us that could feed into the subsequent worldwide social media campaign to save an innocent baby from his criminal parents.

A life of solitude has been a small price for me to pay compared to the sacrifices of my parents and grandparents. If this is my turn to pay a steeper price, so be it, but I will not let my family suffer more because of something I've done. I refuse to let them carry that burden.

I'm ripped from my thoughts at the sound of jingling keys approaching from down the hallway. A young male officer inserts the key in the lock to my cell and opens the door, motioning for me to exit. "You're free to go."

The breath is momentarily stolen from my chest at the man's words. *Free to go.* I owe Robert big for this. It can't have been more than an hour since I called him and he's already paid my bail and secured my freedom.

I try to hide the utter elation I feel inside as I follow the officer down the hallway and back toward the main entrance of the building. An officer inside a glass security booth buzzes us through a locked door that opens into the reception area. I look around for Robert, but my eyes find someone completely unexpected instead.

"Lily?"

Her face blossoms into a smile the moment she glances up at me. She's immediately out of her chair and bolting toward me. "Dante!" She crashes against my chest and presses her lips to mine in a desperate kiss.

I pull her into my arms, confused about why she's here but immensely grateful for her presence nonetheless. "What are you doing here?"

She pulls back from me with a satisfied grin on her face. "I got you out."

"You paid my bail? Lily, I–"

"I didn't pay a dime. I talked to Mitch and convinced him to drop the charges against you."

I stare at her, utterly speechless. My brain and mouth seem to have forgotten how to formulate words.

"Thank you," I finally manage to say even though those two words do nothing to tell her how truly grateful I am for what she's just done for me. She just saved me more than she really knows.

"Sir, we have your belongings here," the escorting officer interjects as he motions me to a nearby window at the security booth. I take my keys, wallet, and phone out of the clear plastic bag on the counter and tuck them away in my pockets as he signs the piece of paper also sitting on the counter. "You just need to sign here, and then you can leave."

I take the pen and sign my name. With a nod to the officer, I quickly turn around and walk away toward the door.

Toward my second chance at freedom.

The moment I step outside into the darkness, it feels like I can breathe again for the first time in hours. I feel different being out here now. The experiences of this evening have changed my perspective, and I can no longer look at the outside world the same way. I don't know if I can continue down this path I've been so content to walk these past few months.

Today has been a wakeup call. Freedom is not something to be careless with. It should be cherished and protected, because to lose it would be to lose everything, and that's not a life worth living.

"The next time you decide to get in a bar fight, try not to do it when there's an off-duty cop around," Lily jokes as she slips her hand into mine, immediately pulling me from my thoughts.

I barely manage a smile at her playful scolding of me as I stop and look around the parking lot. Lily's little red car is nearby, but Robert's green SUV is nowhere in sight. Did he already stop at the station and go to my parents' house to get the bail money?

"What's wrong?" Lily asks as she steps in front of me. When I don't immediately respond, she grabs the side of my face with her free hand and forces me to look at her. "I just gave you a Get Out of Jail Free card and you look like you've lost your puppy or something."

"I was expecting someone," I explain. "He was supposed to be here to pay my bail."

"Well, it's a good thing I got you out first, then," Lily replies proudly.

I quickly pull out my phone and motion it to Lily. "Just give me a minute?"

She nods and lets go of my hand as I dial Robert's number and turn away, anxiously pacing down the parking lot as I wait for the call to connect.

"Hello?" The female voice who answers catches me off guard.

"Um, who is this?"

"Who am I speaking with, please?" the woman says rapidly over a commotion of sound in the background.

"What's going on?" I demand.

"Sir, there's been an accident. This phone was found on the victim. He's been transported to Eastern Maine Medical Center."

My heart feels like it's just jumped to my throat. It seems impossible for my brain and mouth to form words, but they somehow find a way. "Is he okay? What happened?"

"It appears his vehicle was hit by a drunk driver which caused him to go off the road into a tree. I don't have any updates on his condition." She pauses as someone yells something in the background. "Sir, if you're family, I suggest you get the hospital."

I nod even though the woman over the phone can't see me and hang up without another word. As I lower the phone from my ear, I feel like I've just been thrown into some kind of living nightmare. The full weight of what I've done hits me like a bulldozer to my chest.

I caused this. My actions today may have just killed my grandfather.

"Dante?" I hear Lily call to me before her quick steps approach and she stands directly in front of me, grabbing my shoulders softly. "What's wrong?"

Throughout everything I've been through in my life, through years of solitude and living like a fugitive hidden from the world, never have I felt so close to rock bottom as I feel right now. As Lily looks at me with concern, the worry lines of her face highlighted by the orange streetlight nearby, I want nothing more than to crumble right here and give up, because I don't know if I can live with everything I stand to lose today. If there's a risk the police can still figure out my fake identity, I'll have to run, throwing away the only life I've ever known and the promising new beginning I started with Lily. If Robert dies because of my own careless mistakes, I'll never forgive myself. I'll never be able to look my parents in the eyes again, because it will have been all my fault. I will have caused them to lose one of the few people they have left in this world.

"Dante," Lily says forcefully, demanding my attention. "What is it?"

"My grandfather," I choke out, barely able to say the words through the guilt that is constricting my throat. "He was coming to get me. There was an accident."

"Your grandfather?" Lily asks quizzically. "I didn't know you had more family around here."

I step back from Lily and run my hands over my face and through my hair. Let my fuck-ups continue. I'm clearly not thinking straight. The last thing I need to do right now is reveal more details about my life and my family to Lily. "It doesn't matter," I snap, not sure if I'm talking more to Lily or myself. "I just need to get to him."

Lily nods and immediately pulls her keys out of her purse. "Let's go."

It's not too long of a drive to the hospital in Bangor, but it feels like hours go by before we get there in the silence between us and the thoughts and possibilities flooding through my brain. When Lily pulls the car into the parking lot, the adrenaline pulsing through me hits its peak at the thought that I'm about to face whatever it is fate has in store for me.

Lily finds the nearest parking space, and before she can even bring the car to a full stop, I'm already opening the door ready to get to Robert as quickly as possible.

I get out and look back to Lily as she cuts the engine. "Thank you for the ride. Thank you for everything." My heart physically hurts in my chest at the realization that I could never truly thank Lily enough for all she's done for me. "I need to do this part alone, though."

I quickly close the passenger door and start to jog toward the emergency room entrance as I hear another car door slam behind me.

"Dante!" Lily calls to me. By the time I'm at the glass doors of the hospital, she's caught up to me completely, grabbing me by the arm. "I'm not letting you do this alone."

"Lily, I–"

"No." Her response is firm, and from the determined look on her face and the tight grip she has on my arm, I realize there is no point fighting this battle right now.

"Okay," I breathe out. Lily nods and lets go of my arm as we both move into the hospital.

I approach the reception desk and don't even wait for the female nurse behind it to acknowledge me before blurting out, "An older man was just brought in from a car accident. I need to see–"

"Hey, you need to relax," she calmly demands as she meets my crazed expression. "Are you family?"

"Yes."

"You need to take a seat." She looks at her computer screen for only a few seconds, but it's long enough that I feel like to reach for it and flip it around so I can get the information faster. "He's getting a CT scan to check for possible head trauma. Once that's done and he's settled into a room, you can see him."

"Okay." I run a hand through my hair in frustration, not sure how much longer I can take waiting to find out if he's okay. "Please let me know as soon as I can see him."

The nurse smiles in response, somehow managing to maintain her cool despite how demanding and frenzied I'm acting right now. "We'll let you know the moment you can go in."

I nod and turn around to find Lily staring at me with somber eyes. She opens her arms to me, and with nowhere else to go, I take the step into them and let her hold me. My hands snake up her back as we tightly grip each other, and I'm immediately grateful I let her come inside the hospital with me. I'm used to going it alone, to facing my demons and getting through life with only my shadow by my side, but to have a loving and caring girlfriend here supporting me through this is the greatest relief.

"Let's go sit down," Lily suggests as she pulls back from me. In the slight upturn of her lips, I can tell she's trying to put on a positive expression to make me feel better. She knows how much I love to see a smile on her face.

Lily takes my hand and leads me toward the chairs in the waiting area. We sit down next to each other, and for the next excruciating hour, Lily does nothing but comfort me with her touch and soft kisses. With her help, I find a state of calm that I've desperately needed after the potentially life-changing events of today. For at least these moments together with Lily, I can temporarily remain in denial of my mistakes and their awful consequences. It's only temporary, but I'll take it. I need any form of respite at this point even if it's as fleeting as a dream.

An older woman in a white lab coat emerges from the double doors that I've been starting at for the past hour, and it takes a moment for me to truly believe she's there. She heads straight toward me and Lily as we are the only two people left in the waiting room at this late hour.

"I'm Dr. Thompson." She introduces herself with an extended hand as both Lily and I stand up to greet her.

I briefly shake her hand but am ready to move past the introductions to what I need to know. "How is he?"

"He's stable. There's no apparent internal bleeding or significant head trauma, though he does have a mild concussion. We'll continue to monitor for blood flow and pressure issues in the brain. He's bruised up and has a broken arm, but we expect he'll make a full recovery."

I breathe a sigh of relief at the same time Lily takes my hand and squeezes it tightly.

He's going to be fine.

Everything will be okay.

"You can see him now," the doctor says with a smile as she motions to the double doors on the other side of the room. "He's unconscious, but you're welcome to stay with him."

I immediately turn to Lily next to me and pull our connected hands to my chest, hoping I'm not about to upset her with what I'm about to say. "Thank you for being here for me, but I need to see him alone." I see the workings of a refusal on her face and quickly add, "I want you back there with me, but I can't. I just need you to trust me."

Lily opens her mouth to say something but quickly thinks better of it. She nods toward the double doors with an understanding grin. "Go see him."

I kiss the top of her hand before letting go and following the doctor through the doors and down the hallway to Robert's room. Despite knowing the prognosis is good, the moment I walk through the door and see Robert's unconscious body splayed out in the hospital bed, I feel completely shattered inside. My eyes burn with the sting of tears at the sight of the bandages on his wrinkled face and the sling that holds his broken arm. He looks so fragile lying there, and I'm immediately reminded that I'm the one who caused this. It's my fault that he was out driving to begin with. He never should have been on the road when that drunk driver hit him.

It's all my fault.

"I'll leave you alone. Press the call button if you need anything," the doctor says with a gentle smile. I nod at her, unable to manage anything more for fear of letting these emotions inside me emerge and overwhelm me.

Taking a seat in the chair next to the hospital bed, I grasp Robert's free hand in mine, being careful not to disturb the device encompassing his forefinger or the IV in his arm. His skin feels cold, as if death had its grip on him long enough to leave this trace of it behind. I hold his hand and dip my head for a moment, needing to find the courage to look Robert in the face and say what I need to say even though he's not conscious to hear it.

With a deep breath, I look up at him. "I'm sorry. I'm so fucking sorry." The tears I've been holding back finally fall, my body's expression of guilt over what I've done. "This never should have happened. I was selfish and careless, and in the end you paid the price. I let you and our family down, and I'll never do that again. We have so little in life yet so much to lose, and I won't risk it anymore. I can't."

"You have to," Robert whispers in a raspy voice, and if I wasn't watching his lips move as he spoke, I would have thought I was imagining his response. He clears his throat and sluggishly opens his eyes. "There's no actual living in a life without risk. I learned that the hard way with your mother."

I immediately release his hand and stand up at the side of the bed, unsure how to react in my shocked state of seeing Robert awake and speaking. "They said you were unconscious. Hell, you *were* unconscious."

A hint of a smile crosses Robert's bruised and bandaged face. "I've been awake for a while. I just pretended to be asleep. It's a little trick I learned from another elderly gentleman who was part of your life."

My thoughts quickly move past his reference to Jack to ask my burning questions. "What were you listening for? Why didn't you tell me you were awake?"

"I may be old and retired, but I'm still a detective at heart. I was gathering information."

I can't help smiling at Robert's admission. "Even about me?"

"Maybe so," he replies with a sly grin before his face turns more serious. "Are you safe to be here? How did you get out?"

"Lily convinced the guy I beat up to drop the charges. They let me go."

Robert nods just slightly. "That's a good start. You're not completely out of the woods, but the risk is much less now."

It's a huge weight off my shoulders to hear Robert say this. I may not have to run after all. I may actually get through this awful day unscathed.

"I meant what I said," I reaffirm. "I'm really sorry about all this. It's my fault you're in that hospital bed."

Robert raises his free hand in a feeble attempt to stop me from saying more. "You can't control fate. It has a mind of its own."

I shake my head in disagreement. "Fate may have led you to be on that road at the exact moment of the accident, but I'm the one who put you on the road to begin with."

"You can't live in regret, Dante," Robert replies decisively. "I won't let you." He stares at me for a moment, and if I look closely enough, I can almost see the tears forming in the corners of his eyes. "So many things led us to this moment, a lot of them really horrible things, but if they never happened, we may never have reached this point. You may never have existed."

He's describing perfectly the part of my family's story that was the hardest for me to understand when my parents first told me everything as a teenager. It was unfathomable to me that people could find love and happiness while experiencing such pain and absolute darkness. It took some time for me to understand that although we have no control over what's already happened, it's where we end up and what we make of our lives that matter. Our pasts don't define us; they only shape who we are today.

I look away as I can feel my emotions threatening to get the better of me. I need a change in subject or I'm going to lose it here. "I should probably start making phone calls. I couldn't bring myself to call them until I knew you were okay."

"Call your parents. I'll call Cindy. You know I'll need to talk her off the ledge when she finds out where I am."

I nod back to him just as there's a soft knock at the door. A young nurse peeks her head in before walking into the room completely. "You're awake," she says cheerfully to Robert.

She immediately starts fussing over him, adjusting his pillows and checking his IV. In the moment she turns to look at the monitor with his heart rate and other information, Robert gives me a silent look of understanding that I should go make the call that needs to be made while the nurses and doctors tend to him.

"I'll be in the waiting room if you need me." I grasp Robert's free arm lightly and return his warm smile with my own before leaving the room and closing the door behind me.

Relief continues to wash over me as I walk down the hallway back to the waiting room. Robert seems in relatively decent shape and in good spirits, all things considered. The doctor seemed comfortable that a full recovery was likely. I just have one final hurdle to jump over before this painful day is over.

As I'm pulling out my phone and deciding how best to explain to Lily that I need to make this phone call alone, I push through the double doors and enter the waiting area again. Lily's sitting right where she was before, but something's different. There's a look of horror on her face. All color is gone from her skin, and when I get closer to her, I see the tears running silently down her cheeks.

I reach her in just a few more long strides, immediately kneeling down in front of her. "What's wrong? Lily, talk to me."

When her eyes meet mine, they're swirling with a mixture of emotions: fear, shock, pain, and something I can't quite place. Is it pity?

"Dante," she whispers, her voice trembling, "I know who you are."

23

I stare at Lily in shock as she bursts into tears and throws her arms around my neck. I need to ask her about what she said, to understand what happened in the time I was with Robert, but I can't have her making a scene like this here. We need to go somewhere private, so I scoop Lily up in my arms and carry her through the glass sliding doors into the darkness outside.

A bench down the sidewalk near a lamppost catches my attention and I make my way there, carefully setting Lily down on it before taking a seat next to her. My hands move in soothing circles on her back in an attempt to calm her down, but the longer I wait for her tears to subside, the more panicked I become about what she said.

"Lily, I need you to tell me what you meant," I say unsteadily, unable to wait a second longer to find out more from her.

"Robert Whitford," she chokes out quietly, and at the mention of my grandfather's name, my entire body stiffens. "The nurses changed shifts while you were gone. The new nurse at the reception desk asked if I was waiting to see Robert Whitford."

I don't dare move or speak. I don't make any further acknowledgement that I know what Lily's talking about.

She takes a moment to breathe as her tears finally start to slow. "The thing is, I know that name. It came up in my research for a class about social media in journalism. His family's case is the textbook example of viral social media campaigns fueling a news story. For years the entire world was absolutely determined to find that baby."

Lily's eyes meet mine, and my immediate reaction is to run. She's not just looking at me; she's seeing inside me, past the facade I put forth to the world to view all my secrets hidden within.

"I thought the name was just a coincidence," she continues, "but the more I thought about it, the more it made sense. You're about the right age. You've lived here your entire life. You were homeschooled and were barely let out of the house growing up. You have all these secrets about your past." She pauses and waits for me to say something, but I'm too terrified to speak. I feel like I can barely breathe. "You're him, aren't you? You were that missing baby."

I feel like my entire world is collapsing in on me and there's absolutely nothing I can do about it. Lily knows who I am. She knows my family is here.

She's a fucking investigative journalist with the story of the decade in her back pocket.

I don't realize my hands are shaking until Lily grabs them both in hers and squeezes tightly. I'm vaguely aware of her trying to talk to me, but I can't process what she's saying. I can think at all right now as my mind races through the implications of this and the possibilities of what happens next.

I need to get home to my family. We need to run, to abandon this place and get far away from here.

Then I remember where my grandfather is and how I put him there, and suddenly it's all too much. I can't take it anymore. The emotions and pain and guilt build to a breaking point within me, and I shatter apart completely.

"Marini," I whisper, and Lily freezes next to me. "My last name is Marini, and my parents aren't the dangerous criminals the world thinks they are." My voice builds with each word, anger and pent-up frustration seething through each syllable. "They loved me and cared for me since the moment I was born, so fuck the rest of the world for thinking otherwise."

"Dante..." Lily pulls me into her embrace, and I grip her back just as tightly. Silent tears stream down my face, but they're not caused by something I expect. They're fueled by relief. After keeping this secret locked inside for my entire life, it's liberating to finally tell it, even though I don't know what it will mean for my future.

"I don't know what happens now," I admit after a few minutes, immediately prompting Lily to pull back from me.

"What do you mean?"

"I have to tell my parents you know about my family. I have to tell them about my arrest today… and my grandfather's accident." *God, my parents are going to fucking kill me.* "I can't hide these things from them. If they think the risk is high enough, then we'll have to run."

Lily immediately shakes her head. "No. You have to trust that I won't say anything about this. I would never do anything to put you or your family in danger."

I shift in my seat uneasily. "I want to trust you, but look at it from my perspective. You're a damn journalist. That's almost as bad as if you were a cop." A heavy sigh escapes me as I realize the other part of all this that I'll have to tell my parents. "I haven't even told my family that you work for a newspaper. That fact alone will make them want to skip town."

"Then I'll quit."

I look at Lily incredulously. "What?"

"I'll stop writing the column for the paper. I'll send in my resignation tonight, effective immediately."

I'm stunned into silence for a moment by Lily's suggestion. "You can't give up your dreams for this. I don't want you abandoning your career."

Lily shrugs. "Lately I've realized it wasn't all it was cracked up to be, and it doesn't mean I have to stop writing completely. I'll just steer clear of journalism and stick to other forms of writing."

Peering out into the dark and quiet parking lot, I struggle to find the right answer. I don't like the thought of Lily changing the course of her life like this, but it would go a long way toward proving to my parents that she has no intention of selling us out to the public or the authorities.

With a heavy sigh, I reluctantly nod. "I just want you to be happy."

"Being with you makes me happy." A content grin flashes across Lily's face just briefly before a more serious look returns. "I love you. I would do anything to protect you."

I lean in to kiss her, my lips doing all subsequent talking for me as they show her all my love and how deeply I care about her. By the time I pull back from our exchange, I know I can't push this off any longer. It's time to make the phone call I've been dreading.

Lily watches me fish the phone out of my pocket and immediately stands up. "I can go wait inside if you want."

I shake my head and encircle her waist with my free hand to pull her back down to the bench. "I want you next to me. I want to hold on to you for as long as I can." I don't want to acknowledge that this is the end, but it could be. The next five minutes will dictate the course of the rest of my life, and I can only hope that Lily will be a part of it.

As I dial the number, Lily entwines her arm with mine and grasps my free hand, giving me exactly the support I need at this moment. My heart races within my chest as I wait for one of my parents to answer the call.

The call connects, and after a few seconds of muffled shuffling, I hear my dad's raspy voice. "What's wrong?"

"Sorry to wake you." I figure I'll start out small before I really lay this on them. "Did I wake up Mom, too?"

There's silence for a moment before I hear my mom on the line. "I'm here. You're on speaker. What's going on?"

"A lot's happened today," I start out before realizing how much of an understatement that truly is. "Before I say anything else, I need you to know that despite everything that's happened, I truly believe we're going to be okay."

"Dante, you're scaring me," my mom says shakily.

With a deep breath and a glance to my side at Lily's comforting face, I press forward. "I was arrested today. A guy was feeling Lily up at the tavern, and I snapped. They booked me at the station, but Lily convinced the guy not to press charges."

"What were you thinking?" Dad says under his breath. "Jesus Christ, Dante. They could have discovered you."

"But they didn't," I interject. "Robert doesn't think they will, either."

"He already knows about this?"

"That's the next thing I need to tell you." My throat instantly constricts at the memory seared into my brain of Robert stuck in that hospital bed. "I called him from the station. He was coming there to help me, but there was an accident. A drunk driver hit his SUV and ran him off the road. He's got a concussion and some bruises and a broken arm, but they think he'll be fine."

The faint sobs of my mom crying fill the otherwise silence of the call. I can hear my dad speaking in hushed voice to my mom, but I can't make out what he's saying.

"Does Cindy know?" Dad asks calmly.

"Robert's going to call her. He thought he should break the news."

"He's at the hospital now?"

"Yes. We're there with him."

"Who's we?" Dad asks with concern before there's a sharp intake of breath over the line. "You have Lily there with you in the same building as Robert? What the hell are you thinking?"

"Dad, you need to calm down."

"Calm down?" he says in disbelief, his voice escalating. "You've got yourself arrested and landed your grandfather in the hospital all in the same day. How the fuck am I supposed to calm down after hearing that?"

I remove the phone from my ear and close my eyes, finding it physically impossible to continue in this conversation. The tightening in my chest becomes unbearable, and I have to let the emotions out. I burst into a sob, unable to collapse my hand over my mouth in time to prevent its escape. Lily's arms are instantly around me, and while I want nothing more than to find comfort in her presence and her touch, it feels like nothing can make this situation better right now. I've failed my family in every possible way. My dad has every right to be furious with me and disappointed in me.

I ruined everything.

Before I even realize what she's doing, Lily grabs the phone from my hand and puts it to her ear as she stands up and walks away with it. "You need to understand something about your son," she says forcefully into the phone as I get up to chase after her into the parking lot. "He's the kindest, most caring person I know. He protects me and makes me smile and fucking makes life worth living. Sure, he made a mistake or two, but you need to hear him out and cut him some slack."

Lily doesn't wait for a response. She stops in her tracks and hands the phone back to me. Even in the darkness I can tell she has a fiery look on her face.

In the shock of what just happened, my emotions come completely back in check. I reluctantly put the phone back to my ear and clear my throat. "That was Lily, by the way."

Silence fills the line. I begin to wonder if they hung up the phone, but my dad's voice finally comes through again. "She's right. We need to hear you out. You said everything was going to be okay, and we trust you. Just tell us the rest of it."

Pacing back and forth a few steps each way, I work up the courage to tell them the final pieces of my failures today. "Lily knows who we are. She never saw Robert, but a nurse called him by his full name and Lily recognized it. She knows our family's history."

"How did she—"

"She's a journalist," I quickly interject, ready to get this over with. "She writes a monthly column for a newspaper in Bangor."

"A journalist? You've been dating a journalist for the last three months?"

"An investigative journalist, to be exact," I clarify, wincing at my own words. "She has no intention of telling anyone who we are, though. She's even willing to quit her job at the paper to prove it to us."

"But can we trust her?" Dad sighs heavily. "If she turns us in, there are no second chances. It will be the end for us."

"We're in love," I admit simply as my eyes find Lily's. "I don't know what greater level of trust you can have between two people than that."

I wait anxiously as I hear my parents in a hushed discussion on the other end of the line. Lily watches me with concern, and I'm immediately drawn to her, closing the distance between us so that I can pull her against my chest and hold her close to me. I'll hold on to her for as long as I can while my parents decide my fate.

"It's okay, Dante," my mom finally says, though her voice is unsteady. "Everything will be okay. We're just glad you're safe." She takes a deep breath, clearly having a hard time with this, and I wish nothing more than I could be there with her right now to comfort her. A half-laugh, half-sob escapes her. "Tell your grandfather to hurry up and heal already. We can't risk coming to the hospital if they figure out who he is, so tell him we wish we could be there."

"I will. I'm so sorry about all of this."

"Don't be sorry; just be careful," Mom replies. "We love you."

"Love you, too."

As I drop the phone from my ear and end the call, Lily looks up at me from where I still have her held to my chest. "You doing okay?"

I nod in response, pleased to find that despite the trying events of today, I really do feel okay. "I don't have to leave town. We can still be together."

"Thank God." Lily sighs in relief and snuggles into me even more. "You're always protecting me and making me feel safe and loved. It's time you let me do the same for you. I'll protect your secret."

Lily pulls back just enough to look up at me with her loving eyes before she presses her lips to mine. I could stay like this forever, our mouths meeting and our bodies embracing and our souls colliding, but I know I need to go inside the hospital and check on Robert. I pull back from Lily and glance to the emergency room entrance. "I should go back inside."

With a smile and a nod, Lily takes my hand and walks with me back toward the hospital. "Let's get you back to your grandfather."

24

In the few days it's been since the snowballing events that threatened to change the course of my life, I've found myself torn apart internally, and the emotional toll it's taking on me has been utterly exhausting. I'm grateful to have had Lily by my side and the support of my parents when I went to see them the day after everything happened, but despite the encouraging words they've thrown at me and the fact that Robert is out of the hospital and recovering at home, it's hard to push past the guilt I feel over what happened.

No matter what they say, I know it was all my fault. Everything that happened that day was because of me, and no matter how long and hard I think about it, I can never change that. It's a devastating feeling.

"I can't take it anymore," Lily says in frustration as she plops down on the couch next to me. I guess she's caught on to my aimless staring out the window in the living room for the past half-hour. She looks at me with expectation, as if I'm missing my cue to jump in and ask her what she's talking about, before she sighs and demands, "We're going out. I'm taking you somewhere. Well, actually, you're taking me there, because I don't know how to get there."

I give her a sideways glance. "Where is there?"

"Your favorite place in the world. Your special spot in the woods." She looks away and seems to think for a moment. "Though I'm bringing something soft to sit on this time. That damn rock bench is great for serenity but doesn't do much for comfort."

I laugh as Lily grabs my arm with both hands and forcibly pulls on me, though I don't budge an inch. "I don't know."

"I do know. Girlfriend always knows best." She stands up and doubles her efforts to yank me up with her.

When it starts to feel like my arm might come out of its socket, I give in and stand up with her. "Okay. We'll go."

Lily bursts into a smile and kisses me briefly on the cheek. "Perfect. I want you to relax, and if you're a good boy and do just that, maybe we'll have a little fun while we're there."

She winks at me before strutting away, highlighting her backside to me with each step she takes toward the stairs in the snug yoga pants she's wearing.

That alone is enough motivation for me to go along with this.

After getting dressed and packing some drinks, snacks, and a blanket, we head out in my car to my hidden entrance to the waterfall area. It's a beautiful fall day as we drive through the woods, the air's temperature taking on a bit of crispness but maintaining enough heat from the sun to make it feel like earlier in the fall than it really is.

I park the car and grab our supplies before following Lily down the overgrown path painted with fallen leaves into the woods. We've only been here a few times since the day I first brought her here over two months ago, but by the way Lily is taking the trail, you'd think she'd been down this path a million times already.

I have to resist the urge to skip straight to the fun part of this outing as we walk past the grassy area near the waterfall. Making that stop first would defeat the purpose of this trip. Lily's right. My rock bench along the creek is where I'll have the best shot at finding clarity in my thoughts and some amount of peace with what I've done. I need to face that battle first before I move on to other more welcome distractions.

When we arrive at the rock bench, I lay the folded blanket down on it to make the seat more comfortable before helping Lily up onto the rock and taking a seat next to her. The moment I'm seated, I can already feel the calm taking over me. The subtle sounds of nature and the flowing creek play a beautiful soft soundtrack in the background as I close my eyes and focus my thoughts.

Lily wraps her arm around my back and gently rests her head against my shoulder, but she doesn't say anything. We sit like this in silence for a while until I'm alerted by a sound nearby. My eyes shoot open and immediately scan the woods around us.

"What is it?" Lily asks quietly, sitting up with concern.

"Something's out there," I whisper before jumping down from the rock. "Stay here. Let me check it out."

She nods with worry as I pull a switchblade out of my back pocket. I'd rather have my dad's hunting rifle in my hands, but this will have to do.

With soft steps on the dirt, I make my way silently up the path in the direction of the sound I heard. The adrenaline coursing through me hits its peak and my heart skips a beat in my chest when I see the source of the sound.

My parents are walking down the path toward me. They're coming here from the house.

I look behind me to gauge how far I've moved from the rock bench, but it isn't that far. I can see Lily straining her eyes to see where I'm looking in the distance. It's possible she's already spotted my parents' approach.

Bolting into a quick run, I close the distance between me and my parents as quickly as possible, looking up just in time to see their shocked faces at finding me here.

"What are you doing here?" Mom asks as Dad scans the woods around us.

I ignore the question and get straight to the most important point. "Lily's here. She's at the rock bench. She may have seen you."

Mom's hand flies to her mouth as she turns to my dad. They seem to be having some kind of silent conversation between them before Dad nods and addresses me. "Can we meet her?"

"What?" I don't know why I'm questioning him. I've dreamed of introducing Lily to my parents, though I've never let myself acknowledge that it could ever be more than just a dream.

"We've wanted to meet her for a while now," Mom explains, "we just didn't know the right way to go about it. This seems like a good opportunity."

I'm completely stunned. My jaw is hanging open and likely hitting the dirt path below. This isn't how I envisioned this going down. I never saw this happening at all.

"Sure," I blurt out. "We can do this now."

My mom laughs and pulls me to her in a hug. "Don't look so terrified. I promise we won't scare her away."

"Sorry, I just wasn't expecting this. We've never done this before." When we pull away from our embrace, I look back and forth between my parents. "You're sure about this?"

Dad pats me on the shoulder before motioning to the path ahead. "Let's go meet your girlfriend."

It feels a bit like I've entered an alternate reality on the opposite side of the universe as I take the first steps back down the path toward the rock bench, my parents following closely behind me. I can barely process this situation let alone figure out what I'm going to say to Lily when we get to her.

When we emerge about fifty feet away from behind a tree, Lily looks up and spots us. The initial confused expression on her face quickly dissipates into a look of understanding mixed with shock. She hops down from the rock just as we approach.

I clear my throat awkwardly, struggling to find my voice to say the words I never dreamed would leave my mouth. "Lily, these are my parents, Morgan and Leo."

Lily hesitates a moment before extending her hand to my mom. "It's great to meet you."

Mom smiles and takes her hand but pulls her into a hug instead. "And you as well."

When they pull back from each other, my dad steps in with his hand extended and no intention of anything more, which doesn't surprise me given he's never been much of a hugger. Lily glances from his hand all the way up his tattooed arm before finding his face and greeting him in the handshake.

"I don't know how you've kept Dante to one tattoo given how many you have," she says in disbelief.

"He has the only one that's important." My dad maintains his smile, though his expression falters enough for me to notice. If I had even a few minutes to prep Lily for this conversation, I would have warned her that my dad's tattoos are a bit of a sore subject for him. They're more than just ink on his skin. They're the marks of his past, the visual reminders he carries of the pain he went through and the people he lost. I wonder if in her assessment of his arm she noticed the marks he didn't put there himself, the scars that mark him from his years of growing up with a monster for a father figure.

With the introductions complete, my mind quickly works to figure out what happens next. The rock only has enough space for two people, so I grab the folded blanket Lily and I were sitting on and spread it out over a nearby widening in the path.

"Let's have a seat," I offer, though my suggestion is as much for my own benefit as everyone else's. I feel like I need to sit down right now to get me through this conversation.

We settle onto the blanket, Lily sitting next to me with my parents together across from us. After a few moments of awkward silence, I'm about to speak up to save this meeting from turning into a disaster, but Lily beats me to it.

"I want to thank you for trusting me," she says quietly as she looks between each of my parents. "I can't imagine not having Dante in my life. I would never do something to put him or any of you in danger."

"We've been distrustful of the world for too long," Mom admits. "We need to open up more. We're trying to find a better balance of being careful and letting ourselves and Dante truly live."

Lily nods her understanding. "I'm sorry about my little tirade on the phone the other day. I get a little defensive of your son."

"He needs a woman like that in his life," my dad replies with a knowing smile toward my mom. From almost the beginning of the ordeal my parents went through when they first met, my mom was protecting my dad almost as much as he was trying to protect her. It's part of what made them fall so hard for each other.

Lily turns to me with a playful grin before surprising me with a soft kiss to my cheek. "I enjoy being that woman in his life."

I can feel my cheeks flaring with the heat of my embarrassment as I look from Lily to my parents. They're both smiling wildly as Dad holds Mom's hand in his lap.

"I see it now," Lily says with astonishment, and I immediately turn to see what she's looking at. Her eyes are trained on my parents' hands, or more specifically, their wrists. "That's where the symbol comes from."

In recognition of what Lily's trying to say, Mom moves her wrist directly next to Dad's so that their symmetrical black tattoos of an almost completely enclosed circle meet up at the missing parts of the lines to form the symbol of infinity. Mom smiles down at it and says, "There's a long story behind these tattoos." She sighs deeply before lifting her head to look at Lily. "Do you want to hear it?"

The world seems to stop around us at my mom's suggestion. Is she insane? Who is this woman sitting before me? Why isn't my dad freaking out at the very thought of talking about our family's past?

I look back and forth between them, expecting at any moment I'm going to wake up on the couch at Lily's house having just dreamed this conversation and encounter in my head completely, but I'm really here. My mom really did just make that suggestion, and my dad isn't fighting it.

Lily seems almost as taken aback as I am at the offer on the table. She looks to me for guidance. "I've always said this was your story to tell. I don't want this to make you uncomfortable, but I want to understand. I want to know all parts of you and your family."

I'm immediately brought back to the moment on the bench at the hospital a few nights ago when I admitted to Lily that she was right about who I am. Just speaking my real last name to her was an incredibly liberating feeling. It's difficult to imagine the weight that would be lifted from my shoulders if she knew our whole story.

The world will never know my family's story or understand the painful truths behind it, but it doesn't matter. Lily is my world, and I want her to understand. I want her to know me for who I truly am, straight down to the basic clay I was carved from.

I take her hand in mine, ignoring any thoughts of embarrassment as I kiss her lips softly but with every bit of love I have for her. When I pull back, I see she is the one with the reddened cheeks now, and she's absolutely beautiful.

"Yes," I reply with conviction before turning to my parents. "It's time for someone to hear our story."

25

"Damn it. Where's that screwdriver?" I mumble to myself as my eyes scan our bedroom. Lily's shift ends in less than an hour. There's no time to waste looking for tools.

I finally spot the screwdriver on the dresser, it somehow blending in with the containers of makeup Lily has strewn across the wooden surface. After snagging the tool, I jump back up to standing on the bed to finish attaching the new light fixture to the ceiling. It's the final touch on this room I've spent the entire day remodeling, from a fresh coat of vibrant but not too bright yellow paint on the walls to the colorful abstract art on the walls. I even had a local consignment shop deliver a modern chaise lounge with a small side table to give Lily the retreat she was looking for in this bedroom.

When the light fixture is secured in place, I hop down from the bed and stand by the door to inspect my handiwork. The room could still use some more decorating, but it's come miles from its white empty walls that were so wrong for this room given Lily's lively personality.

After a quick shower and getting dressed in a new gray button-up shirt and jeans that Lily helped me pick out recently, I rush to get dinner started, hoping I can at least get the lasagna in the oven before Lily gets home from work. I take care to set the table even though we never do any other day, even setting up candles I found buried in one of the drawers in the kitchen.

Even though I know Lily's shift is just about to end, I breathe a little easier knowing I already have the lasagna cooking. The salad is chopped and on the table, and my fresh Italian bread is sliced and ready to go. I look at the clock and get a little nervous as I realize Lily could be walking in the door any minute now.

I pace around the dining room, glancing at the front door every so often expecting it to open. When the buzzer on the oven goes off for the lasagna, I start to get worried. Lily's shift has been over for a half-hour. She should be home by now.

After taking the lasagna out of the oven, I find that I have to sit down to calm my nerves or I'm going to run ruts into this Pergo flooring with all my pacing back and forth. I give it another ten minutes before I can't take it any longer and I try calling her.

It goes straight to voicemail.

I run my hands through my hair anxiously as an internal debate plays out in my mind. Do I give her more time? Do I go look for her? Is she just working late or could something be wrong?

An idea hits me to call the tavern to see if she's still there. Just as I'm about to grab my phone from the table, the front door opens.

"Thank God," I say with relief as I stand up to meet Lily at the door. She steps in and closes the door behind her before turning around to look at me.

Her eyes look empty.

Her expression is somber.

She is nothing but a shell standing before me.

"What's wrong?" I implore, grabbing her shoulders and searching her brown eyes for any sign of what could be causing this catatonic state she's in. I glance at her neck and notice it's bare even though it wasn't this morning. The infinity necklace I gave her that she wears every day is missing.

"I need to talk to you," she replies with a noticeable thickness to her voice. She sounds on the verge of tears.

"Okay," I respond cautiously as I encircle her waist with my arm and motion her toward the dining room table. She takes a seat as I pull up a chair next to her and take her hands in mine between us.

She glances up at the lit candles and the full dinner I've set up on the table before squinting her eyes closed, forcing silent tears to fall down her cheeks.

"Lily, talk to me," I beg, reinforcing my grip on her hands. "Please tell me what's going on."

"I can't be with you anymore," she blurts out, and my heart stops beating inside my chest.

It takes me a moment to find my voice again. "What are you talking about?"

"We're over," she cries out before breaking into a sob. "We can't be together. I need you to move out. Now."

I'm speechless. I don't know who this woman is in front of me. She's not my Lily. She can't be. Something is off with her. I just need to find out what it is.

"Lily," I plead, my voice shaking. "Please tell me this is some kind of joke."

"It's no joke!" she screams. "This is serious, Dante. I need you out of here tonight, and I never want to see your face again."

Her words pierce into my heart with striking pain unlike I've ever felt in my life. It's devastating. She's absolutely destroying me. "Why? I don't understand."

"There's nothing to understand!" She rips her hands away from mine and stands up from her chair to back away from me. "You just need to leave. It's over, Dante. Do you hear me? It's over!" I stand up and take a step toward her, but she holds her hand out to stop me. "Don't," she warns carefully, and it's the final straw. That one word and the look of hatred and disgust on her face successfully shatter the remainder of my heart within my chest.

Silent tears fall freely from my eyes, my body's expression of the confusion and devastation and grief that are consuming me from within. "I'll do as you ask," I concede, "I just want to know why."

"You really want to know why?" She takes two forceful steps toward me and looks me directly in the eyes. "Because I can't date a fugitive from the law. I'll never mix my DNA with the criminal scum of this Earth."

Whatever bits and pieces of my heart were left in my chest disappear into nothing. I feel completely hollow. I feel worthless. She used her knowledge of my family's story to deliver the lowest possible blow she could, and she succeeded.

I give in.

I can't fucking handle this anymore.

Without another word, I turn and walk up the stairs to our bedroom–Lily's bedroom–and empty my drawer in her dresser into my duffel bag from her closet. I'm barely keeping myself together as I move on to the bathroom and dump my toiletries into the bag.

The constant shaking of my hands makes it difficult to zip up the bag as I walk back downstairs, my walk of shame or misery or whatever the fuck this nightmare is. Out of the corner of my eye I see Lily standing between the dining room and living room with her hands crossed over her chest, but I can't look at her. I can't do any more to acknowledge that the woman I love just turned on a dime out of nowhere and threw me out of her life forever.

I grab my phone from the dining room table and my keys from the kitchen counter. My hand barely touches the doorknob of the front door when I hear Lily say behind me in a low voice, "Your key."

The pain in my chest hits its peak as I drop my bag and struggle to work Lily's house key off my key ring. I set it on the dining room table without looking anywhere else in the room. I don't want to remember my last moments with Lily like this. I can't bear to see her face as I walk out that door and out of her life.

I feel numb as I open the door to the darkness outside and close it behind me. I'm not two steps down the path to the driveway when I hear Lily start wailing from inside the house, her devastation in what just happened apparently hitting her just as hard as it hit me.

By the time I'm seated in my car with the key in the ignition, I feel hopelessly lost. I spent the last few months of my life in a relationship that just crumbled away before my eyes. I trusted Lily with my heart, my past, and my future, and she just threw it all away like it meant absolutely nothing.

When I turn on the car and the classic rock station starts blaring, I scramble to turn off the music that I know to be Lily's favorite. It becomes quickly apparent that I can't stand to be in this driveway a moment longer. The tires screech repeatedly as I back out the car to an abrupt halt and floor the gas to propel me forward. I'm desperate to get far away from here as fast as possible.

I can't go home. I can't face my parents like this. With nowhere else to go, I make my way to the highway and start driving west, making it all the way past Augusta before I realize the futility of this effort.

Pulling off the highway into a service area, I park in a far corner of the lot to put as much space as possible between me and the other travelers at the rest area, though I can't stop looking at them. My eyes remain fixed on the constant coming and going of families and couples and people with lives and happiness that I had a taste of but will never know again. I won't deny the gut-wrenching feeling that festers within me at reverting back to being an observer to the rest of the world, destined to watch from the outside and only ever dream of the lives these people are living that they constantly take for granted.

At some point the flow of cars and people slows considerably, and I realize it must be the middle of the night. I also realize I haven't had anything to eat or drink in hours, so I get out of the car and drag myself into the service station. I stop at the restroom but don't dare look at myself in the mirror while I'm in there. I don't want to see my crumbled appearance or hollow eyes. I've felt enough of my devastation already. I don't need to see it plastered across my face.

I pick up a hot dog and bottle of water at the twenty-four-hour gas station before heading back outside into the cool night air. As I reenter my car, I'm painfully reminded of what I left behind: the homemade dinner I made for Lily and the bed I should be sleeping in with her right now. Instead I'm over seventy miles away about to eat gas station food and sleep in my car.

The pain in my chest is too overwhelming. I abruptly step out of the car and launch the hot dog as far as I can throw it across the almost empty parking lot. Sobs rack my chest as I sit back down and slam the door shut. My fingers press painfully into my forehead as I try to calm myself down.

My mind and body are spent. I need a break from the real world. I need to sleep, even if it means I'll relive portions of this awful evening as nightmares.

I gulp down as much of the water bottle as I can before reclining my seat and turning on my side. It's impossible to look at the passenger seat and not imagine Lily sitting there bobbing her head to classic rock with the window down and her brown hair dancing wildly around her face. I quickly shut my eyes but find it takes a long time to enter the dark depths of sleep. I let it take me away from my reality, though it feels like the darkness has already consumed me.

After a fitful night's sleep in my car at the rest area, I wake up to feeling completely exhausted. With a quick stop inside at the service station, I get back on the road and head east to the only place I have left to go.

It's late morning by the time I make it to my parents' house. When I park the car and kill the engine, absolute stillness surrounds me, a terrifying reminder that this is the life I'm back to, one of silence, solitude, and emptiness.

It's a life I can't live any longer.

I've managed to remain calm this morning and for the entire drive back home, but now that I'm here and facing the life I never wanted to go back to, I can feel my emotions rising uncontrollably within me. My anguish builds to raging anger as I slam my hand against the steering wheel repeatedly, letting it share in the full extent of my pain.

Then I stop, the memory hitting me like a cold bucket of water to the face. This is what brought me to Lily so many months ago. This is what started it all. I was in this car, frustrated and angry with the course of my life and how helpless I felt to direct its path. After all these months, I'm right back here again, alone and helpless with no direction, no purpose.

All my family's suffering and sacrifices were for nothing, because in the end, I am nothing.

There's a knock at my window, scaring the hell out of me. Dad gives me a little wave before stepping back so I can open the door.

As I step out of the car, I immediately notice his face is covered in sweat despite the fall chill in the air. By the looks of his dirty hands and arms, he's likely spent the entire morning chopping wood in the backyard to prepare for the impending winter months.

Months I will spend alone, locked away in this house like I have been for almost my entire life.

"What are you doing here?" Dad asks curiously. When I don't immediately respond, he glances into my car, his eyes widening at the duffel bag on the back seat. "Uh oh. Trouble in paradise?"

I don't laugh at his joke. It only fuels the anger swirling inside me, but it makes me think for a moment. My eyes narrow toward my father as something occurs to me. "Did you threaten her?" I ask in a low voice that sounds nothing like me. The events of last night have turned me into someone I don't recognize, and I hate this person who clearly exists within me.

Dad grabs my shoulder and meets me at eye level. "What are you talking about?"

"Lily." That word that has represented all the joy and vitality and meaning in my life suddenly feels wrong rolling off my tongue. "Did you try to push her away from me? Did you threaten her somehow?"

"Now wait a minute." Dad slowly backs away, looking at me incredulously. "You really think I'd do something like that to her? You think I'd hurt you that way?"

"I don't know, Dad," I snap with frustration. "I don't know what the fuck is going on. It's like someone flipped a switch in her." I throw my hands in the air and pace the length of my car. "She threw me out last night. She doesn't ever want to see me again."

"Last night? Where have you been since then?"

I hear the front door of the house open before Mom calls out to me, "Dante? What's going on?"

She hurries over to us as Dad presses on with his questioning. "What happened with Lily? What did she say?"

"She said we can't be together. She…" The words get caught in the tightening of my throat as I remember her painful jab directed at my family. "She said she'd never mix her DNA with that of a criminal."

Mom immediately extends her arms toward me, but I only back away. I'm not deserving of her love and support. I'm nothing but a worthless human being.

I never should have even existed.

"Dante, please," my mom begs, but my feet only take me further away. "Dante!"

I hear her yelling after me as I break into a run toward the woods, down the path I've helped carve into the cold ground through years of running from my life and hiding from the world in my only refuge from it all. I keep running through the bushes and trees, my lungs barely able to keep up with my need for oxygen, until I hit the small clearing and hear the sound of the nearby creek. My feet don't stop completely until I'm standing next to the rock bench that has witnessed all the highs and lows of my life.

I stare at the ground next to it, to the place where only two weeks ago my parents poured their hearts and souls out to Lily retelling the story of the extraordinary circumstances under which they met, the hell they went through in the time up until my birth, and the life of hiding we've lived ever since. Everything about that memory is clear in my mind: the tears we cried one moment that turned to laughter we couldn't hold back only minutes later, the relief we felt at temporarily stepping out of hiding for the first time, the joy of realizing that the two worlds I was trying to live in could be one in the same. As I stand here staring at the ground where that memory took place, all I want is to go back there, to feel that happiness and contentment again and let it wash over the hollowness and pain eating away at me from the inside out.

Shaking my head vehemently, I bolt into a run across the dirt and continue down the path with no idea where I'm going or what I'm doing. I come to a screeching halt when I hit the cliff's edge at the waterfall. I look down at the pool of water below, and I can almost see us there, Lily and I splashing each other playfully or wrapping our naked bodies around each other. I can almost hear her laughter echoing off the rock wall behind the waterfall as she teases me and dares me to catch her.

As the memories of Lily and I together swirl around in the waters below, a numbness takes over my mind and body, and I like the lack of feeling. As it consumes me, I crave more of it. I take a step forward, my feet within inches of edge of the cliff. With another small movement, the toes of my shoes hang over the edge of the rock. I peer downward over the edge, my mind willing me to forget about the shallow rocks that I know are just beneath the surface around this edge of the pool.

Deep breath. Deep breath.

I step back and wind up my arms behind me.

A hand catches me.

Someone stops me.

Arms grip on to my chest, pulling me against a warm body to the ground. A rapidly thudding heart reverberates against me. Heavy breathing fills my ears. Wet tears drench my skin. A voice is talking to me, begging for me.

I need to listen.

"I won't lose you." It's my dad's voice. He repeats those words over and over again as he cries against me and doesn't let me go.

The numbness is gone, vanishing out into the open air. The pain comes back to me tenfold as I realize what just happened.

I almost gave up. I was ready to throw my life away.

"I'm sorry," I choke out, but I'm not sure my dad can hear me through his forceful sobs.

Mom appears at the path before throwing herself to the ground in front of us. Her arms are shaking as she wraps them around me and my dad. "Oh my God. Are you okay?"

"No," I answer honestly. "I'm losing it, Mom. I've lost my fucking mind."

"I'm here. We're here for you." She grips us even tighter as she begins to cry. "We're always here for you."

I nod against her and let out my own tears to grieve for the loss of the person I was yesterday morning, the man I will never be again.

26

I poke at the scrambled eggs on my plate with my fork but make no attempt to eat them. The couple bites of buttered toast I had were about all I could manage. These simple things like eating and breathing and existing seem pointless now.

My mother's eyes are on me. They have been for at least a few minutes. I know she's worried about my current state, but I can't even find it within me to make an effort to alleviate her concern. Taking a few bites of egg is all I'd need to do to make her feel better at this moment, and I can't even manage that.

"You need to eat something," she finally prods, just as she has said the last three mornings after I've sat at this table and failed to eat more than a few bites of food.

Pushing the plate away from me, I shake my head. "I'm not hungry."

Mom gets up from her chair at the table across from me and circles around until she's hugging me from behind. "You've barely eaten anything in three days. You're hardly sleeping." She kisses me on the side of the head and squeezes me a little tighter. "You need to take better care of yourself."

I sigh heavily. "It's not that easy, Mom." I glance at my cell phone sitting idly on the center of the table, somehow still believing there's a chance it might ring. The device hasn't left my side in days.

Mom lets go of me and takes a seat in the chair next to mine before taking my hand in hers. She seems to take a moment to think, clearly choosing her words carefully before speaking to me. "I don't think she's going to call."

Her words sting as they smack into me, but my mind deflects them away. "She'll call."

"You need to start moving on, Dante."

"No," I counter forcefully.

"I know it's hard, but you can't keep living like this." She looks away, but I can still see the emotion swirling in her expression. "I can't watch my only son wither away before my eyes."

"You won't have to," I say confidently, "because Lily won't give up on me. She'll call."

Mom returns her gaze to me with hopeless tears lining her reddened eyes, and as much as her pained expression makes me want to start believing she may be right about Lily, I'm not ready to give up on her just yet.

She'll call, I think to myself. *She has to.*

But she doesn't call. Another week goes by, and my phone remains silent and I'm stuck in this house and my entire world becomes limited to this tiny, meaningless speck on the Earth. The leaves continue to fall outside and my refuge in the woods calls to me, but I can't even go there alone to think and process and exist because my parents worry I'll try to throw myself off that damn cliff again.

My feet are right here, firmly planted on the ground, yet why does it feel like I'm still falling?

Another week. More silence. I start to neglect my phone, forgetting to carry it with me everywhere like the extra appendage it was before. I'm eating more now, only because I have to in order to survive, because I need to be here and awake and alive when that phone rings. I have to be ready for it. I know it's coming.

But it never does.

Only silence.

Silence and solitude.

Stepping out of my room for the first time since breakfast, I saunter down the hallway, stopping briefly at the bathroom before making my way to the kitchen with my mind set on a glass of water. The moment I step out of the hallway, though, I'm stunned to a stop by the sight I find in the living room: my grandparents sitting on the couch and my parents in the chairs across from them. They're all staring at me expectantly, and suddenly I feel a little ridiculous standing here in sweats with a frazzled head of hair and a week's worth of scruff on my jaw.

My eyes are immediately drawn to Robert. His arm is finally out of its cast and the lacerations and bruising on his face have healed completely. I continue to feel guilty that I've only seen him during his visits to our house and haven't gone to see him recently, but I can't bring myself to make the drive. The thought of driving past the places that remind of me Lily along the only way to my grandparents' house is just too much for me.

"Your arm is healed," I comment as I approach the couch.

Robert nods and smiles, but the expression doesn't reach his eyes. He's not here for small talk or a family visit.

This is an intervention.

"It's been three weeks," Dad says firmly. "It's over, Dante."

Don't say those words. I hate those words.

"We feel like we're losing you," Mom jumps in, her voice thick with emotion. "You've always been strong, not just for yourself, but for your family. Look at what you've accomplished for us." She motions to my grandparents sitting across the room, living reminders of something amazing I did at great risk not just to improve my own life but the lives of my entire family.

"Things don't always work out the way we expect," Robert explains. "Despite everything we had been through, we were the happiest grandparents in the world up until the day the FBI came knocking at our door when you were just a few weeks old. It only took that one day for everything to change, but in the end we made it here. You and your parents stayed safe, and now we're all free. It took years to get here, but ultimately we made it."

Robert takes Cindy's hand in his and they smile at each other before Cindy turns to me. "You'll find your happiness. You have your entire life ahead of you. There's someone for you out there. You just have to find her."

I know this.

I've already found this girl.

Her name is Lily.

I sigh and run my hands through my hair, desperately trying to process all this under the scrutinizing eyes of my entire family. It's hard to face the idea of giving up on the one person who I thought was it for me, but I can't keep living like this. I've neglected my family and my loyalty to them for far too long. I owe it to them to make an effort. Hell, I owe it to myself.

"Okay," I breathe out, that one word sealing my decision. "It's time to move on."

I can almost feel the blanket of relief settling not just over the room but over me as well. Inhaling a deep breath, I feel like oxygen is finding its way to my lungs for the first time in three weeks.

I tuck the pain away inside and try to focus on this moment and the people around me. I pull up a chair and spend the evening in the company of those who will never give up on me, temporarily forgetting all that I lost a few weeks ago.

Little by little the pain lessens. Within hours I find more peaceful slumber. Within days I'm almost back to eating normal meals again. Within a week I'm able to venture into the woods without my parents' watchful eyes on me.

It almost feels like I'm back to my previous life, to the version of me who existed before the force that was Lily came crashing into my world, but it feels different now. Where life seemed empty and hopeless before, I see promise and potential ahead. The view is hazy, the future blurry and unknown to me, but I'll take steps toward it anyway. At least I know something's there waiting for me. I'm rapidly advancing toward it. I have been my entire life without even realizing it, and I know I'll reach it.

Someday.

27

It feels good to have a hammer in my hand again. I realize this more and more each day I spend back on the job volunteering for Habitat for Humanity. It's only been a little over a week since my family's intervention that prompted me to take this transitional step back onto the path toward my future, but I'm already seeing positive results. The pain isn't gone completely, but the overwhelming weight on my chest has lessened. I've accepted what happened, and though I may not embrace this diverted path with as much enthusiasm as the track I was on a month ago, I'm learning to live with it.

I'm slowly learning to live again.

I've spent the last hour nailing up crown molding in the kitchen of this current house project. It seems appropriate that I'm here building something significant and useful from nothing but wooden boards, nails, and drywall, similar to what I'm doing with my life right now. The bits and pieces of me have been strewn all over the place since Lily cut me from her life a month ago. I'm only now starting to put them all back together again, slowly building the new foundation for my life and my future.

When the final piece of crown molding is attached where the wall meets the ceiling above the kitchen cabinets, I step down from the ladder and assess my handiwork. As I take in the room that really just needs appliances at this point, it occurs to me that I've likely worked through lunch already. I pull out my phone to check the time and contemplate taking a thirty-minute break to grab something to eat.

My brow furrows.

I have a missed call.

It looks familiar. I swear I've seen that number before. It only takes a moment for my memory banks to place it though, because that number is tucked away in the forefront of my mind along with all my other memories I'm holding on to so dearly.

It's the number for CJ's Tavern.

My heart begins to race even though I have no idea what this missed call means. Just because the tavern called me doesn't mean it was Lily dialing my number. Why wouldn't she have just used her cell phone?

Unless something happened to her. Maybe she didn't call because she can't. Maybe she's in the hospital right now and the staff at the tavern knew that I'd want to be informed. Maybe it's even worse than that. She could be dead for all I know. That's how truly disconnected I've been from Lily the last month.

I practically run out of the kitchen and down the hallway toward the empty frame that will hold the front door of the house. Brandon, the project coordinator for this house, is working on some electrical wiring in the hallway and gives me a funny look as I go by. "Everything okay, man?"

I stop and grasp the frame of the door with my free hand to look back at Brandon. "I think so. I need to make a quick call."

"Take your time," he says as he gets back to what he was working on. "You've put in more than your fair share of hours today already."

With a quick nod, I take a few extra strides forward onto the dirt that will eventually become a beautifully landscaped yard for whatever family will live here when the house is done. My fingers hover over the keypad on my phone for a moment before I realize I'm not sure whether to call the tavern or Lily's cell phone first.

I take the safer route, dialing the tavern and putting the phone to my ear cautiously as if it might jump out and bite me at any second.

It rings and rings until someone finally picks up. "CJ's Tavern."

It sounds like Jodi. I hope it's her. "Jodi? This is Dante."

A brief moment of silence passes, and for a moment I wonder if she's already forgotten about my existence. "Dante? Wow, long time no talk."

By the surprise in her voice, it's clear to me that she's not the one who called. I doubt any of the kitchen staff would even know how to get me on the phone, so that leaves only one person who could have dialed my number.

"Is Lily there? I had a missed call from the tavern. I think she called me."

"She did?" There's an unusual amount of surprise in Jodi's voice, and I don't know what that means. "Um, hold on a minute. Let me get her when she comes by. She's just running some food to a table right now."

Jodi sounds nervous but excited at the same time. I want nothing more than to unravel that mystery and ask her what the hell is making her act this way on the phone with me, but I keep my mouth shut. I just need to focus on Lily and why she called.

Pacing my way back and forth across the dirt, I anxiously wait in silence for the twenty or thirty seconds that feel like hours it takes for something other than the garbled sound of voices and sharp clinking glass to fill the call.

"Dante?" Lily says my name with hope and light and life and I wish I could wrap myself around that word and hold on to it forever.

"Hey." I pause, half-expecting Lily to burst into some frantic explanation or apology considering how we left things a month ago. When she doesn't say anything, I force myself to speak, unable to stand another moment without knowing why she reached out to me now. "You called me? Is everything okay?"

The background noise of the tavern grows quieter before Lily answers me, her voice just shy of a whisper. "I need to see you."

Warmth envelopes my chest and spreads throughout my entire body. "Okay. Where do I meet you?"

"Come to the tavern," she says quickly, maintaining her hushed voice, "but don't come inside. I'll keep an eye out for you in the parking lot."

I rush to think how long it will take me to get to the tavern from here, suddenly disappointed in myself for purposefully choosing to work on a project that was in the opposite direction of Lily's place and the tavern. "I'm about thirty minutes away, but I'll be there."

"Good." It's such a simple word, but in those four letters and that one syllable, I can hear every bit of Lily's relief that I'm coming to her, and it feels fucking amazing.

The call abruptly ends, but I don't read too much into our non-existent goodbye. I'm still stuck on that four letter word that came out of Lily's mouth.

In a few long strides, I'm back up at the entrance to the house, gripping its frame as I get Brandon's attention. "Hey, I need to head out for the day. Something came up."

Brandon gives me a knowing look but nods his agreement anyway. "No worries. See you tomorrow?"

I nod quickly and dig my keys out of my pocket as I turn and run toward my car. Once I'm inside and on the road, it takes every bit of willpower I have not to double the speed limit to get to the tavern.

By the time I pull into the parking lot and see Lily's car in the far corner, my nerves are shot. I have no idea what to expect. Other than our brief exchange earlier, we haven't spoken since the night she threw me out. I have no idea what state of mind she's in now or why I'm here.

The nerves all quickly melt away, though, because within moments of parking the car in front of the building, Lily emerges from the front door, her wild brown hair shorter than it was the last time I saw her but still hovering around her shoulders. She surveys the parking lot before narrowing her gaze on me with a glowing smile on her face.

I'm up out of the car in record time, anxiously awaiting her next move. Will she kiss me? Will she apologize? Will she explain what the hell happened a month ago and why she called me out of the blue today?

She doesn't do any of these things, though. Instead she grabs my hand and yanks me along to follow her down the length of the tavern and around the corner. We continue along the building until we're entering the woods behind it, taking rushed steps through the heavy brush. She doesn't stop until we reach a small area of grass with plenty of distance between us and the tavern.

"It's not as good of a spot as your place in the woods," she says softly as she pulls me directly in front of her, "but it'll do."

She crashes her lips to mine, her tongue immediately invading my mouth as she devours me as if I'm the only thing that can sustain her at this moment. I meet each movement of her mouth against mine but let her lead the way, enjoying the feeling of her hands in my hair and on my neck. Her fingers continue to roam down my chest as we kiss until they find the button of my jeans.

When she flicks it open and yanks on the zipper, I reluctantly pull my lips from hers. "What are you doing?"

Without a word, Lily encourages us both down to the cold grass and presses my shoulders back so that I'm lying beneath her. She returns to standing just long enough to slip off her shoes and pull off her jeans and panties before falling to her knees straddling my waist. She lowers my jeans and boxers enough to free my erection before she slams herself onto it, taking me into her warmth as deep as I can go as we both gasp at the pleasure of it. She takes me in and out, slowly at first but gradually increasing in speed. If she keeps this up, I know exactly what's going to happen next, and my mind responds before my body lets her go any further.

"I don't have any condoms," I warn with concern as I grasp Lily's hips to try to slow her pace.

She grabs my hands and forcefully pushes them away as she continues to ride me. "Don't worry about it, Dante. Just enjoy it."

I am enjoying it, but alarm bells are going off like crazy inside my head. "I have to worry. I can't… as much as I want to, I can't come inside you."

Lily's eyes meet mine with a reassuring smile on her face. "I'm on the pill. Don't worry about it."

I love that Lily's looking at me.

I love that she's making love to me.

But she just lied to my face.

Somehow finding it within me to deny myself this moment, I firmly grasp Lily's waist and lift her off me. "What's going on, Lily?"

She freezes as shock consumes her entire expression. "What do you mean?"

"Something's off." I look Lily up and down as if her appearance might give me any clue what the hell is causing her to act like this. "You weren't on the pill when we were together. Why would you be on it now?"

Lily continues to stare at me, her expression becoming unreadable. "Why does it matter? All you should care about is that I'm on it."

"You're lying." I say it straight to her face, unafraid to confront her on this. "What's going on?"

When Lily doesn't respond, I reach for her hand to try to communicate a different way with her, but she withdraws it and rolls away from me completely. Within a second she's up to standing and pulling on her panties and jeans.

"Just forget about it," she says with disappointment as she slips into her shoes and starts walking back toward the tavern. "I don't know what I was thinking."

I tuck myself away and zip and button my jeans as I stand up to follow her. When she sees my pursuit, she stops and holds her hand in front of her. "No. Don't follow me." She turns and quickens her pace to move away from me.

"Please, Lily," I call out after her. "Talk to me about this. Help me understand."

"I'll call you," she yells without turning back toward me.

As I stand here in the middle of the woods watching Lily run from me, I'm even more confused than before. When she disappears from my view, I panic at the thought that I may never see her again. I ruined whatever revival of our relationship this was between us just now, and I don't know that she'll give me a second chance after that.

I'm so fucking confused.

After five minutes of unsuccessfully trying to process Lily's latest strange behavior, I slowly make my way back through the brush to the tavern parking lot. When I turn the corner around the front of the building, I immediately notice Lily's car is gone.

I lost her again.

Before my mind even has a chance to catch up and realize what I'm doing, I find myself stepping through the entrance of the tavern to the familiar smell of cigarette smoke and beer. It's unhealthy for me to be in this building that holds such strong memories of me and Lily being together, but I'm not quite ready to let go of those memories just yet. I'll hold on to them for as long as I can. Lily may have walked away from me, but she can't take my memories with her.

My usual table in the corner of the room is taken already, which is just as well as I'm not sure I could emotionally handle sitting there at this moment. I opt to sit at the mostly empty bar instead.

Jodi hands a round of beers to the patrons at the other end of the bar before turning around and noticing me. Her face lights up in a smile. "Dante, my favorite Italian. You're back."

It's impossible not to smile at Jodi's greeting, though I'm not in the right state of mind to come up with a clever response. "Good to see you, Jodi."

"I was hoping this day would come. Please tell me you're here to whisk Lily off her feet again."

My expression falters. "I'd love to, but I'm not sure if that's in the cards for us."

"Damn it." Jodi sighs heavily. "That girl needs to smile more. She's not happy where she's at. She needs you back in her life."

I'm about to bombard Jodi with questions about what she said, but someone yells her name from the back kitchen.

Jodi glances in that direction before returning her gaze to mine with an apologetic look. "Give me a few and I'll get your drink."

As I watch Jodi disappear behind the kitchen doors that I've seen Lily walk through hundreds of times before, I realize that

I'm not ready to let Lily walk away from me this time. I gave her space a month ago when she threw me out of her house. I waited for her to come around even though it absolutely destroyed me, and after her call and this strange meeting with her today, I refuse to believe that there's nothing left between us.

The decision is made.

I'm up off the bar stool and out of the tavern before I can even get my keys out of my pocket. Once I'm in the car, it takes only minutes to make the short drive to Lily's house. I pull up behind her car in the driveway and barely get the engine turned off before I'm out of the vehicle and approaching the front door.

My heart's racing. My palms are sweaty. I'm going into this completely blind with no idea what I'm going to say to her, fueled only by the intense feelings I have for her that never went away. I lift my hand to knock on the door but find the breath knocked out of me instead.

Through the small crack in the window curtain next to the door, I see blood.

Drips of blood. Handprints of blood.

A lifeless body.

I grab the door handle and twist and pull and yank, but it's locked. I slam my shoulder against the wooden surface, using every muscle and whatever force I have and all my being to break down the door, but it doesn't budge. I slam my fists against it, willing the fucking door to open and let me in while simultaneously never wanting to step foot in there to see what's happened because I know it will destroy me.

And the door opens.

Lily stands before me, her entire body shaking, her hair a mess, her shirt ripped at the neckline. Crimson blood covers both of her hands, one brandishing a knife.

Not just any knife.

The switchblade I gave her.

"What happened?" I grasp her hands in mine and look them over for the wound, but I see no openings in her skin.

"Dante," she whispers. "He's dead."

Lily backs away unsteadily, revealing the truth of what happened in the lifeless body on the floor.

Derek's lifeless body.

I rush over to him, crashing to my knees at his side before leaning my ear down close to his mouth to listen for any sound of breath.

Nothing.

I press two fingers to his neck, hopelessly readjusting their position to find a pulse anywhere.

But there is nothing.

I compress the center of his chest with one hand on top of the other repeatedly as I helplessly watch the volcano of blood erupting from the hole near his heart.

"Lily, I need you!" I yell frantically. "Call an ambulance. Put pressure on the wound." After a few more chest compressions, I seal his nose and push two big breaths into his mouth and repeat the process all over again.

Lily doesn't come to me. She doesn't make a sound. Taking only a moment to glance back at her, I see her standing by the closed door with the switchblade still held tightly in her hand. I check for a pulse and any sign of breathing again before doing another round of rescue breathing and chest compressions.

"He's gone, Dante." Lily's tiny voice drifts into the air around us, pulling me out of my state of denial and somehow sealing Derek's fate. My movements begin to slow, and then I stop completely, checking for a pulse one more time even though I know it's not there.

I get off my knees and sit back onto the floor, feeling surrounded by blood and coldness and something I've never had to experience before.

Death.

My gaze find's Lily's whitened face, and only then do I notice the gash just above her left eyebrow. My eyes linger further down her skin to find deep purple bruises forming on her neck.

"Oh my God." I suck in a breath and immediately scramble up and rush to her, the switchblade falling from Lily's grasp to the floor just as I reach her. "Did he do this to you?"

When I reach out to brush Lily's hair to the side so I can see her better, she quickly turns away from me and nods her head. I can see her fighting to hold back her emotions, but within seconds she bursts into uncontrollable tears.

Pulling her gently to my chest, I hold her and wish I could absorb her pain as easily as my shirt absorbs her tears. I do what I can to comfort her, rubbing her back in soft circles and kissing the top of her hair. It takes a few minutes, but Lily's sobs begin to lessen. She eventually pulls back from me and wipes the wetness from her cheeks with a trembling hand.

With my hand on the small of her back, I encourage her toward the dining room table before pulling out a chair for her sit in. She lowers herself unsteadily to it as I pull up a seat directly in front of her, grasping both of her hands in mine. I have to resist the urge to pull her to the kitchen and scrub the dried, sticky blood from her hands. It would do no good, though. Splotches of blood cover her arms and clothes. Between her appearance and crimson red that paints the floor, it feels like blood is everywhere.

"What the hell happened, Lily?" I prod gently while squeezing her hands tighter in mine.

"He was going to kill me," she whispers. "I thought he was going to choke the life right out of me. I tried to stop him, but he was too strong for me. I went for the knife in my back pocket..." As she trails off, she shuts her eyes and seems to relive the painful moment right in front of me. "I just wanted his hands off my neck. I never meant to kill him."

"Why would he hurt you?" I can't fathom Derek hurting the woman he's pined after since they were in college.

"He saw our cars in the tavern parking lot," she replies with an almost palpable fear in her voice. "He was waiting for me when I got home, and he was furious."

"His car isn't here," I point out.

"It's in the garage."

"Why the hell would his car be in your garage?"

A fresh set of tears erupt from Lily's eyes. "Because Derek's practically been living here lately. We were together... as a couple."

The reluctance with which she says these words is the only thing keeping me sane at this moment, otherwise I'd lose it completely. "I don't understand."

"He knew," she says almost inaudibly, and with those two words, my eyes go wide. "He knew your identity was fake. He even knew about the connection to your grandfather." She takes a deep, calming breath. "When I quit my job at the paper, Derek was pissed. He knew it was the end of any shot he had at being with me, and he knew it had everything to do with you. He became obsessed, using all his resources to find anything he could use against you, and he found something that didn't add up in your records. He knew you had to be hiding something, so he expanded his search until he heard about a Dante visiting a Robert Whitford at the hospital, and he put two and two together."

The further Lily gets into her explanation, the more fearful I become of what she's going to say next, not for my own sake, but for Lily's.

"He demanded I break up with you and become his girlfriend or he'd report you to the police," she continues before wincing at her own words. "I hated that night I let you go. I said some really awful things, but I had to. I knew the only way to force you out of my life was to make you hate me."

"I could never hate you." My response is immediate and automatic. No matter how deeply Lily's words cut me that night we broke up, I never stopped loving her.

Lily smiles through her tears, but the expression quickly fades as she looks away from me. "After that, the demands kept coming. Derek wanted to move in, so I let him. Even when he started asking for sex, I gave him what he wanted." Her eyes reluctantly meet mine, her expression swimming in pain as my features flare with the fury building inside me. "When he demanded a baby, though, I couldn't do it anymore. Not completely."

The flames within me extinguish. My heart drops. My dreams evaporate. "A baby?"

She nods slowly. "It was his insurance that I wouldn't leave him, that we'd be tied together forever." Her eyes divert away again, unable to hold my gaze. "I ultimately let him do what he wanted, but I took the morning-after pill the next day. I stopped it once, but I knew I couldn't stop it forever." She covers her mouth with her hand and holds in a sob for a moment before she can speak again. "I remembered your parents' story. I remembered you, and that's why I called you today. The most beautiful human being I know was created out of love to keep a monster from planting his own seed, and I thought it could work for me, too. I could have a piece of you with me forever and keep you safe at the same time."

I lean forward and pull Lily into my embrace, my throat constricting painfully at the thought of how far she was willing to go to protect me. "You didn't have to do that for me. I wouldn't have wanted you to do any of this for me."

"I know," she responds over my shoulder. "That's why I couldn't tell you. I knew you'd turn yourself in before letting me do any of this for you, and I couldn't let that happen. You deserve a happy and full life after everything you've been through. That's all I wanted for you."

My own tears begin to fall as I realize she may have given up too much of her own life trying to protect mine. "You didn't deserve this, though." I pull back from her and glance at Derek's lifeless body on the floor. "I don't know what this means, Lily. I fear what they'll think when we call the police."

Lily's eyes cut to mine. "I'm not letting you be anywhere near here when I call the police. They might think you're involved."

"I'm not running from this. I won't leave you here to face this on your own after all you've done for me."

"Dante, I–"

"I'm tired of hiding," I declare firmly. "Let me be here to support you. Let me help you through this." I take Lily's hand in mine. "If they can see the truth in what happened, we have nothing to worry about."

"And what if they find out about you?"

"They won't," I reassure her with a smile even though I have no idea what they'll do with me. "Let's make the call. They'll be more suspicious the longer we wait."

Lily nods slowly before rising up from the chair and grabbing her cell phone from the table. Her hand is shaking so violently she can barely hit the right numbers. I wrap my arm around her back to give her comfort and support.

It takes just a moment for someone to answer before Lily says the four simple words that will inevitably change the course of our lives. "My boyfriend is dead."

28

I'm trying to focus on the person right in front of me, but my ears are keenly trained on the conversation happening across the room.

"Has he hurt you before?" the officer asks Lily as if it's a completely normal question. She nods as the EMT tips her chin up so that the officer can take a picture of her bruised neck. "How long has this been going on?"

"At least two weeks," she replies with a shaky breath.

She looks uncomfortable as the EMT lifts the bottom of her shirt enough to reveal a deep purple bruise on her side, my blood instantly boiling within my veins at the sight of it. "This is an older wound?" the EMT asks as another picture is taken. When Lily nods in reply, the EMT shares a glance with the officer.

He lets the camera fall to hang around his neck and asks her carefully, "Were you assaulted in any other ways?"

"We had sex," she replies uneasily, "but it was technically consensual. I was too afraid of what he'd do if I didn't give him what he wanted."

Lily glances at me, and in that one look I see all the pain she's holding inside over this. She's speaking the absolute truth to this officer, though he doesn't have the context to realize exactly what she's talking about. She wasn't afraid of what Derek would do to *her* if she didn't comply; she was afraid of what he'd do to *me*.

"Mr. Martes," the officer directly in front of me says for what may be the second or third time in the last ten seconds. "I need you to focus over here, please."

I reluctantly pull away from Lily's gaze to address the man. "Sorry. I'm just worried about her."

"I understand," he replies with hardly a hint of understanding in his voice, "but I need to finish getting your statement."

I nod and steal another glance at Lily. They're inspecting her hands and scraping the contents under the tips of her fingernails into an evidence bag. By the reddened scratches I saw on Derek's hands and arms, it looks like Lily might have got a good piece of him in her struggle to break free from his grasp.

"How would you describe your relationship with Derek Hughes?"

Even the mention of his name causes a torrent of anger to swirl within my chest. It takes everything I have within me not to show it to this officer. "I've only met him a couple times. Our encounters were short and mostly civil, but it was clear he was the jealous type. He didn't like seeing me with Lily."

"How long were you and Lily together?"

"Three months," I reply. *The best three months of my entire life.*

The officer scribbles notes on his notepad, not stopping as he continues his onslaught of questions. "When did you become aware that Lily and Derek were dating?"

"Just today. I had no idea they were together until Lily told me what happened after I couldn't resuscitate Derek."

"She didn't tell you when you met her outside the tavern this afternoon?"

I shake my head. "She didn't tell me much of anything. She seemed worried and seemed like she had something to tell me, but she left before explaining any of it."

The officer continues writing as I take in the scene around me. The pool of red and handprints of blood on the floor are the only haunting reminders of what happened here since they removed Derek's body from the house. It's hard to remember the good times Lily and I shared in this place with those stains across the floor.

My eyes are drawn to the living room as the EMT helps Lily to her feet and holds her hand as she walks unsteadily in my direction. Her eyes meet mine only briefly before she looks away, and it takes all the willpower I have not to spring out of this chair to comfort her.

"Is she okay?" I ask the EMT as they approach, wishing Lily wasn't on the other side of him so I could reach out and at least hold her hand.

"She'll be fine. We're taking her to the hospital just as a precaution."

I'm torn between relief and panic. I don't like the idea of being separated from Lily.

As the EMT continues to walk Lily to the front door, I turn my attention back to the officer that I've completely ignored since the moment Lily stood up in the living room. "Can I go with her to the hospital?"

"I'm afraid not," he replies, and my heart sinks. "We need to bring you to the station for additional questioning."

This man is holding something back from me. I know he is. "Am I a suspect?" I ask out loud even though internally I fear that I already know the answer.

"You're a person of interest. Until we have all the facts and evidence sorted out, we need to keep you at the station."

I nod reluctantly, though I find myself more concerned about the idea of not being with Lily than the realization I'll be spending more time in a police station.

Glancing behind me out the front door, I watch as Lily is helped into the back of an ambulance. As they close its back doors and she disappears from my view, I pray it won't be the last time I ever see her. Both our lives are completely up in the air right now, and when the dust settles after all this, I have no idea where we'll both land.

The officer closes up his notepad and stands up from the chair next to me. He motions his hand toward the front door. "If you'd come with me, I'll take you to the station."

Without another word, I stand up and follow the officer out the front door toward the sea of flashing blue lights from the police cars lined up along Lily's yard. What I find waiting for us outside is something I should have expected but wasn't prepared for at all.

There's a television news crew just down the road from Lily's driveway.

I immediately turn my head away from them, adrenaline shooting through my entire body at the fear that they could have caught my face on camera. I can only imagine what they're thinking as they watch the police officer open the back door of his cruiser to motion me inside.

The moment he closes the door behind me, I lean forward against the steel mesh cage that separates the back seats from the front seats and hide the remaining exposed sides of my face with my hands. I don't move or look up or do anything as the officer gets in the front of the car, turns on the engine, and backs out of the driveway to take me to the station.

This trip in a police cruiser seems twice as long as the last one as my thoughts are consumed by Lily and how she's feeling and what she's going through right now. Even though I'll be under even more scrutiny this time around, I'm not nearly as afraid to go to the police station now as I was after the bar fight simply because my worry for Lily overpowers my fear of being discovered. Lily is all that matters to me right now. She's my other half, and I won't lose her again.

This will all work out, I keep telling myself. *It has to.*

Being a person of interest at the police station is significantly better than being an arrestee. I'm kept in a small locked room with a two-way mirror, but I'm not handcuffed or locked down to the table. I'm given a glass of water, and after a few hours they even offer me a sandwich to eat.

I don't know what time it is, but it has to be getting late by the time a man I don't recognize enters the room. He's dressed in plain clothes–a polo shirt with tan slacks–but by the shiny badge on his belt, I know he's a police officer of some sort.

"I'm Detective Spaulding," he says as he closes the door behind him and takes a seat across the table in front of me. I nod in response, not sure of the proper etiquette for a person of interest greeting a police detective.

My thoughts immediately turn to Lily, though, and I abandon all concern about greetings and ask the question I've asked every single person who has stepped in this room since I was brought here hours ago. "How is Lily?"

"She's shaken up, but she's fine. This was a traumatic experience for her on multiple levels."

I try not to let it show in my face, but I'm holding back the urge to burst into tears at hearing him say this. I've known from the moment I saw Lily's whitened face when she opened the door that she'd never be the same after this, but until this moment, I've successfully suppressed the fear that my Lily may be gone forever. She's been forced into a relationship she didn't want for the last month. She's given her body to a man solely in exchange for his silence about secrets that don't even involve her. She killed a friend as an indirect result of protecting me and my identity. How can she smile after this? How can she ever find happiness again?

"She's been released from the hospital," the detective continues.

My face lights up immediately. "When can I see her?"

"Unfortunately we can't let you see her. She'll be staying in a hotel under police supervision. We need to keep her out of the spotlight until the investigation is complete." At the confused look on my face, he goes on to elaborate. "The media is all over this story. It could go either way. If this truly was a case of self-defense, it's a tragic event. If it was negligent homicide, that's a whole different story."

"Negligent homicide?" The words creep out of my mouth like some strange foreign terms that should have no place in this conversation. "He was going to kill her. How could this possibly be seen as anything more than self-defense?"

"This is part of what I wanted to talk to you about," Detective Spaulding replies with an uneasy sigh. "First off, let me say that you've been cleared of any involvement in Derek's death. Lily's prints on the blade handle and the physical evidence of her struggle against Derek confirm she's the one who stabbed him." He pauses and leans his arms forward on the table before looking me directly in the eyes. "There's no doubt that Lily was assaulted tonight, but the placement of the blade in Derek's chest and the timing surrounding his death call the theory of self-defense into question."

My entire body tenses as I run my hands through my hair in frustration. "This doesn't make any sense."

"Derek was dead for over ten minutes before you even got to the house," he explains. "You made a valiant effort by performing CPR, but there's nothing you could have done to save him. He was already gone."

He's gone, Dante. Lily's words reverberate in my mind. The entire time I was rushing to save Derek's life, she didn't try to help or call for an ambulance. I thought she was just in shock and making worst-case scenario assumptions when she told me he was dead, but she knew it to be the truth.

Did she let him die?

My eyes widen in horror. I can't fathom Lily allowing someone to bleed out on her floor just to ensure that my secrets died with him. She'd never go to those lengths to keep me and my secrets safe.

Would she?

She must have told the police he died before I showed up at her front door. She wanted to ensure that all their attention would be on her and not on me. Regardless of her motivation for not immediately calling for help after she stabbed Derek, there's one indisputable conclusion about what happened today.

Lily was protecting me. Since the moment she broke up with me, that's all she's been doing, and I both love and hate her for it. She never should have gone through any of this. None of this ever should have happened.

I'm tired of the people in my life suffering and making sacrifices for me.

I remain speechless as the detective continues on completely unaware that what he's said just completely turned my life upside down. "She may have been in shock at what happened and unable to form coherent enough thoughts to call the police, or she may have been a victim of abuse purposefully neglecting to make the call immediately after she stabbed him. We may never know the truth, but if the medical examiner determines that he could have been saved by her quick action in calling for help, charges will be filed."

My insides are churning. I feel like at any moment I might lose the contents of my stomach. It's too much to take in at once, the thought of what Lily's done and the lengths she was still willing to go to in order to protect me, the idea that her future is completely in jeopardy and there's nothing I can do about it. I wish I could erase it all for her, even if that meant erasing the good times we shared together. If I've cost her the happiness and freedom she had before she met me, I won't be able to live with myself.

I've ruined her.

"I don't know what to do," I admit out loud, my voice wavering.

"I suggest you go home and rest," the detective advises as he sits back in his chair. "You need to let the investigation play out, and Lily needs to recover."

Lily needs me, I think to myself, but I know with the police presence around her and the media desperate to get their hands on her story, there's no way I could get within two feet of her without drawing attention from the exact people in this world I've been avoiding my entire life.

I reluctantly nod and take a deep breath, willing myself to believe that there's still a happy ending out there somewhere for me and Lily. In the meantime, I'll just have to wait.

29

It's quiet today, even for the forest. There's no wind whisking by, no movement to the trees, no subtle hum of insects in the brush. If not for the sound of the rushing creek at the foot of the rock bench I'm sitting on, I'd wonder if Mother Nature pressed the pause button on all life in the woods this afternoon.

The stillness is peaceful and the calm is relaxing, but there's no denying something is missing from this place.

Or rather, someone.

I've never felt so helpless in my life. Keeping my distance from Lily and the investigation has been challenging, but I know it's my only option. There is no other way. Stepping back into that complicated situation that I was lucky to get out of would only make things worse. As painful as it is, I have to continue to wait it out.

I could only pace the floors of my house and go on aimless drives in the car for so long. Every minute that passed only wound me up tighter, and I finally got a breaking point.

And that was only the first day after Derek's death.

My parents encouraged me to take advantage of my favorite place in the woods to pass the time and find some peace while I wait to learn about Lily's fate. I took them up on the offer, though admittedly I compromised with myself, trying to balance both keeping up on any news about Lily and working on my sanity out here in the woods.

The ancient LCD TV is rarely on in our house, but I've had it tuned to the local news morning, noon, and night for the last three days. All they can talk about is Lily Alistair, but nothing they report gives me comfort. The entire state of Maine is eagerly awaiting the results of the investigation and whether charges will be filed, and until the reporters have definitive answers, all they can do is speculate. Was Lily the victim or the perpetrator? Had she been pushed to the brink of insanity by her abusive boyfriend when she failed to call for help or was it an elaborate plot to steal the job she's always wanted from the man who got it first?

I'm grateful we don't have internet at our house or on our cell phones. Given what they're talking about on the news, I can only imagine what social media has to say about all this.

The speculation and lies floating around about Lily haven't even been the worst part of the last three days. The lack of contact with her has been almost unbearable. I know I've already gone a month without seeing her or talking to her until just a few days ago when this all went down, but the pain I felt in those weeks apart is nothing compared to the difficulty of knowing Lily is out there struggling through this because of me and without me there to comfort her.

The perfect silence of the forest is interrupted by the distant sound of branches cracking. It's the telltale sign of a visitor approaching me, and though I'd usually be frustrated at having my solitude in this place interrupted by someone else, I could really use another human being to talk to at this moment.

My eyes scan the area of the path ahead of me until I see my mom approaching. Her gaze meets mine, and she smiles a brilliant smile that for just a moment reminds me of Lily's similar flashes of happiness that caught my eye from the first day I saw her.

"I thought you could use some company today," Mom says as she hesitates at the bottom of the rock.

"You read my mind," I reply with a small grin as I extend my hand to pull her up to sit with me. With a bit of effort, we manage to get her up onto the rock bench at my side. Being here with her like this is strangely reminiscent of her impromptu interruption of my time alone here back in early spring just before I left for Arizona to pick up Cindy when she was released from prison. It's incredible how much has changed since then.

Mom puts her arm around my back and rubs my arm on the other side, remaining quiet for a moment before she finally says, "You're holding it together really well."

I can't help the small laugh that escapes me. "That's funny considering I feel completely broken inside."

With a soft sigh, Mom leans her head against my shoulder and continues to comfort me with her touch. "You'll get through this. You're strong. You're only twenty-two years old and look at all you've already been through. This is just another rock in your path, but you'll get around it. Lily will, too."

"I wish I could do more for her," I admit, my throat clenching painfully as I hold back the emotions that want to break free from my chest. "She went through so much for me, and I can't do a damn thing to help her. I can't even talk to her." The first tears threaten to fall from my eyes, and I quickly wipe them away before they have a chance. "I can't stand the thought that she did all this for me. All I do is cause the people in my life to suffer because of me. It's not fair."

Mom reinforces her comforting grip around my back. "You can't blame yourself. She made these decisions on her own. She wanted to protect you." Mom pauses a moment, her palm finding the side of my face as she turns my gaze toward hers. "It means she loves you. The people in your life do what they can to help you because they love you."

I inhale a shaky breath and slowly release it, wishing I could expel the pain I feel inside as easily as the air that leaves my lungs.

"Don't give up hope," Mom continues as her eyes begin to water. "This entire family is living proof that where there is hope, there is a way. Even when it's all you have left, it can still be enough." She pauses and looks away briefly as her own tears begin to fall. "I don't know exactly what you're going through, but I've been through enough to know that even through the darkest times, we can survive. Beautiful things can still happen."

"I hope you're right," I respond through the silent tears now freely falling down my cheeks.

"Exactly," Mom replies with a reemergence of her beautiful smile. "You *hope*."

I turn and pull her into my embrace, more grateful than ever to have someone like her in my life. My parents have faced unimaginable circumstances and difficulties that should have broken them completely to pieces, but they survived. The never gave up or lost hope.

And neither will I.

Pulling back from my mom, we sit in silence for some time as I gather my thoughts and regain control of my emotions. After a while I glance up at the fading daylight in the sky. "I should get back to the house. It's almost time."

Mom nods before carefully hopping down from the rock. I lower myself down after her, and we walk together on the path through the woods to our home.

When we arrive, I immediately take my place on the couch and turn on the TV even though the five o'clock news doesn't start for another thirty minutes. The previous show and commercials finally fade into a graphic containing two words that cause my breath to hitch.

Breaking news.

Turning up the volume a few clicks, I sit forward on the couch as if being this much closer will help me hear the sound better.

"We start tonight with breaking news in the Lily Alistair investigation," the female news anchor announces as the dramatic introductory background music begins to fade. "The local authorities issued a statement just moments ago." She fumbles with a piece of paper in her hand as she begins to read from it. "In the case of the death of Derek Hughes, after thorough consideration of the evidence and review of the autopsy report, Lily Alistair has been cleared of all wrongdoing. Mr. Hughes was killed in a tragic case of self-defense during a domestic dispute."

The woman continues to read the rest of the statement, but I'm not listening anymore. My mind is stuck on the four most amazing words in the entire world: *cleared of all wrongdoing*.

Out of the corner of my eye, I see Mom step into the room from the hallway. She turns to look at the TV. "Any news?"

My hand flies to my mouth as I try to hold back the grin erupting on my face. It's all the confirmation she needs. She hurries over to me as I stand to meet her, immediately taking her into my arms. "She's going to be free," I say with a mix of excitement and disbelief over Mom's shoulder. "No charges will be filed. Lily and I can be together."

"I'm so happy for you, Dante." Mom squeezes me tighter before pulling back and grasping the sides of my face. She considers me thoughtfully for a moment just as the front door opens and Dad walks in. He's working a towel over his face and neck but stops when he sees us.

"What'd I miss?" he asks hesitantly.

Mom points at the TV. "Lily's a free woman."

Dad works his way over to me, grasping my shoulder tightly. "Congratulations. This is great news."

"I can't believe it," I reply before glancing back at the TV just to make sure I'm seeing and hearing this all correctly. The video has changed now. It's no longer showing the news anchors in the studio. It's a live feed of an empty podium with a cluster of microphones attached at the top of it.

And then Lily steps into the picture with a man in a gray suit next to her who says, "Lily's going to make a brief statement. She will not be taking any questions." He steps back from the podium and motions Lily toward the microphones.

She steps up to them with her head bowed and a piece of paper clutched in her hand. She places it on the podium in front of her before tipping her chin up to the camera, her gaze somehow directly finding mine through the lens over the TV broadcast.

"I'm deeply saddened by the loss of my good friend, Derek Hughes. My heart goes out to his family. I can never give back to them what I've inadvertently taken away, and I'll have to live with that for the rest of my life." She pauses to wipe the tears from her cheeks. Her chest rises and falls in a deep breath before she continues. "In this time of mourning and recovery, I ask for your cooperation in respecting my privacy." Her eyes leave the paper she's reading as she looks into the camera again, and I swear she's looking directly at me. "I need this time to let things calm down before life can get back to what it was before this all happened." In the deliberate second of silence that follows, I know she's talking to me. She's sending me a message. "I hope my family and friends understand that I am forever grateful for their love and support, and I will reach out to them when I'm ready. Thank you."

The TV speakers blare with the sound of reporters yelling questions toward the now empty podium as Lily and the man in the suit make their way out of view of the camera. The picture changes back to the news anchors at their desk, and they begin to discuss the statement Lily just made.

A statement that was really more of a message to me.

"She was talking to you," Dad says with surprise.

"I know," I reply with a grin, though it quickly fades with the conflicted feelings I have inside. "She's free but afraid to call me or see me with all this attention on her. She wants us to wait." I sigh heavily before looking between both of my parents, reminding myself of their own story and the months they spent apart before my mom was rescued and they were finally reunited. If they could make it through that harrowing time without even knowing whether they'd ever see each other again, I can get through this delay in having Lily back in my arms. "I can wait," I acknowledge with decisiveness and determination. "I can do this."

Mom pulls me into a hug before Dad wraps his arms around both of us. As my parents embrace me and show me their unwavering love and support, I breathe a sigh of relief. For the first time in over a month, I'm looking forward to the future. I'm ready to leave the darkness behind and look to the clearer path ahead.

When Lily says go, I'll be ready.

In the meantime, I'll be waiting.

30

I can see my breath billowing in front of me with each heave of my chest in the cold air as we move, but that doesn't deter me. Brandon and I have unloaded sheet after sheet of drywall from the flatbed truck, determined not to stop until the final materials are unloaded and inside the house.

"You doing okay back there?" Brandon calls out behind him as he navigates the awkwardly large piece of drywall through the open front door.

"I'm good," I reply, loving the burn in my arm muscles as I bring the back end of the drywall through the door. We set it carefully against the wall in the open floorboard space that will become this house's living room before heading back outside into the cold to repeat the process all over again.

It takes four more trips, but we finally empty the flatbed truck and send it on its way before calling it a night. Brandon encourages the few other volunteers still around to head home before he joins me in the partially finished kitchen that has served as our break room on this project.

I toss him a cold bottle of water from the cooler on the floor before returning my attention to my own bottle in my hand, gulping down the rest of the refreshing liquid to renew my parched body.

"Good job today," Brandon compliments between drinks of his water.

I nod in acknowledgement and lean back against the exposed wood that will eventually become the kitchen counter. "It's been a productive day."

"Hell, it's been a productive couple weeks really," Brandon counters.

Internally I'm smiling to myself, knowing exactly what's brought on this recent motivation in my life. I may not have Lily by my side when I wake up each morning, but just knowing that will be my reality someday soon is enough to keep me going. It fuels me more than ever to do better each day, to embrace life and look forward to the next day.

I have a lot to look forward to, and it feels like it's just around the corner.

I'll wait as long as it takes.

Brandon finishes off his bottle of water with a heavy sigh before grabbing the phone from his pocket. He slides his finger across it and checks the screen before tucking it back away. "I better get going. I need to wash up before this date tonight."

Even though I should be jealous of Brandon's uncomplicated and thriving relationship with his girlfriend, I feel nothing but happiness for the guy. I've been in that place before with Lily. I'm just waiting for the chance to go back there again. "Don't stay out too late. We have another full day of work ahead of us tomorrow."

"I thought I was the project coordinator here," he scolds with an amused grin on his face.

I follow him out of the house and part ways with him in the front yard as we walk to our cars.

"I'll catch you tomorrow, Dante," he calls out with a small wave before climbing in his car.

I nod and wave back to him, but my eyes are drawn to something further up the road past the only other two houses on this dead-end street. Something red. Something I'd recognize from a mile away.

Lily's car.

I pretend to get settled in my car and wait for Brandon to drive away before opening my door and bolting into a run down the road. When I'm within feet of Lily's little red hatchback, the driver's-side door opens and the most beautiful person in the world emerges from it.

The other half of my forever.

She runs to me. She connects with me.

I will never let her go again.

We embrace each other with passion and pain and every desperate feeling emerging to the surface between us. She's sobbing into my shoulder, gripping on to me like I'm the only thing that can possibly keep her feet on the ground. I hold her back just as tightly, releasing my own tears at finally being reunited with this lost piece of my heart.

"I missed you," I whisper in her ear, and even though my words only make her sob harder, I continue to say everything that I've waited weeks to tell her. "I love you, Lily Alistair. I know you're hurting and I know this has been hard, but I'm here for you now, every step of the way."

"I love you, Dante Marini," she whispers back, though she can barely get through the words before releasing another wave of tears. "I never stopped loving you."

Though I could stay like this with Lily in my arms forever, I finally decide to pull back from our embrace to gauge her face. Despite the wetness of her cheeks and redness of her eyes, her vibrant smile somehow manages to shine through.

I wipe away her tears with each of my thumbs and press my lips softly to hers. "Tell me what I can do for you," I implore.

"I just need you. Lots of you."

"I'm all yours." I kiss her softly again, but when I pull back this time, her smile has faded.

"I don't know where we'll go or how we'll do this," she says with concern. "I've been living with Jodi these past couple weeks since the investigation wrapped up while I waited for the media coverage to stop. I couldn't bring myself to go back to my place. My belongings are already in storage and the landlord let me out of my lease. There are too many memories there. I can't handle it, Dante."

"Hey, it's okay." Pulling her gently against my chest with her ear hovering near my heart, I quickly realize I'm going to have to play the card available in my back pocket a lot sooner than I intended. "Live with me," I offer to her.

Lily looks up at me in disbelief. "What? Live with you where?"

"My family's house. Come live with us in the woods."

A skeptical look crosses Lily's face. "What do your parents think about that?"

"It was their idea," I reply with a grin before my expression turns more serious. "Come stay with me. I'll keep you safe. I'll help you heal. I want to be there for you. There's no better place to hide from the world than at my house."

Fresh tears spill down Lily's cheeks as she nods. "Yes. I'll come live with you."

Our lips meet again, shy and hesitant at first before quickly building into a fierce exchange of love and emotion. It's impossible to hold back my elation over Lily's acceptance of my offer, so I show her every bit of it through this wild kiss between us.

I feel like I'm on top of the fucking world.

When we finally pull back from each other, Lily's face is still tear-stained but the happiness and relief in her expression has to be a mirror image to my own. I take her hands in mine and pull them to my chest, warming them with my touch and wishing I could do so much more to show her how much I want to make up for not being able to help her until now.

"Can I come with you today?" she asks hesitantly.

"Absolutely."

She breathes a sigh of relief, her exhale clearly visible in the chill of the early winter air around us. "I just need to grab some things from Jodi's apartment. I'll leave my car with her. I won't need it."

"You quit working at the tavern?"

She nods. "I'm ready for the next chapter in my life. I need to leave my old job and house behind."

"And your cell phone," I add, hoping this won't upset her. "We'll get you a burner phone so you can communicate within the family."

She smiles at what I've said, which is confusing given that I've just told her she has to give up her cell phone. "I like how you said 'family.'"

"You'll be part of our family. I know you've been missing out on that since your dad died, but with us I can assure you you'll be cared for and loved. My parents live a simple and secluded life, but that only makes them love the people in their lives more. They want to embrace you as part of the family."

I've made the tears start spilling from Lily's eyes again, but they're accompanied by a grin of excitement and happiness that assures me these are the happiest kind of tears.

Lily glances to the side at her car. "I don't know that I can wait another second. Let's go now."

"Okay," I reply with a laugh. "I'll follow you to Jodi's, then?"

Lily nods and kisses me briefly before maneuvering her way around the front of her car to the driver's side. "I'll see you there."

When she hops inside, I turn around and run back down the street to my car. After getting on the road to follow Lily and calling my parents to tell them what's going on, I find myself still trying to comprehend how significantly life is about to change.

The woman I love is moving in with me.

She's mine. She's safe. We're together.

This is where my life truly begins.

It takes a good hour to get to Jodi's apartment and pack Lily's things into my car. We had no choice but to tell Jodi that Lily was coming to live with me even though I'd prefer that no one knew, but we didn't want her to worry about where Lily disappeared to. It turns out Jodi was thrilled to know we were back together and that Lily was going to live with me. She wouldn't ruin that for us. She assured us she'd never tell anyone where Lily went.

After Lily's tearful goodbye with Jodi, we get on the road in my car to do something I never thought in a million years would happen.

I bring my girlfriend home.

It's almost like we're back to the way it was as we drive, though I know the truth is so much has changed. Classic rock plays softly in the background as Lily leans her head back against the headrest and stares out the window at the endless line of trees passing by. Our hands are connected across the center console, that simple touch doing all the communicating we need between us as we otherwise drive in silence.

By the time we're on the dirt roads, Lily sits up in her seat and looks out the windshield intently. I can tell she knows we're getting close. We haven't seen other cars or houses for miles.

As I make the final turn into our long driveway, my heart begins to race. This is it. We're bringing someone new into our family, letting her fully in on our secluded lives. She's proven to us the lengths she'd go to in order to protect us and our secrets. It's our turn to trust her and reciprocate her loyalty with all the love and support we can give her.

When the small brown house with the pointed roof and white shutters finally comes into view, I say the words that I almost need to hear out loud just to believe they are real. "We're home."

Lily looks at me and smiles as a stray tear falls down her cheek. "I like the sound of that."

By the time we're parked, my parents are already emerging from the front door, Dad's arm wrapped around Mom's shoulder as they approach the car. I hurry out of the vehicle to get Lily's door and offer her a hand to help her up.

Mom beams a smile at Lily before pulling her into a hug. "It's good to see you again."

"Thank you for having me," Lily says over Mom's shoulder with a smile to my dad. He grins back at her with an acknowledging nod.

When Mom and Lily pull back from each other, Mom glances at the house behind her. "It's not much, but it's home."

Lily shakes her head in disagreement. "It's perfect. It's just what I need right now." She turns to me and takes my hand in hers. "You're exactly what I need."

Feelings wash over me that I simply can't ignore. I don't care that my parents are standing right here within feet of us. I pull Lily to my chest and unite our lips, tasting her and loving her with my mouth until we pull back almost gasping for breath.

With an embarrassed glance to my parents, I expect to see some kind of disapproval or shock on their faces, but I only see happiness there. They understand what I'm going through. They recognize passion and true love because they've been there. It's what's kept them together through the darkest times and what keeps them going to this day.

Placing my hand on the small of Lily's back, I encourage her toward the front door. "Welcome to the Marini family."

31

In the week I've given Lily to adjust to her new home, I've been secretly observing her. I want to know every single thing that bothers her, every nightmare she has, anything that makes her frown or show even a sign of being down or upset. If I can understand what's wrong, I can better help with fixing her.

I've learned there's a lot to fix.

I'm grateful to have Lily here in my house constantly at my side. She's happy here, but she's not back to her normal self. The lively, energetic woman who existed before everything that happened with Derek is gone or at least temporarily in hiding. It's become my life's mission to find that person within her again, to bring her back out into the world to brighten it with her presence and personality and life.

Since Lily's arrival here, we haven't talked much about what happened in the time we were apart when she was with Derek or during the investigation and media frenzy. As much as it's easier not to talk about it, I'm beginning to realize that this may be at the core of what's holding Lily back from healing.

"We should talk," I suggest carefully as I roll to my side on the bed to see Lily's face.

She's staring up at the ceiling and doesn't turn to me when she responds. "What do you want to talk about?"

"We should talk about what happened," I clarify. "It would do us both some good, I think. It will help you move on."

"There's nothing to move on from," Lily retorts in an emotionless voice. "I closed that chapter. I'm moving on to the next."

I prop my head up with my elbow on my pillow and stare at her until she finally looks at me. "You were held captive in a relationship for a month by a man who was supposed to be your friend. He took advantage of you. He used your body..." My chest clenches as I can't even finish the thought. "He hurt you in so many ways. You can't just shut yourself off from that and pretend it never happened."

Lily's face contorts into a grimace as she turns her head away from me and rolls to her side. Her silent tears quickly develop into painful sobs, and I immediately feel like an ass for pushing her too far with this conversation. This is exactly what I've been trying to avoid since bringing her here.

Wrapping my arm around her stomach, I conform my body to hers from behind and hold her gently. "I'm sorry. I shouldn't be rushing you like this." I nuzzle my face into her hair, wishing I could get inside her head to know what she's thinking.

We stay like this in silence for a long moment until Lily's sobs diminish. When she's stopping crying completely, she sits up in the bed and wipes away her remaining tears before looking at the small window in our room.

"I need some fresh air," she says in a raspy voice without looking at me.

I'm immediately up out of the bed. "Outside it is, then."

We get dressed in layers of clothing to combat the chill that we know awaits us in the early winter air outside. Lily only manages a quick goodbye to my parents sitting at the dining room table before she walks out the front door. They give me a worried glance, but I return it with as much reassurance in my expression as I can muster before I follow Lily outside.

She's steps ahead of me, already making her way toward the entrance of the path into the woods that we've traveled a few times since her arrival here. As I watch her move one foot in front of the other with no sway to her hips and no bounce in her step, I realize something needs to change today or the Lily I knew will continue to slip away.

I can't let this consume her for a moment longer.

I need to show her it's okay to open up to me.

I need her to understand how dangerous it is to keep it all bottled up inside.

With a few quick strides, I catch up to Lily and grasp her hand in mine as we step onto the path together. I don't push her to talk. I let the sound of the cold wind through the trees fill the otherwise silence between us the entire way to the small clearing in the woods and then to the rock bench along the creek.

Lily approaches the rock, ready to throw herself up onto it but stops when I tug her hand in the opposite direction. She looks at me with confusion.

"Let's keep going," I suggest, encouraging her to continue down the path with me. "There's something I want to show you."

Lily seems hesitant to follow but ultimately complies. The silence firms itself into ice between us the entire way to our destination but finally shatters when we get there.

"The waterfall," Lily whispers as we approach the area where the stream throws itself off the rock cliff into the pool of water below.

I carefully lead her to the small flat area of dirt and withering grass within a few feet of the edge of the rock cliff. We sit down together, sitting cross-legged in front of each other with the edge of the rocks to our side.

I take a deep breath, working myself up to say the words that I hope will help Lily come out of this impenetrable barrier she's put up around herself. In my hesitation, I realize if I wait too long to start talking, I'm not sure I'll be able to get out what I need to say.

"After you threw me out of your house, I was devastated," I begin with a shaky voice, my mind screaming at me to leave these memories locked away inside even though I know I need to let them resurface. "I was lost. My future evaporated before my eyes, and I didn't know how to deal with it. I felt completely worthless again, and I promised myself never to go back to that place in my life."

Lily's eyes are on me, but I can't manage to get through this and hold her gaze. I glance at her only briefly before bowing my head and plowing forward with what I need to tell her.

"My parents tried to help me, offering all their love and support, but I only pushed them away. I ran for it. I came out here to this very spot and was reminded of the amazing times you and I shared together at this waterfall." A tiny smile briefly turns up my lips before I look out toward the rock cliff and feel the expression vanish. "The hopelessness turned to numbness, and I liked the numbness. I thought I could embrace that lack of feeling and make everything else go away." My voice trembles, and I have to will my body to continue talking. "I was going to throw myself off this cliff into the shallow rocks below. I was ready to end it all right here, but my dad stopped me. He grabbed my arm and pulled me back, and when I realized the full extent of his devastation at seeing me almost throw my life away in front of him, I knew I had to let my parents in. I needed their love and support even though every instinct I had told me to push them away. The power of family and love is too great to resist. We have to give in to it. It's the only way to find happiness. It's the only way to be free."

I continue to stare out over the edge of the rocks, the stream rushing by at their side in its own desperate leap off the cliff. I'm surprised by the touch of warm skin to my cheek. A hand forces my head to turn, and my eyes lock on to Lily's and the tiny waterfall of tears pouring out of her eyes. She holds my gaze for only a moment longer before her expression crumbles into deep sobs as she pulls us both to kneeling and envelopes me with her embrace. As her tears come harder and faster, she grips on to me more desperately. Even though I know she's trying to support me right now, I hold her back with just as much strength, wishing I could absorb all her pain through our touch.

"I almost lost you," Lily whispers over my shoulder shakily. "The world can't lose you, Dante."

"I'm not going anywhere," I reassure her, holding on just a little tighter.

She pulls back from me and quickly wipes her eyes with the sleeve of her jacket as we both sit back on the ground. Her face remains tipped downward, but her eyes flicker up to meet mine with the hint of a smile. When she looks away, the brief moment of the reemergence of the Lily I knew fades as her expression turns somber again.

"Derek approached me after work that day," she begins, and I immediately shut out everything else around me to focus on what she's saying. "He said he had something important to tell me. I was worried, so I followed him just down the road from the tavern to a clearing where we could talk."

She swallows hard. With each passing second I can see just how difficult it is for Lily to talk about this with me, so I take her hand between us and give her every bit of support I can through our touch.

"When he told me he knew your identity was fake and you were hiding something, I didn't believe he actually had anything on you. I thought it was just another desperate attempt to mess with my relationship so he could make his own move. It wasn't until he mentioned the connection to your grandfather that I knew he had exactly the leverage he needed over me, and I didn't know what else to do. I was willing to do anything to keep his mouth shut and protect you."

I don't dare interrupt her or move or do anything more to stop Lily's retelling of what happened. I just continue to hold her hand between us, my offered lifeline to keep her from drifting away as she wades further into her difficult memories.

"He demanded I break up with you. He ripped the necklace you gave me from my neck and pulled me against him and gave me the ultimatum that I be his girlfriend or he'd go to the police and the media and anyone else who would listen to tell them of his discovery about you, so I did it. I drove home and walked in that house and broke us both completely to pieces, saying the most vile things I could because I knew the only way I could get you to move on was to have you hate me for what I said. It was the hardest damn thing I ever did in my life."

As the words tumble out of Lily's mouth, the tears come faster from her eyes. I lean forward to try to take her in my arms, but she waves me away, letting me know she can get through this. I take both her hands in mine instead, and she grips me back just as tightly as she continues at a rapid pace.

"It was like we were playing some fucked-up form of house," she cries with the weight of all her pain showing in every single syllable she speaks. "Derek moved in at my place. When I wasn't at work, he expected me home. When I was home, he expected me to cook for him and dote on him and kiss him and love him but it all felt wrong because I didn't want to do any of those things. All I could think about was you and how I had hurt you and how much I wanted to be doing those things with you instead." She pauses and turns completely still, staring at the ground beside us with a completely expressionless and emotionless face. "Eventually he moved on from just wanting kisses. He would touch me, and when I resisted, he'd threaten you again and remind me of my place. The touching quickly turned into wanting more, and that's when it all started to fall apart.

"At first he wouldn't use me for sex. He wanted me to give it to him. He made sure I was the one willingly throwing myself on top of him and letting him inside me, and it broke me. Every time I did it I felt shame and disgust and I couldn't stop crying while I did it. He hated that. He hated my tears more than anything, so he started to take over and pin me beneath him and hit me until I stopped crying. He thought that's what made the tears stop, but it wasn't. The only thing I could do to stop them was to close my eyes and imagine you inside me. It was enough to get me through it each time until the days before I called you. Derek wanted to ensure I was his forever, so he demanded I become pregnant with his child. I tried to resist him. Even when he started to get violent with me, I kept up the fight, but when he dialed the police and had them show up at our door when I continued to deny him, I had no choice but to give in. That night he threw me against the edge of the dresser and fucked me from behind without protection, and I had to let him. There was nothing I could do."

The more I hear of Lily's story, the harder it becomes to keep my breathing under control and my heart rate down. I knew from the beginning I wasn't going to like what she had to say, but this is almost too much. Hearing the full extent of how Derek slowly destroyed the woman I love is almost more than I can bear to hear, but I need to be here for her. She needs to talk about this, and I need to listen.

"I snuck out of work the next day and went to the drugstore. I took a morning-after pill, but I knew that was only a temporary solution. I couldn't keep that up forever. I begged for a double-shift at work that day and made it home late enough that Derek wouldn't ask for sex, and in the middle of that night when I couldn't sleep, an idea popped in my head. I remembered your parents' story and the desperate lengths they went to in order to ensure that psychopath couldn't impregnate your mom."

Lily's pained eyes meet mine, and it only causes my heart to break for us both even more.

"You were created out of their love. An incredible person came out of that horrible situation, and I thought I could accomplish the same thing. I called you to the woods behind the tavern that day because I could think of no better way to protect you and keep a part of you with me than to have your child growing inside me, created out of our love for each other even though we couldn't be together, but you knew I was up to something and wouldn't let me go through with it. That was my only play. I had no backup plan to fall on, so when you rejected me, I left. By the time I got home, I still had no idea what I was going to do next, but it didn't matter. Derek was there waiting for me. He made a surprise stop by the tavern as one of his attempts to keep tabs on me, and when he saw your car there with mine, he immediately went home and waited for me.

"I barely got in the door before he slammed my head against the table and demanded to know what you were doing at the tavern. I tried to play it off with anything I could think of, but he saw right through my lies. He worked himself into a rage, and before I knew it, he had me pinned to the wall with his hands around my neck. I clawed at him and pulled at his arms with everything I had, but they wouldn't budge. By the time I managed to get the switchblade out of my back pocket, my vision was turning red. I opened the blade and plunged it into his chest. His hands immediately let go of my neck and I fell to the floor desperately trying to breathe just before Derek hit the floor next to me. His eyes were wide and his face was white, but everything else was red. There was so much blood coming from his chest. I pressed my hand over the wound, but it did nothing to stop the flow of blood. Derek couldn't speak, but his eyes were pleading with me to help him…"

Lily's voice trails off just as her hands begin to shake within mine. The rest of her body remains completely still as she goes quiet for a long moment, the rushing sound of the nearby waterfall the only thing to fill the silence between us.

"I didn't do anything," she whispers, her words seeming to drift out from her mouth on a breath rather than actually being spoken. "He was bleeding out in front of me, but I didn't call for an ambulance. For a brief moment, I thought I saw the man I used to be friends with lying on the floor in front of me and I wanted nothing more than to save him, then I remembered everything he did to me and threatened to do to you. I thought ahead to my future and how I wasn't sure I could survive living with a monster like him. I watched the life fade out of him right there in front of me with my palm pressed to his chest and the blade that caused his wound still clenched in my other hand. I watched him die. I killed him."

"Lily," I implore, demanding her attention so that she'll actually absorb and understand what I'm going to say to her.

"There's nothing you could have done. The medical examiner confirmed the blade pierced his heart. He bled out in minutes. Even if you called for an ambulance, they never would have arrived in time to save him."

"But I didn't make the call. I let him die right in front of me. What kind of person does that? Who lets that happen?"

"He made you that way. He destroyed you." My chest tightens as I realize just how true that statement is and how all of this happened just because Lily was protecting me. "You went through a lot. He was beating you, practically raping you. You were the victim here, Lily."

She shakes her head vehemently as her words explode from her. "I had the blade in my hand. I drove it through his chest. He's gone forever. How the hell does that make me the victim?"

"The Derek you knew was gone a long time ago. Think about what he did to you. Think about the position he put you in and what he was asking of you. He was a monster attacking you and forcing himself on you. All you did was fight back." My explanation doesn't seem to be getting through to her, so I say the words that I've been afraid to say or even think since the moment I walked into the bloody scene at Lily's house almost a month ago. "He could have killed you."

Lily doesn't immediately move or respond. I can see the debate in her mind playing out on her face. She's torn between guilt and acceptance, and I want nothing more than to make her understand that Derek's death truly was a tragic case of self-defense just as the police and media reported.

With a deep inhale and exhale of breath, Lily looks at me with tears still streaming down her face, but I can see and feel some of the tension releasing from her body. "It's just going to take me time to get over this, to get over everything."

I nod at her with a small but reassuring smile at this sign of progress. "You take all the time you need. Just know I'm here for you. Keep letting me in to help you. I don't want you to have to go through this alone."

"I love you," she says with the most strength I've heard from her in this entire conversation. "That's the one thing that never left me throughout this whole ordeal. I never stopped loving you and never will."

"Come here," I suggest as I motion her to me. She scoots over until she's sitting between my legs with her back pressed up against my chest. I gently encircle my arms around her and bring our heads together with my chin resting on her shoulder. With all the warmth and comfort I can offer, I hold her until her breathing becomes steady and even. When I know she's completely relaxed, I whisper, "I love you, Lily. Every single part of you. You're my forever, and you always will be."

I can't see her face, but I can feel the smile that forms there. I hope it's that signature smile that I've loved since the moment I first saw Lily all those months ago. I'll do anything to make that smile keep appearing more and more each day for the months and years to come.

I have Lily in my arms. Now I just need to bring her back to me completely.

She may be broken, but the pieces are still there and our love is the glue. We can put her back together.

I know we can.

32

My eyes open lazily to the darkness surrounding me, the faint glow from the clock on my nightstand the only source of light in the room. I can tell through the small crack in the curtains that it's still the middle of the night or very early in the morning. The sun has yet to greet this part of the world with its presence, and I'm perfectly happy to go back to sleep until it shows up.

I roll to my other side and reach my arm out to grasp on to the woman who is the source of light in my life, but I stop.

She's not there. The bed is empty next to me.

A surge of adrenaline initially races through me before I realize she could have just slipped out of the room to use the bathroom. Before I let myself panic too much, I give her a few minutes to see if she comes back to bed.

She doesn't.

This is the first night after our talk by the edge of the waterfall, the first time I haven't been consciously able to support her after she poured her heart out to me and divulged every horrifying detail of what she went through with Derek. Maybe she pretended to fall asleep when we came to bed early after dinner last night. I should have stayed awake and made sure she was okay. I should have kept a closer eye on her.

Why am I still in this bed?

I shoot up to standing and run to our bedroom door, throwing it open and racing down the hallway in my boxers. The moment I see Lily hunched over at the dining room table, my heart skips entire beats within my chest. I grasp her shoulders and pull her back, expecting to see tears or blood or lifelessness, but what I find surprises me.

She's scowling at me.

"What the hell are you doing?" she snaps with a look of shock on her face. "Jesus Christ. You scared me to death."

I immediately let go of Lily's shoulders and step back from her, my brain trying desperately to process the scene in front of me. Lily looks perfectly fine. She's not injured. She's not crying. She's sitting in a chair with two simple objects on the table in front of her.

A notebook and pen.

"Sorry," I whisper. "I was worried about you. I thought something happened. I was afraid you…" I can't even finish the thought.

Lily looks me up and down, glances back toward our bedroom, and bursts into a fit of laughter just as the door to my parents' bedroom opens and Dad emerges with an open switchblade in his hand.

Now Dad is looking at me as I stand here wearing nothing but my boxers and a crazed look on my face. When he assesses me and Lily and concludes that there's no threat in the room, he gives me a confused glance and asks, "What's going on out here?"

"We're fine," Lily answers for the two of us, which I'm grateful for as I'm not sure I can properly speak right now. "Sorry to wake you."

Dad nods at her before he returns his attention to me. He gives me a firm look, but it quickly fades into a teasing smile just as he closes the blade and turns around to go back in his room.

When his door clicks shut, I move over to Lily, wrapping my arms around her from behind as I look more closely at the notebook on the table. Both sides of the open face of the notebook are covered in Lily's wild scrawl. This is nothing new to me. Lily had countless similar notebooks stacked in disorderly piles in the office space at her house.

"You're writing," I say quietly with surprise.

"I am, and I promise it's not as dangerous as it looks." When I don't respond to Lily's joke, she turns her head to the side to see my face. "I woke up and couldn't fall back asleep. While I was lying there, an idea popped in my head for a story."

"So you decided to get up in the middle of the night to start writing it?"

She manages a shrug despite my embrace around her. "Why not?"

A small laugh escapes me as I realize this is my spontaneous Lily making a beautiful reappearance. "Sure, why not," I agree.

She gives me a playfully scolding look. "Hey, it's your fault. I remembered you encouraging me to embrace something I love to do as a means to get over everything. It helped you when you got involved with Habitat for Humanity again."

She's right. I told her all about how my parents encouraged me to get back to volunteering after my mental breakdown that tore me to pieces when Lily kicked me out. Having something to apply myself toward and having a purpose again was a huge step in the right direction for me. I hope finding writing again will do the same for Lily.

I kiss Lily's cheek and grasp her just a little tighter as I pick a random line from the notebook and start reading it out loud. "'I hardly recognize him as he's ripping my shorts and underwear off me.'"

"Hey!" Lily quickly wiggles out of my embrace and slams the notebook shut. "No fair reading that."

"This sounds like the kind of book I want to read," I tease just as Lily stands up from the chair, forcing me to take a few steps back from her. She quickly pursues me, grasping the sides of my face with her hands and pulling my lips to hers as her upper body collides with my bare chest. I can feel her nipples poking through the thin material of her shirt as her tongue explores my mouth.

With the way we're pressed together and engaging each other, my hands quickly find their way up the back of Lily's shirt to feel her exposed back. I press her harder against me until I can't tell if the heat I'm feeling is from our physical exchange or from the glowing woodstove in the living room.

Lily suddenly pulls back from our kiss and takes two deep breaths before quietly declaring, "I need a break from writing. Take me to bed."

She doesn't have to ask twice.

I quickly scoop her up in my arms and take her quietly down the hallway to our room, softly nudging the door closed behind us. Using the soft glow of the clock on the nightstand as my guide, I gently lower Lily to the bed before climbing on top of her and claiming her mouth with mine. Our kiss becomes hungry and desperate, and within moments my hands are slipping Lily out of her cotton pants and panties. I separate our lips only long enough to get her shirt over her head and toss it to the side.

Though I'm enjoying her taste and mingling with her tongue, my lips become too tempted by the rest of her naked body beneath me. With one final kiss to the corner of her mouth, my lips find their way down her neck and collarbone all the way to the firm nipple of her breast. Small moans fill the silence around us as my lips enclose around it and my tongue teases it. The moment I suck down hard on it, Lily gasps loudly, but I don't even care if my parents can hear us. My only concern in the entire world right now is eliciting those beautiful sounds from Lily again.

When I've thoroughly worked her up on one breast, my mouth moves to the other, pleasuring it until she's quietly pleading with me for more. I move down the bed with my lips venturing lower on her bare skin until I have her legs spread apart and my lips are devouring her core.

Her hips writhe against each swipe of my tongue across her clit. I tease her there until she's practically gasping for breath then let my tongue focus lower, prodding just inside her opening with tiny flicks of movement before plunging in deeper, causing a primal groan to escape her chest.

"I need you inside me," she pleads in a whisper. "Dante, please."

Though I could keep tasting her like this for hours, I also feel her desperation for more and the need to put myself deep within her. With one final movement of my tongue inside her, I pull away and roll off the bed. In the time it takes me to grab a condom from the nightstand and put it on, Lily's repositioned herself so that she's bent over the bed with her perfect little backside facing me.

I pause in confusion, recalling very clearly our conversation just after Lily moved in with me in which she asked that she be able to see my face when we were having sex. Her request didn't make total sense to me until she told me about Derek forcing her against her dresser and planting his seed inside her from behind.

In response to my hesitation to jump right back in where we left off, Lily gives me a reassuring nod, her face barely lit up by the glow of the clock from the nightstand as she glances back at me. "It's okay. I need to get over this fear. I want you to make love to me like this."

Even with Lily's reassurance, I'm still not completely sure she's ready for this, but I won't deny her this request. I'll make this as pleasurable and wonderful for her as I can. I'll be gentle and loving and treat her the way she deserves to be treated.

Grasping softly at Lily's hips as I press up against her, I take a moment to plant slow and deliberate kisses down the length of her back just before I ease into her. She relaxes her forearms down on the bed as I slowly pump in and out of her, careful to watch and listen for any sign that she's becoming upset.

As Lily's soft moans begin to fill the room again, my pace gradually increases. I lean forward just enough to grasp her breasts that dangle and bounce beneath her as I move inside her. My fingers gently knead them against my palms and occasionally move outward to pinch her hardened nipples before grasping them entirely again.

Lily's hips find perfect rhythm with my thrusts, causing my hands to abandon their play to focus on maintaining this pleasurable pace we've found together. I hold on to Lily's sides as I lose myself inside her, penetrating deep and quick with steady thrusts. Lily's breathing becomes more ragged, and when I hear her cry my name into the bed sheets and feel her warmth clench around my cock, I let it all go, my fluid movements turning my body rigid with each final thrust as I find my own release.

As the height of pleasure works its way out of my body, my movements come to a stop and I lean down to kiss Lily's bare shoulder. I can't see her face. I'm almost afraid to look at her in fear that I may have been too rough or brought back too many horrible memories in what I just did.

"Are you okay?" I whisper cautiously in her ear.

Lily turns her head and nods slightly. For a moment I question how okay she really is until she bites her lip with a playful grin. "I think you parents could have heard us."

I breathe an instant sigh of relief and let loose the smile I was holding in moments before. "Let them hear us. I don't care." At Lily's shocked expression, I lean in to kiss her on the cheek. "They know I love you."

Lily grins. "Okay. I'll make sure to be louder next time."

"Bring it on," I challenge.

"What's got into you?" Lily questions with a soft laugh.

"You. This is what you do to me."

Slipping out of her, I crawl up onto the bed and lie down sideways. Lily scoots herself up further so that she's on her side facing me. We're close enough that my adjusted eyes can see her curious expression even in the darkness.

"You've changed me," I explain. "I used to be some lost and lonely kid content to hide from the world forever, but you brought me out of that empty existence. You showed me life and love and filled me with a sense of meaning and purpose. You've taught me how to live, and I'm so lucky to have you. I'll thank God or Fate or whoever every day for the rest of my life for giving me this beautiful, incredible woman to be my other half."

"The other half of your forever," Lily clarifies for me, and with those words, I have to kiss her for understanding just how much it means to me that she understands that.

When our lips finally part, Lily nuzzles her head into mine and wraps her arm around my back. We remain still and silent for a long moment before Lily whispers, "Thank you for listening to me and being there for me yesterday. It helped to let it all out."

"I'm just sorry you've been alone in this for so long."

Lily smiles at me, her beautiful, brilliant smile. "I'm not alone anymore, and neither are you. That's all that matters."

She's completely right.

I'm no longer alone, and I never will be again.

33

Sunlight billows through the sheer curtains of our hotel room. It's too beautiful outside to stay in bed a moment longer. I have to see it. I need to enjoy this view for what little time I have left with it.

My body rises from the crisp white sheets and plush mattress carefully so as not to disturb the beautiful woman still sleeping soundly there. Lily looks peaceful with her mouth barely pursed open and her brown hair spread wildly over the pillow. It takes all the willpower I have not to lean down and kiss her, but I don't want to risk waking her.

With a few quiet steps across the room, I find myself staring out the window at the towering cityscape of Boston. From the height of our hotel room from the ground, the view makes it look like we're living in the sky among the clouds. All I see are buildings and streets and cars before me, a vast landscape of concrete and brick to temporarily replace the forests and natural beauty of the Earth that I'm used to. It's a welcome change of scenery, though. After four long months of living through yet another harsh winter in the backwoods of Maine, I was ready for this trip to experience late April in the city of Boston.

It's felt strange for me to be here since our arrival a few days ago, like I don't belong in this busy urban environment, but I've enjoyed every minute of this attempt to mark another item off my bucket list. Lily and I have walked the city from Fenway Park to the Charles River to Boston Harbor. We've done every possible touristy attraction we can find: riding the Swan Boats in Boston Common and catching sunset at the Skywalk Observatory at the top of the Prudential Center. We shared a few beers at an Irish pub downtown and went to a show in the Theatre District. It's been an amazing trip with the woman I love and an experience I'll never forget, but it's also been a wakeup call.

It's reminded of something I want more than anything in the world, but I don't know if it will ever happen.

It physically hurts inside my chest to know that I can never legally make Lily my wife. She can never have my real last name, and I would never ask her to take on my fake last name. Even though Lily has supported me and protected me ever since learning about my real identity, she should never get tangled up in this precarious web my family's been weaving since they went on the run so many years ago. I want Lily's life and identity to remain pure and unaffected by my family's continuing struggle to remain anonymous and hidden. I won't get her involved in any of that.

It's always been enough for my parents to not be legally married and for my mom to not share my dad's real last name. I can only hope that will be enough for Lily, too.

The gentle touch of hands slipping around me from behind startles me out of my thoughts, causing me to jump slightly. I glance over my shoulder to see Lily's soft smile beaming toward me. She places a kiss on my shoulder. "Sorry, didn't mean to scare you."

I want to turn around and return her kiss, but I'm enjoying the warmth of her arms around me just a little too much to make the move. "It's okay. It's my own fault getting lost in thought over here. How are you?"

"I'm wonderful. Going to miss that bed and this view."

"Are you saying you don't like our bed at home?" I tease.

Lily's arms release me just before she slaps me playfully on the shoulder. "Don't go putting words in my mouth. I like our bed just fine. Our room doesn't have anything on this view, though."

She moves in front of me, brushing aside the curtains so there's nothing to block the skyscrapers painted across the pristine blue sky canvas outside our window. It's hard to focus on the view when she's standing there in that tiny tank top and panties that conform perfectly to her body.

I take Lily's hand in mine and join her right up at the window, my heart swelling within my chest as I savor this moment with her knowing that we'll be packing our bags and heading back to Maine within hours. As I'm holding her hand, though, I realize she's still wearing a couple of the rings she put on for our formal dinner date last night, the final splurge of our vacation. The silver bands around her fingers only remind me that I can never properly get down on one knee and offer her a ring to bind us together in marriage. She may be part of the Marini family, but she will never bear the Marini name.

"Hey." Lily's eyes are on me. She's facing me, holding both of my hands now and pulling them tightly to her. "What's wrong?"

The pain in my chest is back again, only this time I feel it bubbling up within me and threatening to come out because the woman I love is right here asking me about it.

"It's nothing. I'm fine." I brush it off as best I can, but by the skepticism in Lily's face, I can tell she doesn't believe me.

"Talk to me, Dante. I owe it to you after all you've done to help me these past months."

"You don't owe me a thing," I respond automatically. "I told you I'd be there for you every step of the way after what happened last year, and I meant it."

"Regardless," Lily interjects, "I can tell something's bothering you, and I want you to talk to me about it. If there's anything I've learned from days and weeks of being snowed in at the house this past winter, it's that we can't keep this stuff bottled up. You need to talk to me."

She's right. I know she is, but I also know that I'm not ready to have this conversation. We've both enjoyed these months of living together, even through the hardships of dealing with frigid winter nights and surviving on limited supplies until the roads were passable again, but we haven't talked much about our future. I know we have a future together, I just don't know what it will look like. I want to promise Lily the world, but I know I only have so much to give.

In a lot of ways, it's absolutely terrifying.

I take Lily's left hand and gently grasp the base of her ring finger between my thumb and forefinger. "I want to put a ring here," I whisper almost inaudibly. "I want to make you my wife. I want you to have the Marini name. I want you to bear my children." My throat clenches on those last words, the verbalization of the most devastating part of what I fear we'll never have together. "I want all these things with you, and if I were anyone but who I really am, we could have them all together without question, but it's not as simple as that because of me and my past."

"It is simple," Lily replies, glancing from her left hand up to my face with a fiery look of determination in her eyes. "I love you. I don't need a ring on my finger or a certain last name attached to me to prove it." Her free hand reaches for the side of my face. "I don't need to be married to you to bear your children."

I swallow hard, willing myself not to let the emotions pour out of me at hearing Lily say these things. It takes a few deep breaths before I feel confident enough that I can get my voice out again without breaking apart completely. "You have no idea how much it means to me to hear you say that."

Lily wraps her arms around me, pulling me to her and enveloping me with her warmth and love as I hold her back just as tightly. After a few calming breaths, we pull back from each other, but Lily keeps my left hand between both of hers. She turns my wrist over, exposing my small black tattoo of the symbol of infinity. Pulling my wrist to her lips, she kisses the tattoo lightly then brings my wrist to her chest right next to her heart.

"This thing between us is forever, Dante. It's persistent and endless, and nothing can change that. Nothing can stand in its way."

I nod to her. It's all I can do. There are no words to properly express my relief and joy and absolute disbelief that I could be so lucky to have this incredible, supportive woman by my side.

A curious look crosses Lily's face as she pulls my wrist away from her just enough to inspect the tattoo. She traces the lines of the symbol with her forefinger before looking up at me with an excited gleam in her eye. "This is what I need," she says softly, almost in disbelief at her own words. "Just like your parents."

I stare at Lily and try to process her suggestion. "You want a matching tattoo?"

She nods, her smile only broadening. "The exact same tattoo. Same tattoo artist and everything."

I can't help laughing at Lily's excitement over the prospect of permanently branding her body to match me. "If that's what you want, I'll take you there."

"Today," she insists. "On the way home. Let's stop there today and do this."

"Today it is, then." I kiss Lily's cheek and pull her against me as my gaze drifts out the window at the Boston skyline. Suddenly I don't feel as sad about leaving this place. There's excitement ahead, a future for me and Lily to embrace. Our lives together are only just beginning, and we have so much to look forward to.

It all starts today.

Epilogue

Three years later...

I can't stop pacing.

"I need to get back in there," I insist, making my way across the living room toward the closed bedroom door.

"Relax, Dante," Dad says as he blocks my way. "You need a break. She's in good hands."

I know she's in good hands. I know there's nothing to worry about and everything's progressing exactly as it should be, but I feel like I need to do something.

"This all looks very familiar to me," Robert says from the rocking chair in the corner of the room. Both Dad and I turn to look at him, our combined confused faces apparently causing a wide grin to overtake Robert's features. "I'll never forget the expression on your face, Leo, when I pulled up to the house in Arizona the day Morgan went into labor. You looked just as lost and worried as Dante looks now."

Dad rolls his eyes at Robert's tease but manages a laugh. "I seem to remember Cindy saying something that day about me looking as much of a wreck as you were before Morgan was born."

Robert nods at Dad, looking impressed. "Touché. I guess this is a family trait, then."

This little back and forth between my dad and grandfather is doing nothing to make me feel better, but Dad's original point was right. I need to relax. It's imperative I be on my A-game by the time I go back in to see Lily.

Taking a seat on the couch, I lower my head into my hands and focus on the unstained hardwood beneath my feet. It reminds me of the few projects I have yet to complete in this house that

Lily I share together. When she legitimately purchased the small foreclosure at an auction a few months ago using her own savings from her last couple years as a freelance writer and self-published author, I never would have thought we'd complete the majority of the rebuild and renovations in time for this day, but we managed to pull it off.

I guess it's good motivation to have a baby on the way.

The couch cushion sinks next to me just before I feel a firm hand on my shoulder. "You're doing just fine, son."

I glance to my side and give my dad as much of a smile as I can manage. "I'm glad someone thinks so."

"Don't worry. When your mom was in labor with you, I got kicked out of the room for a while, too."

Dad's trying to bring some humor into this and make me feel better, but it's not enough to cut through my worry over what's going on elsewhere in the house behind that closed door.

"I know you feel helpless right now," Dad continues, "but you'll quickly realize women have superpowers when it comes to having children. All you have to do is be there for Lily and she'll do the rest. Everything's going to be just fine."

The bedroom door suddenly opens, bringing me immediately to my feet. Mom and Cindy walk out of the room with glowing expressions on their faces that give me a momentary feeling of relief.

"She's asking for you," Mom says with a warm smile as she pulls me in for a hug. I embrace her back tentatively, my hands trembling a bit despite all attempts to steady them.

When we pull back from each other, I give my mom and the rest of my family a quick glance and a nod. It's all the appreciation I can manage right now for their support as I face the most terrifying part of this incredible day in my life.

With a few quick steps, I'm inside the bedroom and closing the door behind me. The scene has changed significantly since I was last in here. The chair and birthing ball Lily was using to get through the contractions have been shoved to the side. There's towels and plastic sheeting everywhere around the bed where Lily's already lying down on her back with her knees in the air. Rebecca, the midwife, is in position at the end of the bed.

"We're pushing already?" I ask in a mix of disbelief and horror.

"She's ready," Rebecca replies cheerily, still maintaining the peaceful, calm exterior she's put forth since the moment we called her when Lily's water broke early this morning.

Rushing to the side of the bed, I take Lily's hand in mine and kiss her briefly before taking in the rest of her face. Beads of sweat rest on her forehead and her hair is a little wilder than it was before, but other than that she looks perfectly fine.

"Are you doing okay?" I ask her, not even bothering to strip the worry out of my voice. "I haven't heard a peep from in here. How is it you're pushing already?"

"I've tried to be quiet," she breathes out, though I can hear the discomfort in each syllable she speaks. "I didn't want to worry you."

I'm about to open my mouth to argue when Rebecca interjects, "I want you to push hard with the next contraction."

Lily nods and takes a few deep breaths before her eyes squeeze shut and her face twists into a grimace. She grips my hand tightly as her entire body seems to shake with the force of her pushing.

"That's great, Lily," Rebecca encourages. "A few more of those and I bet we'll see the head soon."

By the time we get through a few more of those, though, Lily's panting for breath after each contraction and the baby's head is nowhere in sight. Lily's hair is matted to the sides of her head in sweat from the sheer exertion her body's going through.

I keep a tight hold on her hand and do my best to whisper words of encouragement and let her know I'm here for her, but it doesn't seem like enough. After an hour of her pushing, I begin to wonder if anything will be enough to get this baby out of her.

"Big push," Rebecca calls from the end of the bed, and Lily responds with exactly what she asked for. She's still mid-push when Rebecca announces, "The baby's crowning. You're almost there."

When the contraction is over, Lily exhales a heavy breath and looks at me. It's really horrible timing considering Rebecca's words just caused a look of terror on my face. I quickly try to recover and plaster my supportive, worry-free expression back on, but by the look Lily's giving me, I'm far too late.

"You're going to be a great father," Lily says to me breathlessly, somehow managing to smile despite the exhaustion and pain that lace her every feature. "Don't be afraid."

I laugh to myself and shake my head in disbelief. Lily's about to give birth to our child and she's more concerned about me than anything else. There seem to be only two words to properly respond to her. "Thank you."

She gives me a confused look. "For what?"

Leaning in close to her ear, I whisper, "For everything you've done for me and for us. For what you're doing at this moment for us."

"I love you. It's what I do." She pauses and grins for a moment before her expression turns more serious. "You've done just as much for me."

Despite every instinct I feel to look away from her in the guilt that still plagues me, I manage to hold her gaze. "I've changed your life in a lot of ways, not all of them good."

"Don't say that. My life has been so much better with you in it." She removes her hand from mine to cup the side of my face, brushing my cheek with her thumb. "I'm happy, Dante. You've shown me how to feel true happiness again, something that's been missing in my life since my dad died."

Lily's hand drops from my face as she takes a couple deep breaths. I grasp her hand tightly as she enters the next contraction with a firm look of determination on her face.

"Give it all you've got, Lily," Rebecca calls from the end of the bed just as Lily closes her eyes and grits her teeth and seems to put the focus of her entire body toward this push. My heart rate soars to a rapid pace as I watch her then comes to a complete halt at the most beautiful sound to greet my ears.

A baby's cries.

There's a tiny human being in Rebecca's arms.

A piece of me. A piece of Lily.

Our son.

Seeing him in the flesh and breathing and flailing his tiny limbs is too much for me. I can't hold back my tears as Rebecca wraps him loosely in a blanket and immediately places him on Lily's chest. Lily's crying and smiling and laughing all at once, her face aglow with the same adoration and love I feel inside at seeing our beautiful creation for the first time. She gently places a hand behind his back and head and holds him to her as his cries begin to diminish.

"He's perfect," Lily whispers as she glances over to me.

I nod in agreement, unable to find my voice in the chaos of emotions swirling through me.

Lily removes her hand from his head and takes my palm to place it there instead. Though his skin is still damp, I can feel the softness of the fuzz of dark hair that covers his head. He feels so warm, and it makes me realize that seeing him and touching him are two completely different things. I could gaze at him all day and know he's here with us, but feeling his warmth against my skin is what makes this so real. He's actually here, our own flesh and blood.

Our small family just got a little bit bigger.

Rebecca directs me through cutting the umbilical cord and takes a few minutes to check the baby and clean him up. By the time he's in a diaper and wrapped in a clean blanket, Rebecca's ready to hand him off to Lily, but Lily points at me instead.

"He needs to meet his daddy," she explains, "and daddy needs to introduce him to the family."

"Now?" I say in disbelief, and Lily nods.

I feel both completely out of my element and one hundred percent content as Rebecca places my son in my arms. His eyes are closed, but by the slight movements of his head and wiggling of his body, I know he must be awake. I look to Lily one more time, her grinning face wet with tears as she watches me cradle our son, before I carefully open the door.

The quiet chatter in the living room immediately ceases as I walk into the room. Mom's hands cover her mouth as she sees me, and she already has tears falling down her cheeks. Dad stands next to her with his arm around her back and a proud look of approval on his face. Cindy and Robert are sitting on the couch, hand in hand, both beaming smiles at me.

"I want you to meet our son," I announce, "Jack Pearce Alistair."

Mom immediately bursts into a smile, though her tears seem to double at hearing the name Lily and I chose for our son. Despite Dad's attempts to hold himself together, I can see the emotions overtaking his face. It only seemed appropriate to name our son after the man who did so much for my parents and ultimately saved my life when I was just an infant. The only thing he's missing is my family's last name.

"Hello, Jack," Mom says quietly as she brushes her fingers lightly across his temple.

Dad wraps his arms around Mom's stomach from behind as he watches the baby, a spark of admiration in his watering eyes. He glances at me and smiles. "Jack was a great man. You couldn't have picked a better name for your son."

Cindy and Robert approach us together. Cindy's expression is beaming as she takes in the baby in my arms. Robert's gaze remains stoic, but I can see the elation in his eyes.

With my entire family surrounding me and my son, it becomes exceptionally clear to me that regardless of where we've been and what came before this, all that matters is we're here. My parents suffered through the worst kinds of pain and separation before they could finally be together and embrace their future with me. We've been through a lot together since then. Life hasn't been easy or free of hardships, and I've battled plenty of my own demons over the years, but in the end I've found happiness and something to look forward to in my life.

The light at the end of the tunnel always seemed out of reach for me, constantly visible in the distance but always too far ahead of my path no matter how hard I tried to reach it. Now I'm right there in the midst of it, basking in the light and joy of having a supportive family around me, an incredible woman by my side, and a son in my arms.

My future is resting comfortably in my arms.

"Don't let us keep you both from Lily," Mom insists as she wipes at her eyes. "You should be with her."

Cindy nods in agreement. "Little Jack needs some time with his parents. We'll have plenty of time for visiting later."

I nod appreciatively to the circle of family around me, still a little speechless that I just introduced them to their newest member of the family, before making my way back to the bedroom.

As I walk in, a tired but beaming smile emerges on Lily's face as she's sitting up in the bed with a sheet pulled over her. Rebecca is busy cleaning up but abandons her efforts when she sees me walk in the room.

"Let me give you both some privacy," she offers as she heads to the door. "I'll be outside if you need me."

Before we can even say another word, she slips out the door and closes it behind her, leaving our little family alone together for the first time since Jack's arrival.

I carefully take a seat on the bed next to Lily and offer the baby to her. She takes him from me and holds him in her arms as if she's done this a million times already, and it only causes me to smile more.

"You're a natural," I compliment, prompting Lily to look up at me with a shy but playful smirk.

"You're not doing too bad yourself," she replies before returning her gaze to the tiny bundle in her arms. She contemplates him quietly for a few moments before saying, "You know what this means, right?"

Lily's excited eyes reach my confused gaze as I give her a sideways glance. "We're not sleeping soundly again for the next eighteen years?"

With a slight roll of her eyes, Lily tries and fails to keep a straight face. "You're lucky Jack's in my arms or I'd smack you," she scolds. "I'm trying to be serious here. Something significant just happened and I don't think you even realize it."

I readjust on the bed so that I'm facing Lily directly, doing everything I can to maintain a serious face. "Okay. Enlighten me."

"You just completed your bucket list," she whispers with excitement, and the moment the words leave her lips, I find my mouth agape.

She's right. Starting a family was last on my original bucket list that Lily coaxed out of me years ago before we were even officially dating. At the time I wasn't sure it would ever be in the cards for me. I couldn't imagine asking a woman to bear my children without knowing my past and the truth behind the identity I've had to live by and put forth to the world.

But Lily knows my past. I never intended for her to learn of it or meet my family or know every part of me, but none of it scared her away. If anything, it only made her support me and love me even more. It ultimately brought us closer together, and in the end we were able to start a family. We created a beautiful son who has his entire future ahead of him, the horizon endless, the possibilities boundless.

"My bucket list is complete," I acknowledge out loud as I laugh to myself at the more important realization behind this development in my life.

My bucket list never mattered. It's not about me or my lost childhood or the loneliness and difficulties I endured growing up hidden away in the backwoods of Maine with my parents and the forest as my only companions. None of that matters now that I have Lily and Jack in my life. I can't undo my past, but I can shape Jack's future. He can have everything I didn't have, and in the end, that's all that counts.

We may not live in a busy neighborhood embedded in society, but we have a house of our own much closer to civilization than my parents' house. Jack will have a real birth certificate with his actual name that he can stand behind and live by for his entire life. He'll attend school and grow up with friends and be part of society just like any other kid. He won't have to hide from the world. He won't have to grow up like I did. Someday he may learn of his family's history, but he'll never know that life.

"You okay?" Lily prods cautiously as she places her hand on mine, pulling me from my thoughts.

I nod and lift Lily's hand to my lips, placing a soft kiss over the black infinity tattoo on her wrist that is identical to mine. "He's going to have a good life."

"We all are," Lily replies reassuringly. "You, me, your entire family… Look how far we've all come, and look who we have with us now."

Movement from the bundle in Lily's arms catches our attention just before Jack opens his eyes, gracing us with his brilliant dark irises as he looks up toward his mother.

"Hey, little buddy," Lily says in disbelief, her entire face lighting up in an exquisite smile. "Welcome to the world."

I move back against the headboard and wrap my arm around Lily's shoulder, pulling myself as close to her as possible. My movement seems to catch Jack's attention and he looks at me, his eyes full of innocence and purity and what seems like an endless amount of hope and potential.

No one's life is easy or perfect, and I can't guarantee Jack's life will ever be either of those things, but I know he has this incredible clean slate to work with. He is a fresh start for this family, and though he may not share my family's name, he is my son.

He is a Marini.

Author Notes and Acknowledgements

It's simple. This book never would have existed if not for the outpouring of support I've received from readers who loved this series enough to want more. I owe this book entirely to you. Thank you for your amazing support and feedback. Thank you for inspiring me to do this.

I'm not going to lie. Writing *Beyond Resistance* has been the hardest project I've worked on thus far, but not because of difficulty figuring out the story or developing the characters or anything like that. This book was written over the course of three months in the middle of being pregnant with my second child, and I've learned the hard way that pregnancy makes for a whole new ballgame when it comes to writing.

You'd be surprised just how important the liquid fuels of coffee and alcohol can be to the writing process.

In the end, it was completely worth it, though. I'm so glad to have put this book down on paper. I hope the fans of The Ransom Series enjoy reading this book as much as I enjoyed writing it. It's hard to say goodbye to these characters and their stories, but I can only look ahead at this point.

I have a lot more writing to do. There are more stories to be told, more challenges to be tackled, and more blank pages to be filled. I'm ready for the next step in this journey, wherever it takes me.

I'm absolutely ready.

Other Books by this Author

Someone to Listen

New Adult Contemporary Romance

Abby wanted a fresh start, a new life thousands of miles away from her four difficult years of high school and the rumors that followed her. As she begins her college experience in Boston, she finds friendship and love she didn't expect, people who show her that she doesn't have to be alone.

She is torn between two paths, inexplicably drawn to two completely different guys. One understands her and reminds her of who she used to be, the broken shadow of a person wandering through life but not truly living. The other is the key to her future, the guiding hand that she waited for years to pull her out of the darkness and into the light.

When Abby's newfound happiness and renewed existence are threatened, everything changes. She can fall back to that dark place within her or fight to save her future.

She faces the same struggle she has all along: getting someone to hear her, finding someone to believe her.

All she ever needed was someone to listen.

About the Author

A.T. Douglas embraced her renewed passion for reading by diving into the self-publishing world in 2013. Fueled by her love of music and her addiction to the Young Adult/New Adult genres, she strives to turn daydreams and the realities of life into words the world can read. She lives in New Hampshire, USA, with her husband and sons and wishes desperately that there were more hours in the day for family, reading, and writing.

Follow her news and random musings online:

Facebook: www.facebook.com/a2tdouglas

Twitter: @a2tdouglas

Goodreads: www.goodreads.com/atdouglas

Blog: atdouglas.wordpress.com